Ouida

Wanda

Vol. I.

Ouida

Wanda
Vol. I.

ISBN/EAN: 9783337002244

Printed in Europe, USA, Canada, Australia, Japan

Cover: Foto ©Andreas Hilbeck / pixelio.de

More available books at **www.hansebooks.com**

WANDA

BY

OUIDA

'Doch!—alles was dazu mich trieb;
Gott!—war so gut, ach, war so lieb!' Goethe

IN THREE VOLUMES

VOL. I.

London

CHATTO & WINDUS, PICCADILLY

1883

LONDON: PRINTED BY
SPOTTISWOODE AND CO., NEW-STREET SQUARE
AND PARLIAMENT STREET

TO

'A PERFECT WOMAN, NOBLY PLANN'D'

WALPURGA, LADY PAGET

NÉE

COUNTESS VON HOHENTHAL

.

𝕿𝖍𝖎𝖘 𝕭𝖔𝖔𝖐 𝖎𝖘 𝕴𝖓𝖘𝖈𝖗𝖎𝖇𝖊𝖉

IN ADMIRATION AND AFFECTION

WANDA.

PROEM.

OWARDS the close of a summer's day in Russia a travelling carriage was compelled to pause before a little village whilst a smith rudely mended its broken wheel. The hamlet was composed of a few very poor dwellings grouped around a large low horse-shoe shaped building, which was the manorial mansion of the absent proprietor. It was gloomy, and dropping to decay; its many windows were barred and shuttered; the grass grew in its courts, and flowering weeds had time to seed and root themselves on its whitewashed walls.

Around it the level ground was at this season covered with green wheat, spreading for leagues on leagues, and billowing and undulating under the wind that blew from the steppes, like the green sea which it resembled. Farther on were woods of larch and clumps of willow; and in the distance, across the great plain to the westward, rolled a vast shining river, here golden with choking sand, here dun-coloured with turbid waves, here broken with islets and swamps of reeds, where the singing swan and the pelican made their nests.

It was in one of those far-off provinces through which the Volga rolls its sand-laden and yellow waves. The scene was bleak and mournful, though for many leagues the green corn spread and caught the timid sunshine and the shadow of the clouds. There were a few stunted willows near the house, and a few gashed pines; a dried-up lake was glittering with crystals of salt; the domes and minarets of a little city rose above the sky line far away to the south-east; and farther yet northward towered the peaks of the Ural Mountains; the wall of stone that divides Siberia from the living world. All was desolate, melancholy, isolated, even though the season was early summer ; but the vastness of the view, the majesty of the river, the suggestion of the faint blue summits where the Urals rose against the sky, gave solemnity and a melancholy charm to a landscape that was otherwise monotonous and tedious.

Prince Paul Ivanovitch Zabaroff was in Russia because he was on the point of marriage with a great heiress of the southern provinces, and was travelling across from Orenburg to the Krimea, where his betrothed bride awaited him in the summer palace of her fathers. Russia, with the exception of Petersburg, was an unknown and detested place to him ; his errand was distasteful, his journey tedious, his temper irritated ; and when a wheel of his *telegue* came off in this miserable village of the Northern Volga district, he was in no mood to brook with patience such an accident. He paced to and fro restlessly as he looked round on the few and miserable cabins of a district that had been continually harried and fired through many centuries by Kossack and Tartar.

'Whose house is that ?' he said to his ser- vant, pointing to the great white building.

The servant humbly answered, 'Little father, it is thine.'

'Mine.!' echoed Paul Zabaroff. He was astonished ; then he laughed, as he remembered

that he had large properties around the city of
Kazán.

The whole soil was his own as far as his eyes
could reach, till the great river formed its
boundary. He did not even know his steward
here ; the villagers did not know him. He had
been here once only, a single night, in the late
autumn time, long, long before. He was a man
in whose life incidents followed each other too
rapidly for remembrance to have any abiding-
place or regret any home in his mind. He had
immense estates, north, south, east, west ; his
agents forwarded him the revenues of each, or
as much of the revenues as they chose him to
enjoy, when they themselves were satisfied with
their gains.

When he was not in Paris he was in
Petersburg, and he was an impassioned and very
daring gamester. These great silent houses,
in the heart of fir woods, in the centre of grass
plains, or on the banks of lonely rivers, were all
absolutely unknown to and indifferent to him.
He was too admired and popular at his Court
ever to have had the sentence passed upon him
to retire to his estates ; but had he been forced to
do so he would have been as utterly an exile in
any one of the houses of his fathers as if he
had been consigned to Tobolsk itself.

He looked around him now, an absolute

stranger in the place where he was as absolutely
lord.   All these square leagues he learned were
his, all these miserable huts, all these poor lives ;
for it was in a day before the liberation of the
serfs had been accomplished by that deliverer
whom Russia rewarded with death.   A vague
remembrance came over him as he gazed
around : he had been here once before.   The
villagers, learning that it was their master who
had arrived thus unexpectedly in their midst,
came timidly around and made their humble
prostrations : the steward who administered the
lands was absent that day in the distant town.
He was entreated to go within his own deserted
dwelling, but he refused : the wheel was nearly
mended, and he reflected that a house abandoned for so long was probably damp and
in disorder, cold and comfortless.   He was
impatient to be gone, and urged the smith
to his best and quickest by the promise of
many roubles.   The *moujiks*, excited and
frightened, hastened to him with the customary offerings of bread and salt ; he touched
the gifts carelessly ; spoke to them with
good-humoured, indifferent carelessness ; and
asked if they had any grievances to complain of,
without listening to the answer.   They had
many, but they did not dare to say so, knowing
that their lord would be gone in five minutes,

but that the heavy hand of his steward would lie for ever upon them.

Soon the vehicle was repaired, and Paul Zabaroff ceased his restless walk to and fro the sandy road, and prepared to depart from this weary place of detention. But, from an *isba* that stood apart, beneath 'one of the banks of sand that broke the green level of the corn, the dark spare figure of an old woman came, waving bony hands upon the air, and crying with loud voice to the *barine* to wait.

'It is only mad Maritza,' said the people; yet they thought Maritza had some errand with their lord, for they fell back and permitted her to approach him as she cried aloud: 'Let me come! Let me come! I would give him back the jewel he left here ten years ago!'

She held a young boy by the hand, and dragged him with her as she spoke and moved. She was a dark woman, once very handsome, with white hair and an olive skin, and a certain rugged grandeur in her carriage; she was strong and of strong purpose; she made her way to Paul Zabaroff as he stood by the carriage, and she fell at his feet and touched the dust with her forehead, and forced the child beside her to make the same obeisance.

'All hail to my lord, and heaven be with

him ! The poor Maritza comes to give him back what he left.'

Prince Zabaroff smiled in a kindly manner, being a man often careless, but not cruel.

'Nay, good mother, keep it, whatever it be : you have earned the right. Is it a jewel, you say ? '

'It is a jewel.'

'Then keep it. I had forgotten even that I was ever here.'

'Ay! the great lord had forgot.'

She rose up with the dust on her white hair, and thrust forward a young boy, and put her hands on the boy's shoulders and made him kneel.

'There is the jewel, Paul Ivanovitch. It is time the Gospodar kept it now.'

Paul Zabaroff did not understand. He looked down at the little serf kneeling in the dust.

'A handsome child. May the land have many such to serve the Tsar. Is he your grandson, good mother ? '

The boy was beautiful, with long curling fair hair and a rosy mouth, and eyes like the blue heavens in a night of frost. His limbs were naked, and his chest. He had a shirt of sheepskin.

Old Maritza kept her hands on the shoulders of the kneeling child.

' He is thy son, O lord ! '

' My son ! '

' Ay. The lord has forgotten. The lord tarried but one night, but he bade my Sacha serve drink to him in his chamber, and on the morrow, when he left, Sacha wept. The lord has forgotten ! '

Paul Zabaroff stood silent, slowly remembering. In the boy's face looking up at him, half-sullenly, half-timidly, he saw the features of his own race mingled with something much more beautiful, oriental, and superb.

Yes : he had forgotten ; quite forgotten ; but he remembered now.

The people stood around, remembering better than he, but thinking it no wrong in him to have forgotten, because he was their ruler and lord, and did that which seemed right to him ; and when he had gone away, in Sacha's bosom there had been a thick roll of gold.

' Where is—the mother ? ' he said at length.

Old Maritza made answer :

' My Sacha died four summers ago. Always Sacha hoped that the lord might some day return.'

Prince Zabaroff's cheek reddened a little with pain.

' Fool ! why did you not marry her ? ' he said

with impatience. 'There were plenty of men.
I would have given more dowry.'

'Sacha would not wed.   What the lord had
honoured she thought holy.'

'Poor soul!' muttered Paul Zabaroff; and he
looked again at the boy, who bore his own face,
and was as like him as an eaglet to an eagle.

'Do you understand what we say?'

The boy answered sullenly, 'I understand.'

'What is your name?'

'I am Vassia.'

'And what do you do?'

'I do nothing.'

'Are you happy?'

'What is that?   I do not know.'

Prince Zabaroff was silent.

'Rise up, since you are my son,' he said
at length.

The boy rose.

He was sullen, shy, tameless, timid, like a
young animal from the pine woods.   The old
woman took her hands off his shoulders.

'I have delivered the jewel to the lord
that owns it.   I have done Sacha's will.'

Then she turned herself round and covered
her face, and went towards her home.

The child stood, half-fierce, half-fearful, like
a dog which an old master drives away, and
which fears the new one.

'These jewels are as many as the sands of the sea, and as worthless,' said Paul Zabaroff with a slight smile.

Nevertheless, he resolved, since Maritza spoke truth, that the boy should be cared for and well taught, and have all that gold could get for him, and be sent away out from Russia; for in Russia he was a serf.

The boy's hair hung over his eyes, which were hungrily watching the dark lean figure of the woman as it went away through the tall corn to the white wood hut that stood alone in the fields. He dimly understood that his life was being changed for him, but how he knew not. He wanted to go home with Maritza to his nest of moss, where his bear-cubs slept with him by night and played with him at dawn.

'Farewell,' said Paul Zabaroff, and he touched his son's cheek with his hand.

'You are magnificently handsome, my poor child; indeed, who knows what you will be?—a jewel or only a toad's eye?' he said dreamily; then he sprang up behind his horses, and was borne away through the fast-falling shades of the evening, leaving behind him the boy Vassia and a little rough mound of nameless grass, which he had never seen, and which was Sacha's grave.

The four fiery horses that bore the *telegue* dashed away with it in the sunlight, scattering the sand in yellow clouds, and the village on the Volga plains beheld its lord never more in life. The boy stood still, and looked after it with a sombre anger on his beautiful fair Circassian face.

'You will go and be a prince far away, Vassia,' said the men to him with envy. The child could not have expressed the vague mute wrath and shame that stirred together in him, but he turned from them without a word, and ran fleet as a roe in the path which Maritza had taken. He loved his great-grandmother with a strong affection that was almost passion, though it was silent and almost unconscious of itself. She never checked him, beat him, or cursed him as the other women often did their children. She did her best by him, though they dwelt in a miserable little *isba*, that often in winter time was covered up with the snow like a bear's hole, and in summer, the fierce brief parching summer of north-east Russia, was as hot as a scorched eye under a sun-glass. Life was barren and wretched to her, but not to him. He was loved and he was free : childhood wants nothing more.

Maritza was a Persian woman. Years and years before, when she had been in her youth,

she had come from the Caspian shore, where
the land and the sea are alike alive with
the leaping naphtha of the Ghebir worship:
she had been born within the iron gates of
Derbent, of Persian parentage, and she had
known war and capture and violence, and had
had many troubles, many privations, many
miseries before she had found herself stranded
in her old age, with her grandchild, in this
little desolate village on the sand-bank by the
Volga.

She was very poor; she had an evil reputa-
tion: nothing evil was ever really traced to her,
but she had Oriental faiths and traditions and
worshipped fire, or so said her enemies the
black clergy of the scattered villages and their
ready believers. Never did Maritza light a
lamp at nightfall, but her neighbours saw in
the act a devil worship.

She was silent, proud, fierce, calm, exceedingly poor; she was hated accordingly. When
her granddaughter Sacha bore a child that was
the offspring of Prince Paul Zabaroff, though
she cursed him, the neighbours envied her and
begrudged her such an honour.

Maritza had brought up the young Vassia
with little tenderness, yet with a great yearning
over the boy, with his pure Persian face and
his beautiful fair body, like a pearl. The utter-

most she wished for him was that he should grow up a raftsman or a fisherman on the Volga water; all that she dreaded was that the Kossacks would take him and put a lance in his hand and have him slain in war, as in the old stern days of her youth her lovers had been taken by the battle-god, that devoured them one by one, and her sons after them.

She never gave a thought to the boy's parentage as of possible use to him, but she always said to herself, 'If Paul Zabaroff ever come back, then shall he know his son,' and meanwhile the boy was happy, though he had not known the meaning of the word. He would plunge in the tawny Volga in the summer-time, and watch the slow crowd of rafts go down it, and the iron pontoon pass by, closed like a bier, which took the condemned prisoners to Siberia. Now and then a gang of such captives would go by on foot and chained; miserable exceedingly, wounded, exhausted, doomed to twelve months' foot-sore travel ere they reached the endless darkness of the mines or the blindness of the perpetual frost. He watched them; but that was all. He felt neither curiosity nor pity as he lay on the tall rough grass, and they moved by him on the dusty, flint-strewn, ill-made road towards that chain of blue hills which marked their future home and their eternal grave.

For sport the boy had the bear, the wolf, the blue fox, the wild hare, in the long winter-time; in the brief summer he helped chase the pelican and the swan along the sand-banks of the Volga or upon its lime-choked waves. He was keen of eye and swift of foot: the men of his native village were always willing to have his company, child though he was. He was fond of all beasts and birds, though fonder still of sport; once he risked his own life to save a stork and her nest on a burning roof. When asked why he did it, he who choked the cygnet and snared the cub, he could not say: he was ashamed of his own tenderness.

He wanted no other life than this rude freedom, but one day, a month or more after Paul Zabaroff had passed through the country, there came to the door of Maritza's hut a stranger, who displayed to her eyes, which could not read, a letter with the Prince's seal and signature. He said: 'I am sent to take away the boy who is called Vassia.'

The Persian woman bowed her head as before a headsman's glaive.

'It is the will of God,' she said.

But the time came when Vassia, grown to man's estate, thought that devils rather than gods had meddled with him then.

'Send him to a great school; send him out of

Russia; spare no cost; make him a gentleman,'
Paul Zabaroff had said to his agents when he
had seen the son of Sacha, and he had been
obeyed. The little fierce half-naked boy who
in frost was wrapped in wolf-fur and looked
like a little wild beast, had been taken from
the free, headstrong, barbaric life of the Volga
plains, where he was under no law and knew
no rule, and passionately loved the river and
the chase, and the great-silent snow-wrapt world
of his birth, and was sent to a famous and
severe college near Paris, to the drill, and the
class, and the uniform, and the classic learning,
and the tape-bound, hard, artificial routine
of mechanical education. The pride, of the
Oriental and the subtlety of the Slav were all
he brought with him as arms in the unequal
combat with an unsympathetic crowd.

For a year's time he was insulted, tor-
mented, ridiculed; in another twelve months
he was let alone; in a third year he was admired and feared. All the while his heart was
bursting within him with the agony of home-
sickness and revolt; but he gave no sign of
either. Only at nights, when the others of
his chamber were all sleeping, he would slip
out of bed and stare up at the stars, which
did not look the same as he had known, and
think of Maritza and of the bear-cubs, and of

the Volga's waters bearing the wild white swans upon their breast; and then he would sob his very soul out in silence.

He had been entered upon the books of the college under the name of Vassia Kazán; Kazán having been the place at which he had been baptised, the golden-domed, many-towered, half Asiatic city which was seen afar off from the little square window in Maritza's hut. High influence and much gold had persuaded the principal of a great college—the Lycée Clovis, situated between Paris and Versailles—not to inquire too closely into the parentage of this beautiful little savage from the far north. Russia still remains dim, distant, and mysterious to the western mind; among his tutors and comrades it was taken for granted that he was some young barbarian noble, and the child's own lips were shut as close as if the ice of his own land had frozen them.

Eight years later, on another day when wheat was ripe and willows waved in summer sunshine, a youth lay asleep with his head on an open Lucretius in the deserted playground of a French college. The place of recreation was a dusty gravelled square; there were high stone walls all round it, and a few poplars stood in it white with dust. It was August, and all the other scholars were away; he alone had

been forgotten; he was used to being forgotten. He was not dull or sorrowful, as
other lads are when left in vacation time
alone. He had many arts and pastimes, and
he was a scholar by choice, if a capricious one,
and he had a quick and facile tact which
taught him how to have his own way always;
and on many a summer night, when his teachers
believed him safe sleeping, he was out of college, and away dancing and singing and laughing at students' halls, and in the haunts of
artists, and at the little theatre beyond the
barrier, and he had never been found out, and
would have cared but little if he had been.
And he slept now with his fair forehead leaning on Lucretius, and a drowsy, heavy heat
around him, filled with the hum of flies and
gnats. He did not dream of the heat and the
insects; he did not even dream of the saucy
beauty at the barrier ball the night before,
who had kicked cherries out of his mouth with
her blue-shod feet, and kissed him on his curls.
He dreamt of a little, low, dark hut; of an old
woman that knelt before a brazen image; of
slumbering bear-cubs in a nest of hay; of
a winter landscape, white and shining, that
stretched away in an unbroken level of snow to
the sea that half the year was ice. He dreamed
of these, and, dreaming, sighed and woke. He

thought he stood on the frozen sea, and the ice broke, and the waters swallowed him.

It was nothing; only the voice of his tutor calling him. He was summoned to the Principal of the Lycée: a rare honour. He rose, a slender, tall, beautiful youth, in the dark close-fitting costume of the institute. He shook the dust off his uniform and his curls, shut his book, and went within the large white prison-like building which had been his home since he had left the lowly *isba* among the sandhills and the blowing corn by Volga.

The Principal was sitting in one of his private chambers, a grim, dark, book-lined chamber; he held an open letter in his hand, which he had read and re-read. He was a clever man, and unscrupulous and purchasable; but he was not without feeling, and he was disquieted, for he had a painful office to fulfil.

When the youth obeyed his summons he looked up and shaded his eyes with his hand. He hesitated, looking curiously at the young man's attitude, which had an easy grace in it, and some hauteur visible under a semblance of respect.

The Principal took up the open letter: 'I regret, I grieve, to tell you,' he said slowly, 'your patron and friend, the Prince Zabaroff, has died suddenly!'

The face of Vassia Kazán grew very pale, but very cold.   He said nothing.

'He died quite suddenly,' continued the director of the college; 'a blood-vessel broke in the brain, after great fatigue in hunting; he was upon one of his estates in White Russia.'

The son of Paul Zabaroff was still silent. His master wished that he would show some emotion.

'It was he who placed you here—was at all costs for your education.   I suppose you are aware of that?' he continued, with some embarrassment.

Vassia Kazán bowed and still said nothing. He might have been made of ice or of marble for any sign that he gave.   He might only have heard that an unknown man had died in the street.

'You were placed here by him—at least, by his agents; you were the son of a dead friend, they said.   I did not inquire closer—payments were always made in advance.'

He passed his hand a little confusedly over his eyes, for he felt a little shame; his college was of high repute, and the agents of Prince Zabaroff had placed sums in his hands, to induce him to deviate from his rules, larger than he would have cared to confess.

The boy was silent.

'If he would only speak!' thought his master. 'He must know—he must know.'

But the son of the dead Zabaroff did not speak.

'I am sorry to say,' resumed his master, still with hesitation, 'I am very sorry to say that the death of the Prince being thus sudden and thus unforeseen, his agents write me that there are no instructions, no arrangement, no testament, in short—you will understand what I mean; you will understand that, in point of fact, there is nothing for you, there is no one to pay anything any longer.'

He paused abruptly; the fair face of the boy grew a shade paler, that was all. He bore the shock without giving any sign.

'Is he made of ice and steel?' thought the old man, who had been proud of him as his most brilliant pupil.

'It pains me to give you such terrible intelligence,' he muttered; 'but it is my duty not to conceal it an hour. You are quite—penniless. It is very sad.'

The boy smiled slightly; it was not a smile for so young a face.

'He has given me learning; he need not have done that,' he said carelessly. The words sounded grateful, but it was not gratitude that glanced from his eyes.

'I believe I am a serf in Russia?' he added, after a short silence.

'I do not know at all,' muttered the Principal, who felt ill at ease and ashamed of himself for having taken for eight years the gold of Prince Paul.

'I cannot tell—lawyers would tell you—I am not sure at all; indeed, I know nothing of your history; but you are young and friendless. You are a brilliant scholar, but you are not fit for work. What will you do, my poor lad?'

The boy did not respond to the kindness that was in the tone, and he resented the pity there was in it.

'That will be my affair alone,' he said, still carelessly and very haughtily.

'All is paid up to the New Year,' said his master, feeling restless and dissatisfied. 'There is no haste—I would not turn you from my roof. You are a brilliant classic—you might be a teacher here, perhaps?'

The youth smiled; then he said coldly:

'You are very good. I had better go away at once. I should wish to be away before the others return.'

'But where will you go?' said the old man, staring at him with a dull and troubled surprise.

The boy shrugged his shoulders.

'The world is large—at least it looks so when one has not been over it. Can you tell me who inherits from Prince Paul Zabaroff?'

'His eldest son by his marriage with a Princess Kourouassine. If he had only left some will, some sort of command or direction—perhaps if I wrote to the Princess, and told her the facts, she——'

'Pray do not do that,' said the boy coldly. 'I thank you for all I have learned here, and I will leave your house to-night. Farewell to you, sir.'

The boy's eyes were dry and calm; the old man's were wet and dim. He rose hurriedly, and laid aside his stern habit of authority for a moment, as he put his hand on the lad's shoulder.

'Vassia, do not leave us like that. I do not like to see you so cold, so quiet, so unnaturally indifferent. You are left friendless and nameless—and after all he was your father.'

The boy drew himself away gently, and shrugged his shoulders once more with his slight gesture of contempt.

'He never called me his son. I wish he had left me by the Volga with the bear-cubs: that is all. Adieu, sir.'

'But what do you mean to do?'

' I will do what offers.'

'But few things offer when one is friendless ; and you have many faults, Vassia, though you have many talents. I fear for your future.'

' Adieu, sir.'

The boy bowed low, with composure and grace, and left the room. The old man sat in the shadow by his desk, and blamed himself, and blamed the dead. The young collegian went out from his presence with a firm step and a careless carriage, and ascended the staircase of the college to his dormitory. The large long room, with its whitewashed walls, its barred casements, its rows of camp bedsteads, looked like a barrack-room deserted by the soldiers. The aspen and poplar leaves were quivering outside the grated windows; the rays of the bright August sun streamed through and shone on the floor. The boy sat down on his bed. It was at the top of the row of beds, next one of the casements. The sun-rays touched his head ; he was all alone. The clamour, the disputes, the mirth, the wrong-doing with which he and his comrades had consoled themselves for the stern discipline of the day, were all things of the past, and he would know them no more. In a way he had been happy here, being lord and king of the rebellious band that had filled this chamber, and knowing so little of his own fate or of his own future that any greatness or glory might be possible to him.

Three years before he had been summoned to a château on the north coast of France in the full summer season. It had entered into the capricious fancy of Prince Zabaroff that he should like to see what the wild young wolf-cub of the Volga plains had become. He had found in him a youth so handsome, so graceful, so accomplished, that a certain fibre of paternal pride had been touched in him; whilst the coldness, the silence, and the disdainfulness of the boy's temper had commanded his respect. No word of their relationship had passed between them, but by the guests assembled there it had been assumed that the young Vassia Kazán was near of kin to their host, whose lawfully-begotten sons and daughters were far away in one of his summer palaces of the Krimea.

The boy was beautiful, keen-witted, precocious in knowledge and tact; the society assembled there, which was dissolute enough, dazzled and indulged him. The days had gone by like a tale of magic. There had been always in him the bitter, mortified, rebellious hatred of his own position; but this he had not shown, and no one had suspected it. These three summer months of unbridled luxury and indulgence had made an indelible impression on him. He had felt that life was not worth the living unless it could be passed in the same manner. He had known that away there in Russia there were young Zabaroff princes, his brethren, who would not have owned him; but the remembrance of them had not dwelt on him. He had not known definitely what to expect of the future. Though he was still there only Vassia Kazán, yet he had been treated as though he were a son of the house. When the party had broken up he had been sent back to his college with many gifts and a thousand francs in gold. When he reached Paris he had given the presents to a dancing girl and the money to an old professor of classics who had lost his sight. Not a word had been said as to his future. Measuring both by the indulgences and liberalities that were conceded to him, he had always dreamed of it vaguely but gorgeously, as sure to bring recognition and reverence, pomp and power, to him from the world. He had vaguely built up ambitious hopes. He had been sensible of no ordinary intelligence, of no common powers; and it had seemed legitimate to suppose that so liberal and princely an education meant that some golden gates would open to him at manhood:

why should they rear him so if they intended to leave him in obscurity?

This day, as he had sat in the large white courtyard, shadowed by the Parisian poplar trees, he had remembered that he was within a few weeks of the completion of his eighteenth year, and he had wondered what they meant to do with him. He had heard nothing from Prince Zabaroff since those brilliant, vivid, tumultuous months which had left on him a confused sense of dazzling though vague expectation. He had hoped every summer to hear something, but each summer had passed in silence; and now he was told that Paul Zabaroff was dead.

He had been happy, being dowered with facile talents, quick wit, and the great art of being able to charm others without effort to himself. He had been seldom obedient, often guilty, yet always successful. The place had been no prison to him; he had passed careless days and he had dreamed grand dreams there; and now——

He sat on the little iron bed, and knew that in a few nights to come he might have to make his bed with beggars under bridge arches and in the dens of thieves.

Tears gathered in his eyes, and fell slowly one by one. A sort of convulsion passed over

his face.   He gripped his throat with his hand,
to stifle a sob that rose there.

The intense stillness of the chamber was not
broken even by the buzzing of a gnat.

He sat quite motionless, and his thoughts
went back to the summer day in the cornfields
by the Volga; he saw the scene in all its little
details: the impatient good-humour of the
great lord, the awe of the listening peasants,
the blowing wheat, the wooden cross, the
stamping horses, the cringing servants; he
heard the voice of his father saying, 'Will you
be a jewel or a toad's eye?'

'Why could he not leave me there?' he
thought; 'I should have known nothing; I
should have been a hunter; I should have done
no harm on the ice and the snow there, with
old Maritza.'

He thought of his grandmother, of the little
hut, of the nest of skins, of the young bears at
play, of the glittering plains in winter, of the
low red sun, of the black lonely woods, of the
grey icy river, of the bright virgin snow—
thought, with a great longing like that of thirst.
Why had they not let him be? Why had they
not left him ignorant and harmless in the clear,
keen, solitary winter world?

Instead of that they had flung him into
hell, and now left him in it, alone.

There was a far-off murmur on the sultry summer air, and a far-off gleam of metal beyond the leaves of the poplar trees; it was the murmur of the streets, and the glisten of the roofs of Paris.

About his neck there hung a little silver image of St. Paul. His mother had hung it there at birth, and Maritza had prayed him never to disturb it. Now he took it off, he spat on it, he trod on it, he threw it out to fall into the dust.

He did this insult to the sacred thing coldly, without passion. His tears were no more on his cheeks, nor the sobs in his throat.

He changed his clothes quickly, put together a few necessaries, leaving behind nearly all that he possessed, because he hated everything that the dead man's money had bought; and then, without noise and without haste, looking back once down the long empty chamber, he went through the house by back ways that he knew and had used in hours of forbidden liberty, and opening the gate of the courtyard, went out into the long dreary highway, white with dust, that stretched before him and led to Paris.

He had made friends, for he was a beautiful bold boy, gay of wit, agile, and strong, and of many talents; but these friends were artists little known in the world, soldiers who liked pleasure, young dramatists without theatres, pretty frail women who had taught him to eat the sweet and bitter apple that is always held out in the hand of Eve. These and their like were all butterfly friends of a summer noon or night; he knew that very well, for he had a premature and unerring knowledge of the value of human words. They would be of no use in such a strait as his; and the colour flushed back for one instant into his pale cheeks, as he thought that he would die in a hospital before he was twenty rather than ask their aid.

As the grey dust, the hot wind, the nauseous smell of streets in summer smote upon him, leaving the poplar-shadowed court of his old school, he felt once more the same strange yearning of home-sickness for the winter world of his birth, for the steel-grey waters, the darkened skies, the forests of fir, the howl of the wolves on the wind, the joys of the fresh fierce cold, the feel of the ice in the air, the smell of the pines and the river. The bonds of birth are strong.

'If Maritza were not dead I would go back,' he thought. But Maritza had been long dead, laid away under the snow by her daughter's side.

The boy went to Paris.

Would it be any fault of his what he became?

He told himself, No.

It would lie with the dead; and with Paris.

CHAPTER I.

IN the heart of the Hohe Tauern, province of lakes and streams, there lies one lake called the Szalrassee; known to the pilgrim, to the fisher, to the hunter, but to the traveller little, for it is shut away from the hum and stir of man by the amphitheatre of its own hills and forests. To the south-east of it lies the Iselthal, and to the north-west the Wilde Gerlos; due east is the great Glöckner group, and due west the Venediger. Farther away are the Alps of Zillerthal, and on the opposite horizon the mountains of Karinthia.

Here, where the foaming rivers thunder through their rocky channels, and the ice bastions of a thousand glaciers glow in the sunrise and bar the sight of sunset; here, where a thousand torrents bathe in silver the hillsides, and the deep moan of subterranean waters sounds for ever through the silence of the gorges, dark with the serried pines; here, in the green and cloudy Austrian land, the merry trout have many a joyous home, but none is fairer or more beloved by them than this lovely lake of Hohenszalras; so green that it might have been made of emeralds dissolved in sunbeams, so deep that at its centre no soundings can be taken, so lonely that of the few wanderers who pass from S. Johann im Wald or from Lienz to Matrey, even of those few scarce one in a summer will know that a lake lies there, though they see from afar off its great castle standing, many-turreted and pinnacled, with its frowning keep, backed by the vast black forests, clothing slopes whose summits hide themselves in cloud, whilst through the cold clear air the golden vulture and the throated eagle wing their way.

The lake lies like a crystal bedded in rock, lovely and lonely as the little Gosausee when the skies are fair; perilous and terrible as the great Königs-See in storm, when the north wind is racing in from the Bœhmervald and the Polish steppes, and the rain-mists are dark and dense, and the storks leave their home on the chapel roof because the winter draws nigh. It is fed by snow and ice descending from a hundred hills, and by underground streams and headlong-descending avalanches, and in its turn feeds many a mountain waterfall, many a mountain tarn, many a woodland brook, and many a village fountain. The great white summits tower above it, and the dense still woods enshroud it ; there are a pier and harbour at either end, but these are only used by the village people, and once a year by pilgrims who come to the Sacred Island in its midst; pilgrims who flock thither from north, south, east, and west, for the chapel of the Szalrassee is as renowned and blessed as the silver shrine of holy Mariazell itself.

On the right bank of its green glancing water, looking towards the ice-peaks of the Glöckner on the east, and on the south towards the Kitchbull mountains and the limestone Alps, a promontory juts out into the lake and soars many hundred feet above it. It is of hard granite rock. Down one of its sides courses a torrent, the other side is clothed with wood ; on the summit is the immense building that is called the Hohenszalrasburg, a mass of towers and spires and high metal roofs and frowning battlements, with a huge square fortress at one end of them : it is the old castle of the Counts of Szalras, and the huge donjon keep of it has been there twelve centuries, and in all these centuries no man has ever seen its flag furled or its portcullis drawn up for a conqueror's entry.

The greater part of the Schloss now existing is the work of Meister Wenzel of Klosterneuburg, begun in 1350, but the date of the keep and of the foundations generally are much earlier, and the prisons and clock tower are Romanesque. Majestic, magnificent, and sombre, though not gloomy, by reason of its rude decoration and the brilliant colours of its variegated roofs, it is scarcely changed since its lords dwelt there in the fourteenth century, when their great banner, black vultures on a ground of gold and red, floated then high up amongst the clouds, even as it now shakes its heavy folds out on the strong wind that blew so keenly from the Prussian and the Polish plains due north.

It is a fortress that has wedded a palace; it is majestic, powerful, imposing, splendid, like the great race of which it so long has been the stronghold and the birthplace. But it is as lonely in the quiet heart of the everlasting hills as any falcon's or heron's nest hung in the oak branches.

And this loneliness seemed its sweetest charm in the eyes of its châtelaine and mistress, the Countess Wanda von Szalras, as she leaned one evening over the balustrade of her terrace, watching for the after-glow to warm the snows of the Glöckner. She held in her hand an open letter from her Kaiserin, and the letter in its conclusion said: 'You have sorrowed and tarried in seclusion long enough—too long; longer than he would have wished you to do. Come back to us and to the world.'

And Wanda von Szalras thought to herself: 'What can the world give me? What I love is Hohenszalras on earth, and Bela in heaven.'

What could the world give her indeed? The world cannot give back the dead. She wanted nothing of the world. She was rich in all that it can ever give.

In the time of Ferdinand the Second those who were then Counts of Szalras had stitched the cloth cross on their sleeves and gone with the Emperor to the Third Crusade. In gratitude for their escape, father and son, from the perils of Palestine and the dangers of the high seas and of the treacherous Danube water, from Moslem steel, and fever of Jaffa, and chains of swarming Barbary corsairs, they, returning at last in safety to their eyrie above the Szalrassee, had raised a chapel on the island in the lake, and made it dedicate to the Holy Cross. A Szalras of the following generation, belonging to the Dominican community, and being a man of such saintly fervour and purity

that he was canonised by Innocent, had dwelt
on the Holy Isle, and given to it the benediction
and the tradition of his sanctity and good works.
As centuries went on the holy fame of the
shrine where the Crusader had placed a branch
from a thorn-tree of Nazareth grew, and gained
in legend and in miracle, and became as adored
an object of pilgrimage as the Holy Phial of
Heiligenblut. All the Hohe Tauern, and throngs
even from Karinthia on the one side and Tirol
on the other, came thither on the day of
Ascension.

The old faith still lives, very simple, warm,
and earnest, in the heart of Austria, and with
that day-dawn in midsummer thousands of
peasant-folks flock from mountain villages and
forest châlets and little remote secluded towns, to
speed over the green lake with flaming crucifix
and floating banner, and chaunted anthem echoed
from hill to hill. One of those days of pilgrimage had made her mistress of Hohenszalras.

It was a martial and mighty race this which
in the heart of the green Tauern had made of
fealty to God and the Emperor a religion for
itself and all its dependants. The Counts of
Szalras had always been proud, stern, and noble
men : though their records were often stained
with fierce crimes, there was never in them any
single soil of baseness, treachery, or fear. They

had been fierce and reckless in the wild days
when they were for ever at war with the Counts
of Tirol and the warlike Archbishops of Salzburg.
Then with the Renaissance they had become no
less powerful, but more lettered, more courtly,
and more splendid, and had given alike friendship and service to the Habsburg. Now, of all
these princely and most powerful people there
was but one descendant, but one representative;
and that one was a woman.

Solferino had seen Count Gela fall charging
at the head of his own regiment of horse;
Magenta had seen Count Victor cut in two by
a cannon-shot as he rode with the dragoons of
Swartzenberg; and but a few years later the
youngest, Count Bela, had been drowned by
his own bright lake.

Their father had died of grief for his eldest
son; their mother had been lost to them in infancy; Bela and Wanda had grown up together,
loving each other as only two lonely children
can. She had been his elder by a few years,
and he younger than his age by reason of his
innocent simplicity of nature and his delicacy
of body. They had always thought to make
a priest of him, and when that peaceful future
was denied him on his becoming the sole heir,
it was the cause of bitter though mute sorrow
to the boy, who was indeed so like a young

saint in church legends that the people called him tenderly *der Heilige Graf.* He had never quitted Hohenszalras, and he knew every peasant around, every blossom that blew, every mountain path, every forest beast and bird, and every tale of human sorrow in his principality. When he became lord of all after his brother's death he was saddened and oppressed by the sense of his own overwhelming obligations. 'I am but the steward of God,' he would say, with a tender smile, to the poor who blessed him.

One Ascension Day the lake was, as usual, crowded with the boats of pilgrims ; the morning was fair and cloudless, but, after noontide, wind arose, the skies became overcast, and one of the sudden storms of the country burst over the green waters. The little lord of Hohenszalras was the first to see the danger to the clumsy heavy boats crowded with country people, and with his household rowed out to their aid. The storm had come so suddenly and with such violence that it smote, in the very middle of the lake, some score of these boats laden with the pilgrims of the Pinzgau and the Innthal, women chiefly ; their screams pierced through the noise of the roaring winds, and their terror added fresh peril to the dangers of the lake, which changed in a few moments to a

seething whirlpool, and flung them to and fro like.
coots' nests in a flood. The young Bela with
his servants saved many, crossing and recrossing
the furious space of wind-lashed, leaping,
foaming water; but on the fourth voyage back
the young Count's boat, over-burdened with
trembling peasants, whose fright made them
blind and restive, dipped heavily on one side,
filled, and sank. Bela could swim well, and
did swim, even to the very foot of his own
castle rock, where a hundred hands were out-
stretched to save him; but, hearing a drowning
woman's moan, he turned and tried to reach
her. A fresh surge of the hissing water, a
fresh gust of the bitter north wind, tossed him
back into a yawning gulf of blackness, and
drove him headlong, and with no more resistance in him than if he had been a broken
bough, upon the granite wall of his own rocks.
He was caught and rescued almost on the
instant by his own men, but his head had
struck upon the stone, and he was senseless.
He breathed a few hours, but he never spoke
or opened his eyes or gave any sign of conscious life, and before the night had far advanced his innocent body was tenantless and
cold, and his sweet spirit lived only in men's
memories. His sister, who was absent at that
time at the court of her Empress, became by

—his death the mistress of Hohenszalras and the last of her line.

When the tidings of his heroic end reached her at the imperial hunting-place of Gödöllö all the world died for her; that splendid pageant of a world, whose fairest and richest favours had been always showered on the daughter of the mighty House of Szalras. She withdrew herself from her friends, from her lovers, from her mistress, and mourned for him with a grief that time could do little to assuage, nothing to efface. She was then twenty years of age.

She was thinking of that death now, four years later, as she stood on the terrace which overhung the cruel rocks that had killed him.

His loss was to her a sorrow that could never wholly pass away.

Her other brothers had been dear to her, but only as brilliant young soldiers are to a little child who sees them seldom. But Bela had been her companion, her playmate, her friend, her darling. From Bela she had been scarce ever parted. Every day and every night, herself, and all her thoughts and all her time, were given to such administration of her kingdom as should best be meet in the sight of God and his angels. 'I am but Bela's almoner, as he was God's steward,' she said.

She leaned against the parapet, and looked across the green and shining water, the open letter hanging in her hand.

The Countess Wanda von Szalras was a beautiful woman; but she had that supreme distinction which eclipses beauty, that subtle, indescribable grace and dignity which are never seen apart from some great lineage with long traditions of culture, courtesy, and courage. She was very tall, and her movements had a great repose and harmony in them; her figure, richness and symmetry. Her eyes were of a deep brown hue, like the velvety brown of a stag's throat; they were large, calm, proud, and meditative. Her mouth was very beautiful; her hair was light and golden; her skin exceedingly fair. She was one of the most beautiful women of her country, and one of the most courted and the most flattered; and her imperial mistress said now to her, 'Come back to us and to the world.'

Standing upon her terrace, in a gown of pale grey velvet that had no ornament save an old gold girdle with an enamelled missal hung to it, with two dogs at her side, one the black hunting-hound of St. Hubert, the other the white sleuth-hound of Russia, she looked like a châtelaine of the days of Mary of Burgundy or Elizabeth of Thuringia. It seemed as if the dark cedar boughs behind her should lift and admit to her presence some lover with her glove against the plume of his hat, and her ring set in his sword-hilt, who would bow down before her feet and not dare to touch her hand unbidden.

But no lover was there. The Countess Wanda dismissed all lovers; she was wedded to the memory of her brother, and to her own liberty and power.

She leaned on the stone parapet of her castle and gazed on the scene that her eyes had rested on since they had first seen the light, yet of which she never wearied. The intense depth of colour, that is the glory of Austria, was deepening with each moment that the sun went nearer to its setting in the dark blue of thunder-clouds that brooded in the west, over the Venediger and the Zillerthal Alps. Soon the sun would pass that barrier of stone and ice, and evening would fall here in the mountains of the Iselthal, whilst it would be still day for the plains of the Ober Pinzgau and Salzkammergut. But as yet the radiance was here; and the dark oak woods and birch woods, the purple pine forests, the blue lake waters, and the glaciers of the Glöckner range, had all that grandeur which makes a sunset in these highlands at once so splendid and so peaceful. There is an infinite sense of peace in those cool, vast, unworn mountain solitudes, with the rain-mists sweeping like spectral armies over the level lands below, and the sun-rays slanting heavenward, like the spears of an angelic host. There is such abundance of rushing water, of deep grass, of endless shade, of forest trees, of heather and pine, of torrent and tarn; and beyond these are the great peaks that loom through breaking clouds, and the clear cold air, in which the vulture wheels and the heron sails; and the shadows are so deep, and the stillness is so sweet, and the earth seems so green, and fresh, and silent, and strong. Nowhere else can one rest so well; nowhere else is there so fit a refuge for all the faiths and fancies that can find a home no longer in the harsh and hurrying world: there is room for them all in the Austrian forests, from the Erl-King to Ariel and Oberon.

The Countess Wanda leaned against the balustrade of the terrace and watched that banquet of colour on land and cloud and water; watched till the sun sank out of sight behind the Venediger snows, and the domes of the Glöckner, and all the lesser peaks opposite were changing from the warmth, as of a summer rose, to a pure transparent grey, that seemed here and there to be pierced as with fire.

'How often do we thank God for the

mountains?' she thought; 'yet we ought
every night that we pray.'

Then she sighed as her eyes sank from the
hill-tops to the lake water, dark as iron,
glittering as steel, now that the radiance of the
sun had passed off it.   She remembered Bela.

How could she ever forget him, with that
murderous water shining for ever at her feet?

The world called her undiminished tenderness for her dead brother a morbid grief, but
then to the world at large any fidelity seems so
strange and stupid a waste of years : it does not
understand that *tout casse, tout lasse, tout passe,*
was not written for strong natures.

'How could I ever forget him, so long as
that water glides there?' she thought, as her
eyes rested on the emerald and sparkling lake.

'Yet her Majesty is so right! So right
and so wise!' said a familiar voice at her side.

And there came up to her the loveliest little
lady in all the empire; an old lady, but so
delicate, so charming, so pretty, so fragile, that
she seemed lovelier than all the young ones;
a very fairy godmother, covered up in lace
and fur, and leaning on a gold-headed cane,
and wearing red shoes with high gilt heels, and
smiling with serene blue eyes, as though she
had just stepped down out of a pictured copy of
Cinderella, and could change common pumpkins

into gilded chariots, and mice into horses, at a wish.

She was the Princess Ottilie of Lilienhöhe, and had once been head of a religious house.

'Her Majesty is so right!' she said once more, with emphasis.

The Countess Wanda turned and smiled, rather with her eyes than with her lips.

'It would not become my loyal affection to say she could be wrong. But still, I know myself, and I know the world very well, and I far prefer Hohenszalras to it.'

'Hohenszalras is all very well in the summer and autumn,' said Princess Ottilie, with a glance of anything but love at the great fantastic solemn pile; 'but for a woman of your age and your possessions to pass your days talking to farmers and fishermen, poring over books, perplexing yourself as to whether it is right for you to accept wealth that comes from such a source of danger to human life as your salt mines— it is absurd, it is ludicrous. You are made for something more than a political economist; you should be in the great world.'

'I prefer my solitude and my liberty.'

'Liberty! Who or what could dictate to you in the world? You reigned there once; you would always reign there.'

'Social life is a bondage, as an empress's

is. It denies one the greatest luxury of life—
solitude.'

'Certainly, if you love solitude so much,
you have your heart's desire here. It is an
Alvernia! It is a Mount Athos! It is a snow-
entombed paraclete, a hermitage, only tempered
by horses!' said the Princess, with a little
angry laugh.

Her grand-niece smiled.

'By many horses, certainly. Dearest aunt,
what would you have? Austrians are all cen-
taurs and amazons. I am only like my Kaiserin
in that passion.'

The Princess sighed.

She had never been able to comprehend the
forest life, the daring, the intrepidity, the open-
air pastimes, and the delight in danger which
characterised all the race of Szalras. Daughter
of a North German princeling, and with some
French blood in her veins also, reared under
the formal etiquette of her hereditary court,
and at an early age canoness of one of those
great semi-religious orders which are only open
to the offspring of royal or of most noble lines,
her whole life had been one moulded to form
and conventional habit, and only her own
sweetness and sprightliness of temper had saved
her from the narrowness of judgment and the
chilliness of formality which such a life begets.

The order of which until late years she had
been superior was one for magnificence and
wealth unsurpassed in Europe ; but, semi-secular
in its privileges, it had left her much liberty,
and never wholly divorced her from the world,
which in an innocent way she had always loved
and enjoyed.   After Count Victor's death she
had resigned her office on plea of age and
delicacy of health, and had come to take up her
residence at Hohenszalras with her dead niece's
children.   She had done so because she had
believed it to be her duty, and her attachment
to Wanda and Bela had always been very great;
but she had never learned to love the solitude of
the Hohe Tauern, or ceased to regard Hohenszalras as a place of martyrdom.   After the minute
divisions of every hour and observances of every
smallest ceremonial that she had been used to
at her father's own little court of Lilienslüst,
and in her own religious house, where every
member of the order was a daughter of some
one of the highest families of Germany or
of Austria, the life at Hohenszalras, with its
outdoor pastimes, its feudal habits, its vast
liberties for man and beast, and its long frozen
winters, when not a soul could come near it from
over the passes, seemed very terrible to her.
She could never understand her niece's passionate attachment to it, and she in real truth

only breathed entirely at ease in those few
weeks of the year which to please her niece
she consented to pass away from the Hohe
Tauern.

'Surely you will go to Ischl or go to
Gödöllö this autumn, since Her Majesty wishes
it ?' she said now, with an approving glance at
the imperial letter.

'Her Majesty is so kind as always to wish it,'
answered the Countess Wanda. 'Let us leave
time to show what it holds for us. This is
scarcely summer. Yesterday was the fifteenth
of May.'

'It is horribly cold,' said the Princess,
drawing her silver-grey fur about her. 'It is
always horribly cold here, even in midsummer.
And when it does not snow it rains; you cannot
deny *that.*'

'Come, come! we have seen the sun all day
to-day. I hope we shall see it many days, for
they have begun planting-out, you see—the
garden will soon be gorgeous.'

'When the mist allows it to be seen, it will
be, I dare say,' said Princess Ottilie, somewhat
pettishly. 'It is tolerable here in the summer,
though never agreeable ; but the Empress is so
right, it is absurd to shut yourself longer up
in this gloomy place ; you are bound to return

to the world. You owe it to your position to be seen in it once more.'

'The world does not want me, my dear aunt ; nor do I want the world.'

'That is sheer perversity——'

'How am I perverse? I know the world very well, and I know that no one is necessary to it, unless it be Herr von Bismarck.'

'I do not see what Herr von Bismarck has to do with your going back to your natural manner of life,' said the Princess, severely, who abhorred any sort of levity in regard to the mighty minister who had destroyed the Lilien-höhe princes one fine morning, as indifferently as a boy plucks down a cranberry bough. 'In summer, or even autumn, Hohenszalras is en- durable, but in winter it is—hyperborean— even you must grant that. One might as well be jammed in a ship, amidst icebergs, in the midst of a frozen sea.'

'And you were born on the Elbe, oh fie! But indeed, my dearest aunt, I like the frozen sea. The white months have no terrors for me. What you call, and what calls itself, the great world is far more narrow than the Iselthal. Here one's fancies, at least, can fly high as the eagles do ; in the world who can rise out of the hot-house air of the salons, and see beyond the doings of one's friends and foes?'

'Surely one's own friends and foes—people like oneself, in a word—must be as interesting as Hans, and Peter, and Katte, and Grethel, with their crampons or their milkpails,' said the Princess, with impatience. 'Besides, surely in the world there are political movement, influence, interests.'

'Oh, intrigue?—as useful as Mdme. de Laballe's or Mdme. de Longueville's? No! I do not believe there is even that in our time, when even diplomacy itself is fast becoming a mere automatic factor in a world that is governed by newspapers, and which has changed the tyranny of wits for the tyranny of crowds. The time is gone by when a "Coterie of Countesses" could change ministries, if they ever did do so outside the novels of Disraeli. Drawing-room cabals may still do some mischief perhaps, but they can do no good. Sometimes, indeed, I think that what is called Government everywhere is nothing but a gigantic mischief-making and place-seeking. The State is everywhere too like a mother who sweeps her doorstep diligently, and scolds the neighbours, while her child scalds itself to death unseen within.'

'In the world,' interrupted the Princess oppositely, 'you might persuade them that the sweeping of doorsteps is not sufficient——'

'I prefer to keep my own house in order.
It is quite enough occupation,' said the Countess
Wanda, with a smile. 'Dear aunt, here amongst
my own folks I can do some real good, I have
some tangible influence, I can feel that my life
is not altogether spent in vain. Why should
I exchange these simple and solid satisfactions.
for the frivolities and the inanities of a life of
pleasure which would not even please me?'

'You are very hard to please, I know,'
retorted the Princess. 'But say what you will,
it becomes ridiculous for a person of your age,
your great position, and your personal beauty,
to immure yourself eternally in what is virtually
no better than confinement to a fortress!'

'A court is more of a prison to me,' said
Wanda von Szalras. 'I know both lives, and
I prefer this life. As for my being very hard to
please, I think I was very gay and mirthful
before Bela's death. Since then all the earth has
grown grey for me.'

'Forgive me, my beloved!' said Princess
Ottilie, with quick contrition, whilst moisture
sprang into her limpid and still luminous blue
eyes.

Wanda von Szalras took the old abbess's
hand in her own, and kissed it.

'I understand all you wish for me, dear
aunt. Believe me, I envy people when I hear

them laughing light-heartedly amongst each other.   I think I shall never laugh *so* again.'

'If you would only marry——' said the Princess, with some hesitation.

'You think marriage amusing?' she said, with a certain contempt.   'If you do, it is only because you escaped it.'

'Amusing!' said the Princess, a little scandalised.   'I could speak of no Sacrament of our Holy Church as "amusing."   You rarely display such levity of language.   I confess I do not comprehend you.   Marriage would give you interests in life which you seem to lack sadly now.   It would restore you to the world. It would be a natural step to take with such vast possessions as yours.'

'It is not likely I shall ever take it,' said Wanda von Szalras, drawing the soft fine ear of Donau through her fingers.

'I know it is not likely.   I am very sorry that it is not likely.   Yet what nobler creature does God's earth contain than your cousin Egon?'

'Egon?   No: he is a good and brave and loyal gentleman, none better; but I shall no more marry him than Donau here will wed a forest doe.'

'Yet he has loved you for ten years.   But if not he there are so many others, men of high enough place to be above all suspicion of mercenary motive. No woman has been more adored than you, Wanda. Look at Hugo Landrassy.'

'Oh, pray spare me their enumeration. It is like the Catalogue of Ships!' said the Countess Wanda, with some coldness and some impatience on her face.

At that moment an old man, who was major-domo of Hohenszalras, approached and begged with deference to know whether his ladies would be pleased to dine.

The Princess signified her readiness with alacrity; Wanda von Szalras signed assent with less willingness.

'What a disagreeable obligation dining is,' she said, as she turned reluctantly from the evening scene, with the lake sleeping in dusk and shadow, while the snow summits still shone like silver and glowed with rose.

'It is very wicked to think so,' said her great-aunt. 'When a merciful Creator has appointed our appetites for our consolation and support it is only an ingrate who is not thankful lawfully to indulge them.'

'That view of them never occurred to me,' said the châtelaine of Hohenszalras. 'I think you must have stolen it, aunt, from some abbé galant or some chanoinesse as lovely as yourself in the last century. Alas! if not to care to eat be ungrateful I am a sad ingrate. Donau and Neva are more ready subscribers to your creed.'

Donau and Neva were already racing towards the castle, and Wanda von Szalras, with one backward lingering glance to the sunset, which already was fading, followed them with slow steps to the grand house of which she was mistress.

In the north alone the sky was overcast and of a tawny colour, where the Pinzgau lay, with the green Salzach water rushing through its wooded gorges, and its tracks of sand and stone desolate as any desert.

That slender space of angry yellow to the north boded ill for the night. Bitter storms rolled in west from the Bœhmerwald, or north from the Salzkammergut, many a time in the summer weather, changing it to winter as they passed, tugging at the roof-ropes of the châlets, driving the sheep into their sennerin's huts, covering with mist and rain the mountain sides, and echoing in thunder from the peaks of the Untersburg to the snows of the Ortler Spitze. It was such a sudden storm which had taken Bela's life.

'I think we shall have wild weather,' said the Princess, drawing her furs around her, as she walked down the broad length of the stone terrace.

'I think so too,' said Wanda. 'It is coming very soon; and I fear I did a cruel thing this morning.'

'What was that?'

'I sent a stranger to find his way over our hills to Matrey, as best he might. He will hardly have reached it by now, and if a storm should come——'

'A stranger?' said Princess Ottilie, whose curiosity was always alive, and had also lately no food for its hunger.

'Only a poacher; but he was a gentleman, which made his crime the worse.'

'A gentleman, and you sent him over the hills without a guide? It seems unlike the hospitality of Hohenszalras.'

'Why he would have shot a *kuttengeier*!'

'A *kuttengeier* is a horrible beast,' said the Princess, with a shudder; 'and a stranger, just for an hour or so, would be welcome.'

'Even if his name were not in the Hof-Kalender?' asked her niece, smiling.

'If he had been a pedlar, or a clockmaker, you would have sent him in to rest. For a gentlewoman, Wanda, and so proud a one as you are, you become curiously cruel to your own class.'

'I am always cruel to poachers. And to shoot a vulture in the month of May!'

CHAPTER II.

THE dining-hall was a vast chamber, panelled and ceiled with oak. In the centre of the panels were emblazoned shields bearing the arms of the Szalras, and of the families with which they had intermarried; the long lancet windows had been painted by no less a hand than that of Jacob of Ulm; the knights' stalls which ran round the hall were the elaborate carving of Georges Syrlin; and old gorgeous banners dropped down above them, heavy with broideries and bullion.

There were upper servants in black clothes with knee breeches, and a dozen lacqueys in crimson and gold liveries, ranged about the table. In many ways there were a carelessness and ease in the household which always seemed lamentable to the Princess Ottilie, but in matters of etiquette the great household was ruled like a small court; and when sovereigns became guests there little in the order of the day needed change at Hohenszalras.

The castle was half fortress, half palace; a noble and solemn place, which had seen many centuries of warfare, of splendour, and of alternate war and joy. Strangers used to Paris gilding, to Italian sunlight, to English country-houses, found it too severe, too august, too dark, and too stern in its majesty, and were awed by it. But she who had loved it and played in it in infancy changed nothing there, but cherished it as it had come to her; and it was in all much the same as it had been in the days of Henry the Lion, from its Gothic Silber-kapelle, that was like an ivory and jewelled casket set in dusky silver, to its immense Rittersaal, with a hundred knights in full armour standing down it, as the bronze figures stand round Maximilian's empty tomb in Tirol. There are many such noble places hidden away in the deep forests and the mountain glens of Maximilian's empire.

In this hall there were some fifteen persons standing. They were the priest, the doctor, the high steward, the almoner, some dames de compagnie, and some poor ladies, widows or spinsters, who subsisted on the charities of Hohenszalras. The two noble ladies bowed to them all and said a few kind words; then passed on and seated themselves at their own table, whilst these other persons took their seats noiselessly at a longer table, behind a low screen of carved oak.

The lords of Hohenszalras had always thus adhered to the old feudal habit of dining in public, and in royal fashion, thus.

The Countess Wanda and her aunt spoke little; the one was thinking of many other things than of the food brought to her, the other was enjoying to the uttermost each *bouchée*, each *relevée*, each morsel of quail, each mouthful of wine-stewed trout, each succulent truffle, and each rich drop of crown Tokaï.

The repast was long, and to one of them extremely tedious; but these formal and prolonged ceremonials had been the habit of her house, and Wanda von Szalras carefully observed all hereditary usage and custom. When her aunt had eaten her last fruit, and she herself had broken her last biscuit between the dogs, they rose, one glad that the most tiresome, and the other regretful that the most pleasant, hour of the uneventful day was over.

With a bow of farewell to the standing household, they went by mutual consent their

divers ways; the Princess to her favourite blue
room and her after-dinner doze, Wanda to her
own study, the chamber most essentially her
own, where all were hers.

The softness and radiance of the after-glow
had given place to night and rain; the mists
and the clouds had rolled up from the Zillerthal Alps, and the water was pouring from the
skies.

Lamps, wax candles, flambeaux, burning
in sconces or upheld by statues or swinging
from chains, were illumining the darkness
of the great castle, but in her own study only
one little light was shining, for she, a daughter
of the mystical mountains and forests, loved the
shadows of the night.

She seated herself here by the unshuttered
casement. The full moon was rising above
the Glöckner range, and the rain-clouds as
yet did not obscure it, though a film of
falling water veiled all the westward shore
of the lake, and all the snows on the peaks
and crests of the Venediger. She leaned her
elbows on the cushioned seat, and looked out
into the night.

'Bela, my Bela! are you content with me?'
she murmured. To her Bela was as living as
though he were present by her side; she lived in
the constant belief of his companionship and

his sight. Death was a cruel—ah, how cruel!—
wall built up between him and her, forbidding
them the touch of each other's hands, denying
them the smile of each other's eyes; but none
the less to her was he there, unseen, but ever
near, hidden behind that inexorable, invisible
barrier which one day would fall and let her
pass and join him.

She sat idle in the embrasure of the oriel
window, whilst the one lamp burned behind
her. This, her favourite room, had scarcely
been changed since Maria Theresa, on a visit
there, had made it her bower-room. The
window-panes had been painted by Selier of
Landshut in 1440; the stove was one of Hirsch-
vögel's; the wood-carvings had been done by
Schuferstein; there was silver *repoussé* work of
Kellerthaler, tapestries of Marc de Comans,
enamels of Elbertus of Köln, of Jean of Limoges,
of Leonard Limousin, of Penicaudius; embroidered stuffs of Isabeau Maire, damascened
armour once worn by Henry the Lion, a
painted spinet that had belonged to Isabella
of Bavaria, and an ivory Book of Hours, once
used by Carolus Magnus; and all these things,
like the many other treasures of the castle, had
been there for centuries; gifts from royal
guests, spoils of foreign conquest, memorials of
splendid embassies or offices of state held by

the lords of Szalras, or marriage presents at
magnificent nuptials in the old magnificent
ages.

In this room she, their sole living representative, was never disturbed on any pretext.
In the adjacent library (a great cedar-lined
room, holding half a million volumes, with
many missals and early classics, and many an
editio princeps of the Renaissance), she held all
her audiences, heard all petitions or complaints,
audited her accounts, conversed with her ten-
ants or her stewards, her lawyers or her
peasants, and laboured earnestly to use to the
best of her intelligence the power bequeathed
to her.

'I am but God's and Bela's steward, as my
steward is mine,' she said always to herself, and
never avoided any duty or labour entailed on
her, never allowed weariness or self-indulgence
to enervate her. *Qui facit per alium, facit per se*
had been early taught to her, and she never
forgot it. She never did anything vicariously
which concerned those dependent upon her.
And she was an absolute sovereign in this her
kingdom of glaciers and forests; her frozen sea
as she had called it. She never avoided a duty
merely because it was troublesome, and she
never gave her signature without knowing why
and wherefore. It is easy to be generous; to be

just is more difficult and burdensome. Generous by temper, she strove earnestly to be always just as well, and her life was not without those fatigues which a very great fortune brings with it to anyone who regards it as a sacred trust.

She had wide possessions and almost incalculable wealth. She had salt mines in Galicia, she had Vosläuer vineyards in the Salzkammergut, she had vast plains of wheat, and leagues on leagues of green lands, where broods of horses bred and reared away in the steppes of Hungary. She had a palace in the Herrengasse at Vienna, another in the Residenzplatz of Salzburg; she had forests and farms in the Innthal and the Zillerthal; she had a beautiful little schloss on the green Ebensee, which had been the dower-house of the Countesses of Szalras, and she had pine-woods, quarries, vineyards, and even a whole riverain town on the Danube, with a right to take toll on the ferry there, which had been given to her forefathers as far back as the days of Mathias Carvin, a right that she herself had let drop into desuetude. 'I do not want the poor folks' copper kreutzer,' she said to her lawyers when they remonstrated. What did please her was the fact coupled with this right that even the Kaiser could not have entered her little town without his marshal thrice knocking at the gates, and receiving from

the warder the permission to pass, in the words,
'The Counts of Idrac bid you come in peace.'

All these things and places made a vast
source of revenue, and the property, whose title-
deeds and archives lay in many a chest and
coffer in the old city of Salzburg, was one of the
largest in Europe. It would have given large
portions and dowries to a score of sons and
daughters and been none the worse. And it
was all accumulating on the single head of one
young and lonely woman! She was the last of
her race; there were distant collateral branches,
but none of them near enough to have any title
to Hohenszalras. She could bequeath it where
she would, and she had already willed it to her
Kaiserin, in a document shut up in an iron
chest in the city of Salzburg. She thought the
Crown would be a surer and juster guardian
of her place and people than any one person,
whose caprices she could not foretell, whose
extravagance or whose injustice she could not
foresee. Sometimes, even to the spiritual mind
of the Princess Ottilie, the persistent refusal of
her niece to think of any marriage seemed
almost a crime against mankind.

What did the Crown want with it?

The Princess was a woman of absolutely
loyal sentiment towards all ancient sovereign-
ties. She believed in Divine right, and was as

strong a royalist as it is possible for anyone to be whose fathers have been devoured like an anchovy by M. de Bismarck, and who has the sympathy of fellow feeling with Frohsdorf and Gmünden. But even her devotion to the rights of monarchs failed to induce her to see why the Habsburg should inherit Hohenszalras. The Crown is a noble heir, but it is one which leaves the heart cold. Who would ever care for her people, and her forests, and her animals as she had done? Even from her beloved Kaiserin she could not hope for that. 'If I had married?' she thought, the words of the Princess Ottilie coming back upon her memory.

Perhaps, for the sake of her people and her lands, it might have been better.

But there are women to whom the thought of physical surrender of themselves is fraught with repugnance and disgust; a sentiment so strong that only a great passion vanquishes it. She was one of these women, and passion she had never felt.

'Even for Hohenszalras I could not,' she thought, as she leaned on the embrasure cushions, and watched the moon, gradually covered with the heavy blue-black clouds. The Crown should be her heir and reign here after her, when she should be laid by the side of Bela in that

beautiful dusky chapel beneath the shrines of
ivory and silver, where all the dead of the
House of Szalras slept. But it was an heir
which left her heart cold.

She rose abruptly, left the embrasure, and
began to examine the letters of the day and put
down heads of replies to them, which her
secretary could amplify on the morrow.

One letter her secretary could not answer
for her; it was a letter which gave her pain,
and which she read with an impatient sigh. It
urged her return to the world as the letter of
her Empress had done, and it urged with
timidity, yet with passion, a love that had been
loyal to her from her childhood. It was
signed ' Egon Vàsàrhely.'

' It is the old story,' she thought. ' Poor
Egon ! If only one could have loved him, how
it would have simplified everything; and I do
love him, as I once loved Gela and Victor.'

But that was not the love which Egon
Vàsàrhely pleaded for with the tenderness of
one who had been to her as a brother from her
babyhood, and the frankness of a man who
knew his own rank so high and his own fortunes
so great, that no mercenary motive could be
attributed to him even when he sought the
mistress of Hohenszalras. It was the old story :
she had heard it many times from him and from

others in those brilliant winters in Vienna which had preceded Bela's death. And it had always failed to touch her. Women who have never loved are harsh to love from ignorance.

At that moment a louder crash of thunder reverberated from hill to hill, and the Glöckner domes seemed to shout to the crests of the Venediger.

'I hope that stranger is housed and safe,' she thought, her mind reverting to the poacher of whom she had spoken on the terrace at sunset. His face came before her memory: a beautiful face, oriental in feature, northern in complexion, fair and cold, with blue eyes of singular brilliancy.

The forests of Hohenszalras are in themselves a principality. Under enormous trees, innumerable brooks and little torrents dash downwards to lose themselves in the green twilight of deep gorges; broad, dark, still lakes lie like cups of jade in the bosom of the woods; up above, where the Alpine firs and the pinus cembra shelter him, the bear lives and the wolf too; and higher yet, where the glacier lies upon the mountain side, the merry steinbock leaps from peak to peak, and the white-throat vulture and the golden eagle nest. The oak, the larch, the beech, the lime, cover the lower hills, higher grow the pines and firs, the lovely drooping Siberian pine foremost amidst them. In the lower wood grassy roads cross and thread the leafy twilight. A stranger had been traversing these woods that morning, where he had no right or reason to be. Forest-law was sincerely observed and meted out at Hohenszalras, but of that he was ignorant or careless.

Before him, in the clear air, a large, dark object rose and spread huge pinions to the wind and soared aloft. The trespasser lifted his rifle to his shoulder, and in another moment would have fired. But an alpenstock struck the barrel up into the air, and the shot went off harmless towards the clouds. The great bird, startled by the report, flew rapidly to the westward; the Countess Wanda said quietly to the poacher in her forest, 'You cannot carry arms here.'

He looked at her angrily, and in surprise.

'You have lost me the only eagle I have seen for years,' he said bitterly, with a flush of discomfiture and powerless rage on his fair face.

She smiled a little.

'That bird was not an eagle, sir; it was a white-throated vulture, a *kuttengeier*. But had it been an eagle—or a sparrow—you could not have killed it on my lands.'

Pale still with anger, he uncovered his head.

'I have not the honour to know in whose presence I stand,' he muttered sullenly. 'But I have Imperial permission to shoot wherever I choose.'

'His Majesty has no more loyal subject than myself,' she answered him. 'But his dominion does not extend over my forests. You are on the ground of Hohenszalras, and your offence——'

'I know nothing of Hohenszalras!' he interrupted, with impatience.

She blew a whistle, and her head forester with three jägers sprang up as if out of the earth, some great wolf-hounds, grinning with their fangs, waiting but a word to spring. In one second the rangers had thrown themselves on the too audacious trespasser, had pinioned him, and had taken his rifle.

Confounded, disarmed, humiliated, and stunned by the suddenness of the attack, he stood mute and very pale.

'You know Hohenszalras now!' said the mistress of it, with a smile, as she watched his seizure seated on a moss-grown boulder of granite, black Donau and white Neva by her side. He was pale with impotent fury, conscious of an indefensible and absurd position.

The jäger looked at their mistress; they had
slipped a cord over his wrists, and tied them
behind his back; they looked to her for a sign
of assent to break his rifle. She stood silent,
amused with her victory and his chastisement;
a little derision shining in her lustrous eyes.

'You know Hohenszalras now!' she said
once more. 'Men have been shot dead for what
you were doing. If you be, indeed, a friend
of my Emperor's, of course you are welcome
here; but——'

'What right have you to offer me this indignity,' muttered the offender, his fair features
changing from white to red, and red to white,
in his humiliation and discomfiture.

'Right!' echoed the mistress of the forests.
'I have the right to do anything I please with
you! You seem to me to understand but little
of forest laws.'

'Madame, were you not a woman, you
would have had bloodshed.'

'Oh, very likely. That sometimes happens,
although seldom, as all the Hohe Tauern knows
how strictly these forests are preserved. My
men are looking to me for permission to break
your rifle. That is the law, sir.'

'Since 'Forty-eight,' said the trespasser,
with what seemed to her marvellous insolence,

'all the old forest laws are null and void. It is scarcely allowable to talk of trespass.'

A look of deep anger passed over her face. 'The follies of 'Forty-eight have nothing to do with Hohenszalras,' she said, very coldly. 'We hold under charters of our own, by grants and rights which even Rudolf of Habsburg never dared meddle with. I am not called on to explain this to you, but you appear to labour under such strange delusions that it is as well to dispel them.'

He stood silent, his eyes cast downward. His humiliation seemed to him enormously disproportioned to his offending. The hounds menaced him with deep growls and grinning fangs; the jägers held his gun; his wrists were tied behind him. 'Are you indeed a friend of the Kaiser?' she repeated to him.

'I am no friend of his,' he answered bitterly and sullenly. 'I met him a while ago zad-hunting on the Thorstein. His signature is in my pocket; bid.your jäger take it out.'

'I will not doubt your word,' she said to him. 'You look a gentleman. If you will give me your promise to shoot no more on these lands I will let them set you free and render you up your rifle.'

'You have the law with you,' said the trespasser, moodily. 'Since I can do no less—I promise.'

'You are ungracious, sir,' said Wanda, with a touch of severity and irritation. 'That is neither wise nor grateful, since you are nothing more or better than a poacher on my lands. Nevertheless, I will trust you.'

Then she gave a sign to the jägers and a touch to the hounds: the latter rose and ceased their growling; the former instantly, though very sorrowfully, untied the cord off the wrists of their prisoner, and gave him back his un-loaded rifle.

'Follow that path into the ravine; cross that; ascend the opposite hills, and you will find the high road. I advise you to take it, sir. Good-day to you.'

She pointed out the forest path which wound downward under the arolla pines. He hesitated a moment, then bowed very low with much grace, turned his back on her and her foresters and her dogs, and began slowly to descend the moss-grown slope.

He hated her for the indignity she had brought upon him, and the ridicule to which she forced him to submit; yet the beauty of her had startled and dazzled him. He had thought of the great Queen of the Nibelungen-Lied, whose armour lies in the museum of Vienna.

'Alas! why have you let him go, my Countess!' murmured Otto, the head forester.

'The Kaiser had made him sacred,' she answered, with a smile; and then she called Donau and Neva, who were roaming, and went on her way through her forest.

'What strange and cruel creatures we are!' she thought. 'The vulture would have dropped into the ravine. He would never have found it. The audacity, too, to fire on a *kuttengeier*; if it had been any lesser bird one might have pardoned it.'

For the eagle, the gypæte, the white-throated pygargue, the buzzard, and all the family of falcons were held sacred at Hohen-szalras, and lived in their mountain haunts rarely troubled. It was an old law there that the great winged monarchs should never be chased, except by the Kaiser himself when he came there. So that the crime of the stranger had been more than trespass and al-most treason! Her heart was hard to him, and she felt that she had been too lenient. Who could tell but that that rifle would bring down some free lord of the air?

She listened with the keen ear of one used to the solitude of the hills and woods; she thought he would shoot something out of bravado. But all was silent in that green defile beneath whose boughs the stranger was wending on his way. She listened long, but she heard no shots, although in those still heights the slightest noise echoed from a hundred walls of rock and ice. She walked onward through the deep shadow of the thick growing beeches; she had her alpenstock in her right hand, her little silver horn hung at her belt, and beside it was a pair of small ivory pistols, pretty as toys, but deadly as revolvers could be. She stooped here and there to gather some lilies of the valley, which were common enough in these damp grassy glades.

'Where could that stranger have come from, Otto?' she asked of her jäger.

'He must have come over the Hündspitz, my Countess,' said Otto. 'Any other way he would have been stopped by our men and lightened of his rifle.'

'The Hündspitz!' she echoed, in wonder, for the mountain so called was a wild inaccessible place, divided by a parapet of ice all the year round from the range of the Gross Glöckner.

'That must he,' said the huntsman, 'and for sure if an honest man had tried to come that way he would have been hurled headlong down the ice-wall——'

'He is the Kaiser's *protégé*, Otto,' said his mistress, with a smile, but the old jäger muttered that they had only his own word for that. It had pierced Otto's soul to let the poacher's rifle go.

She thought of all this with some compunction now, as she sat in her own warm safe chamber and heard the thunder, the wind, the raising of the storm which had now fairly broken in full fury. She felt uneasy for the erring stranger. The roads over the passes were still perilous from avalanches and half melted snow in the crevasses ; the time of year was more dangerous than midwinter.

'I ought to have given him a guide,' she thought, and went out and joined the Princess Ottilie, who had awakened from her after-dinner repose under the loud roll of the thunder and the constantly recurring flashes of lightning.

'I am troubled for that traveller whom I saw in the woods to-day,' she said to her aunt. 'I trust he is safe housed.'

'If he had been a pastry-cook from the Engadine, or a seditious heretical *colporteur* from Geneva, you would have sent him into the kitchens to feast,'said the Princess, contentiously.

'I hope he is safe housed,' repeated Wanda. 'It is several hours ago ; he may very well have reached the posthouse.'

'You have the satisfaction of thinking the *kuttengeier* is safe, sitting on some rock tearing a fish to pieces,' said the Princess, who was irritable because she was awakened before her time. 'Will you have some coffee or some tea? You look disturbed, my dear; after all, you say the man was a poacher.'

'Yes. But I ought to have seen him safe off my ground. There are a hundred kinds of death on the hills for anyone who does not know them well. Let us look at the weather from the hall; one can see better from there.'

From the Rittersäal, whose windows looked straight down the seven miles of the lake water, she watched the tempest. All the mountains were sending back echoes of thunder, which sounded like salvoes of artillery. There was little to be seen for the dense rain mist; the beacon of the Holy Isle glimmered redly through the darkness. In the upper air snow was falling; the great white peaks and pinnacles ever and again flashed strangely into view as the lightning illumined them; the Glöckner-wanda towered above all others a moment in the glare, and seemed like ice and fire mingled.

'They are like the great white thrones of the Apocalypse,' she thought.

Beneath, the lake boiled and seethed in blackness like a witches' cauldron.

A storm was always terrible to her, from the memory of Bela.

In the lull of a second in the tempest of sound it seemed to her as if she heard some other cry than that of the wind.

'Open one of these windows and listen,' she said to Hubert, her major-domo. 'I fancy I hear a shout—a scream. I am not certain, but listen well.'

'There is some sound,' said Hubert, after a moment of attention. 'It comes from the lake. But no boat could live long in that water, my Countess.'

'No!' she said, with a quick sigh, remembering how her brother had died. 'But we must do what we can. It may be one of the lake fishermen caught in the storm before he could make for home. Ring the alarm-bell, and go out, all of you, to the water stairs. I will come, too.'

In a few moments the deep bell that hung in the chime tower, and which was never sounded except for death or danger, added its sonorous brazen voice to the clang and clamour of the storm. All the household paused, and at the summons, coming from north, south, east, and west of the great pile of buildings, grooms, gardeners, huntsmen, pages, scullions, underlings, all answered to the metal tongue, which told them of some peril at Hohenszalràs.

With a hooded cloak thrown over her, she

went out into the driving rain, down the terrace
to the head of what were called the water stairs ;
a flight of granite steps leading to the little quay
upon the eastward shore of the Szalrassee, where
were moored in fair weather the pleasure boats,
the fishing punts, and the canoes which belonged to the castle : craft all now safe in the
boat-house.

'Make no confusion,' she said to them.
'There is no danger in the castle. There is
some boat, or some swimmer, on the lake.
Light the terrace beacon and we shall see.'

She was very pale. There was no storm on
those waters that did not bring back to her, as
poignant as the first fresh hours of its grief, the
death of Bela.

The huge beacon of iron, a cage set on high
and filled with tow and tar and all inflammable
things, was set on fire, and soon threw a scarlet
glare over the scene.

The shouts had ceased.

'They may be drowned,' she said, with her
lips pressed tightly together. 'I hear nothing
now. Have you the rope and the lifeboat
ready? We must wait for more light.'

At that moment the whole of the tar caught,
and the beacon blazed at its fiercest in its iron
cage, as it had used to blaze in the ages gone
by as a war signal, when the Prelates of Salz-

burg and Birchtesgaden were marching across the marshes of Pinzgau in quarrel or feud with the lords of the strongest fortress in the Hohe Tauern.

In the struggling light which met the blue glance of the lightning they could see the angry waters of the lake as far as the Holy Isle, and near to land, only his head above the water, was a man drowning, as the pilgrims had drowned.

'For the love of God—the rope!' she cried, and almost before the words had escaped from her her men had thrown a lifebuoy to the exhausted swimmer, and pushed one of the boats into the seething darkness of the lake. But the swimmer had strength enough to catch hold of the buoy as it was hurled to him by the *fischermeister's* unerring hand, and he clung to it and kept his grasp on it, despite the raging of the wind and waters, until the boat reached him. He was fifty yards off the shore, and he was pulled into the little vessel, which was tossed to and fro upon the black waters like a shell; the *fohn* was blowing fiercely all the time, and flung the men headlong on the boat's bottom twice ere they could seize the swimmer, who helped himself, for, though mute and almost breathless, he was not insensible, and had not lost all his strength. If he had not been so near the land he and the boat's crew would all have sunk, and dead bodies would once more have been washed on the shore of the Szalrassee with the dawn of another day.

Drenched, choked with water, and thrown from side to side as the wind played with them as a child with its ball, the men ran their boat at last against the stairs, and landed with their prize.

Dripping from head to foot, and drawing deep breaths of exhaustion, the rescued man stood on the terrace steps bareheaded and in his shirt-sleeves, his brown velvet breeches pulled up to his knees, his fair hair lifted by the wind, and soaked with wet.

She recognised the trespasser of the forest.

'Madame, behold me in your power again!' he said, with a little smile, though he breathed with labour, and his voice was breathless and low.

'You are welcome, sir. Any stranger or friend would be welcome in such a night,' she said, with the red glow of the beacon light shed upon her. 'Pray do not waste breath or time in courtesies. Come up the steps and hurry to the house. You must be faint and bruised.'

'No, no,' said the swimmer; but as he spoke his eyes closed, he staggered a little; a deadly faintness and cold had seized him, and cramp came on all his limbs.

The men caught him, and carried him up the stairs; he strove to struggle and protest, but Otto the forester stooped over him.

'Keep you still,' he muttered. 'You have the Countess's orders. Trespass has cost you dear, my master.'

'I do not think he is greatly hurt,' said the mistress of Szaravola to her house physician. 'But go you to him, doctor, and see that he is warmly housed and has hot drinks.' Put him in the Strangers' Gallery, and pray take care my aunt is not alarmed.'

The Princess Ottilie at that moment was alternately eating a *nougat* out of her sweet-meat box and telling the beads of her rosary. The sound of the wind and the noise of the storm could not reach her in her favourite blue-room, all *capitonnée* with turquoise silks as it was; the only chamber in all Szaravola that was entirely modern and French.

'I do hope Wanda is running no risk,' she thought, from time to time. 'It would be quite like her to row down the lake.'

But she sat still in her lamp light, and told her beads.

A few moments later her niece entered. Her waterproof mantle had kept her white gown from the rain and spray.

There was a little moisture on her hair,

that was all. She did not look as if she had
stirred further from her drawing-room than the
Princess had done.

Now that the stranger was safe and sound
he had ceased to have any interest for her; he
was nothing more than any flotsam of the
lake; only one other to sleep beneath the roofs
of Hohenszalras, where half a hundred slept
already.

The castle, in the wild winters that shut out
the Hohe Tauern from the world, was often-
times a hospice for travellers, though usually
those travellers were only pedlars, colporteurs,
mule-drivers, clock-makers of the Zillerthal or
carpet weavers of the Defreggerthal, too late in
the year to pursue their customary passage over
the passes in safety. To such the great beacon
of the Holy Isle and the huge servants' hall of
Szaravola were well known.

She sat down to her embroidery frame
without speaking; she was working some
mountain flowers in silks on velvet, for a
friend in Paris. The flowers stood in a glass
on a table.

'It is unkind of you to go out in that mad
way on such a night as this, and return looking so unlike having had an adventure!' said
the Princess, a little pettishly.

'There has been no adventure,' said Wanda

von Szalras, with a smile. 'But there is what may do as well—a handsome stranger who has been saved from drowning.'

Even as she spoke her face changed, her mouth quivered; she crossed herself, and murmured, too low for the other to hear:

'Bela, my beloved, think not that I forget!'

The Princess Ottilie sat up erect in her chair, and her blue eyes brightened like a girl of sixteen.

'Then there *is* an adventure! Tell it me quick! My dear, silence is very stately and very becoming to you; but sometimes—excuse me—you do push it to annoying extremes.'

'I was afraid of agitation for you,' said the Countess Wanda; and then she told the Princess what had occurred that night.

'And I never knew that a poor soul was in peril!' cried the Princess, conscious-stricken. 'And is that the last you have seen of him? Have you never asked—— ?'

'Hubert says he is only bruised; they have taken him to the Strangers' Gallery. Here is Herr Greswold—he will tell us more.'

The person who entered was the physician of Hohenszalras. He was a little old man of great talent, with a clever, humorous, mild countenance; he had, coupled with a love for rural life, a passion for botany and natural history,

which made his immurement in the Iselthal
welcome to him, and the many fancied ailments of the Princess endurable. He bowed
very low alternately to both ladies, and refused
with a protest the chair to which the Countess
Wanda motioned him. He said that the stranger
was not in the least seriously injured; he had
been seized with cramp and chills, but he had
administered a cordial, and these were passing.
The gentleman seemed indisposed to speak,
shivered a good deal, and was inclined to
sleep.

'He is a gentleman, think you?' asked the
Princess.

The Herr Professor said that to him it appeared so.

'And of what rank?'

The physician thought it was impossible to
say.

'It is always possible,' said the Princess, a
little impatiently. 'Is his linen fine? Is his
skin smooth? Are his hands white and
slender? Are his wrists and ankles small?'

Herr Greswold said that he was sorely
grieved, but he had not taken any notice as to
any of these things; he had been occupied
with his diagnosis of the patient's state; for,
he added, he thought the swimmer had been
long in the water, and the Szalrassee was of

very dangerously low temperature at night, being fed as it was from the glaciers and snows of the mountains.

'It is very interesting,' said the Princess; 'but pray observe what I have named, now that you return to his chamber.'

Greswold took the hint, and bowed himself out of the drawing-room. Frau Ottilie returned to her nougâts.

'I wish that one could know who he was,' she said regretfully. To harbour an unknown person was not agreeable to her in these days of democracies and dynamite.

'What does it matter?' said her niece. 'Though he were a Nihilist or a convict from the mines, he would have to be sheltered to-night.'

'The Herr Professor is very inattentive,' said the Princess, with an accent that from one of her sweetness was almost severe.

'The Herr Professor is compiling the Flora of the Hohe Tauern,' said her niece, 'and he will publish it in Leipzig some time in the next twenty years. How can a botanist care for so unlovely a creature as a man? If it were a flower indeed!'

'I never approved of that herbarium,' said the Princess, still severely. 'It is too insignificant an occupation beside those great questions of human ills which his services are retained to study. He is inattentive, and he grows even impertinent : he almost told me yesterday that my neuralgia was all imagination !'

'He took you for a flower, mother mine, because you are so lovely ; and so he thought you could have no mortal pain !' said Wanda, tenderly.

Then after a pause she added :

'Dear aunt, come with me. I have asked Father Ferdinand to have a mass to-night for Bela. I fancy Bela is glad that no other life has been taken by the lake.'

The Princess rose quickly and kissed her.

In the Strangers' Gallery, in a great chamber of panelled oak and Flemish tapestries, the poacher, as he lay almost asleep on a grand old bed, with yellow taffeta hangings, and the crown of the Szalras Counts in gilded bronze above its head, he heard as if in his dream the sound of chanting voices and the deep slow melodies of an organ.

He stirred and opened his drowsy eyes.

'Am I in heaven?' he asked feebly. Yet he was a man who, when he was awake and well, believed not in heaven.

The physician, sitting by his bedside, laid his hand upon his wrist. The pulse was beating strongly but quickly.

'You are in the Burg of Hohenszalras,' he answered him. 'The music you hear comes from the chapel; there is a midnight mass. A mass of thanksgiving for you.'

The heavy lids fell over the eyes of the weary man, and the dreamy sense of warmth and peace that was upon him lulled him into the indifference of slumber.

CHAPTER III.

WITH the morning, though the storm had ceased and passed away, the clouds were dark, the mountains were obscured, and the rain was pouring down upon lake and land.

It was still early in the day when the stranger was aroused to the full sense of awaking in a room unknown to him; he had slept all through the night; he was refreshed and without fever. His left arm was strained, and he had many bruises; otherwise he was conscious of no hurt.

'Twice in that woman's power,' he thought, with anger, as he looked round the great tapestried chamber that sheltered him, and tried to disentangle his actual memories of the past night from the dreams that had haunted

him of the Nibelungen Queen, who all night
long he had seen in her golden armour, with
her eyes which, like those of the Greek nymph,
dazzled those on whom they gazed to madness.
Dream and fact had so interwoven themselves
that it was with an effort he could sever the
two, awaking as he did now in an unfamiliar
chamber, and surrounded with those tapestries
whose colossal figures seemed the phantoms of
a spirit world.

He was a man in whom some vein of
superstition had outlived the cold reason and
the cynical mockeries of the worldly experiences and opinions in which he was steeped.
A shudder of cold ran through his blood
as he opened his eyes upon that dim, tranquil, and vast apartment, with the stories of
the Tannhäuser legend embroidered on the
walls.

'I am he! I am he!' he thought inco-
herently, watching the form of the doomed
knight speeding through the gloom and snow.

'How does the most high and honourable
gentleman feel himself this morning?' asked
of him, in German, a tall white-haired woman,
who might have stepped down from an old
panel of Metzu.

The simple commonplace question roused
him from the mists of his fancies and fears, and

realised to him the bare fact that he was a guest, unbidden, in the walls of Szaravola.

The physician also drew near his bed to question him; and a boy brought on a tray Rhine wine and Tokayer Ausbruck, coffee and chocolate, bread and eggs.

He broke his fast with a will, for he had eaten nothing since the day before at noon; and the Professor Greswold congratulated him on his good night's rest, and on his happy escape from the Szalrassee.

Then he himself said, with a little confusion:

'I saw a lady last night?'

'Certainly, you saw our lady,' said Greswold, with a smile.

'What do you call her?' he asked, eagerly.

The physician answered:

'She is the Countess Wanda von Szalras. She is sole mistress here. But for her, my dear sir, I fear me you would be now lying in those unfathomed depths that the bravest of us fear.'

The stranger shuddered a little.

'I was a madman to try the lake with such an overcast sky; but I had missed my road, and I was told that it lay on the other side of the water. Some peasants tried to dissuade me from crossing, but I am a good rower and swimmer too; so I set forth to pull myself over your lake.'

'With a sky black as ink! I suppose you are used to more serene summers. Midsummer is not so different to midwinter here that you can trust to its tender mercies.'

• The stranger was silent.

'She took my gun from me in the morning,' he said abruptly. The memory of the indignity rankled in him, and made bitter the bread and wine.

The physician laughed.

'Were you poaching? Oh, that is almost a hanging matter in the Hohenszalras woods. Had you met Otto without our lady he would most likely have shot you without warning.'

' Are you savages in the Tauern?'

'Oh no; but we are very feudal still, and our forest laws have escaped alteration in this especial part of the province.'

'She has been very hospitable to me, since my crime was so great.'

'She is the soul of hospitality, and the Schloss is a hospice,' said the physician. 'When there is no town nearer than ten Austrian miles, and the nearest posting-house is at Windisch-Matrey, it is very necessary to exercise the primitive virtues; it is our compensation for our feudalism. But take some tokayer, my dear sir; you are weaker than you know. You have had a bath of ice; you had best lie still, and I will send you some journals and books.'

'I would rather get up and go away,' said the stranger. 'These bruises are nothing. I will thank your lady, as you call her, and then go on my way as quickly as I may.'

'I see you do not understand feudal ways, though you have suffered from them,' said the doctor. 'You shall get up if you wish; but I am certain my lady will not let you leave here to-day. The rains are falling in torrents; the roads are dangerous; a bridge has broken down over the Burgenbach, which you must cross to get away. In a word, if you insist on departure, they will harness their best horses for you, for all the antique virtues have refuge here, and amongst them is a grand hospitality; but you will possibly kill the horses, and perhaps the postillions, and you will not even then get very far upon your way. Be persuaded by me. Wait at least until the morning dawns.'

'I had better burden your lady with an unbidden guest than kill her horses, certainly,' said the stranger. 'How is she sole mistress here? Is there a Count von Szalras? Is she a widow?'

'She has never married,' answered Greswold;

and gave his patient a brief sketch of the tragic
·fates of the lords of Hohenszalras, amongst
whom death had been so busy.'

'A very happy woman to be so rich, and so
free!' said the traveller, with a little impatient
envy; and he added, 'She is very handsome
also; indeed, beautiful. I now remember to
have heard of her in Paris. Her hand has
been esteemed one of the great prizes of
Europe.'

'I think she will never marry,' said the old
man.

'Oh, my dear doctor, who can make such
a prophecy for any woman who is still young—
at least she looks young. What age may she
be?'

'She was twenty-four years of age on
Easter Day. As for happiness, when you know
the Countess Wanda, you will know that she
would go out as poor as S. Elizabeth, and self-
dethroned like her, most willingly, could she by
such a sacrifice see her brothers living around
her.'

The stranger gave a little cynical laugh of
utter incredulity, which dismayed and annoyed
the old professor.

'You do not know her,' he said angrily.

'I know humanity,' said the other. 'Will
you kindly take all my apologies and regrets to

the Countess, and give her my name; the
Marquis de Sabran.   She can satisfy herself
as to my identity at any embassy she may care
to consult.'

When he said his name, the professor gave
a great cry and started from his seat.

'Sabran!' he echoed.   'You edited the
" Mexico "!' he exclaimed, and gazed over
his spectacles in awe and sympathy com-
mingled at the stranger, who smiled and
answered—

'Long ago, yes.   Have you heard of it?'

'Heard of it!' echoed Greswold.   'Do you
take us for barbarians, sir?   It is here, both in
my small library, which is the collection of a
specialist, and in the great library of the castle,
which contains a million of volumes.'

'I am twice honoured,' said the stranger,
with a smile of some irony.   The good professor was a little disconcerted, and his enthusiasm
was damped and cooled.   He felt as much embarrassment as though he had been the owner
of a discredited work.

'May I not be permitted to congratulate
you, sir?' he said timidly.   'To have produced
that great work is to possess a title to the gratitude and esteem of all educated men.'

'You are very good,' said Sabran, somewhat
indifferently; 'but all that is great in that book

is the Marquis Xavier's.   I am but the mere
compiler.'

'The compilation, the editing of it, required
no less learning than the original writer displayed, and that was immense,' said the physician, and with all the enthusiasm of a
specialist he plunged into discussion of the
many notable points of a mighty intellectual
labour, which had received the praise of all the
cultured world.

Sabran listened courteously, but with visible
weariness. 'You are very good,' he said at
last. 'But you will forgive me if I say that I
have heard so much of the "Mexico" that I am
tempted to wish I had never produced it. I
did so as a duty; it was all I could do in
honour of one to whom I owed far more than
mere life itself.'

Greswold bowed and said no more.

'Give me my belt,' said the stranger
to the man who waited on him; it was
a leathern belt, which had been about his
loins; it was made to hold gold and notes, a
small six-chambered revolver, and a watch;
these were all in it, and with his money was
the imperial permission to shoot, which had
been given him by Franz Josef the previous
autumn on the Thorstein.

'Your Countess will doubtless recognise her

Emperor's signature,' he said, as he gave the paper to the physician. 'It will serve at least as a passport, if not as a letter of presentation.'

Réné, Marquis de Sabran-Romaris, was one of those persons who illustrate the old fairy tale, of all the good gifts at birth being marred by the malison of one godmother. He had great physical beauty, personal charm, and facile talent; but his very facility was his bane. He did all things so easily and well, that he had never acquired the sterner quality of application. He was a brilliant and even profound scholar, an accomplished musician, a consummate critic of art; and was endowed, moreover, with great natural tact, taste, and correct intuition.

Being, as he was, a poor man, these gifts should have made him an eminent one or a wealthy one, but the perverse fairy who had cursed when the other had blessed him, had contrived to make all these graces and talents barren. Whether it be true or not that the world knows nothing of its greatest men, it is quite true that its cleverest men very often do nothing of importance all their lives long. He did nothing except acquire a distinct repute as a *dilettante* in Paris, and a renown in the clubs of being always serene and fortunate at play.

He had sworn to himself when he had been a youth to make his career worthy of his name; but the years had slipped away, and he had done nothing. He was a very clever man, and he had once set a high if a cold and selfish aim before him as his goal. But he had done worse even than fail; he had never even tried to reach it.

He was only a *boulevardier*; popular and admired amongst men for his ready wit and his cool courage, and by women often adored and often hated, and sometimes, by himself, thoroughly despised: never so much despised as when by simple luck at play or on the Bourse he made the money which slid through his fingers with rapidity.

All he had in the world were the wind-torn oaks and the sea-washed rocks of a bleak and lonely Breton village, and a few hundred thousand francs' worth of pictures, porcelains, arms, and *bibelots*, which had accumulated in his rooms on the Boulevard Haussmann, bought at the Drouot in the forenoons after successful play at night. Only two things in him were unlike the men whose associate he was: he was as temperate as an Arab, seldom even touching wine; and he was a keen mountaineer and athlete, once off the asphalte of the Boulevards. For the rest, popular though he was in the society he frequented, no living man could boast of any real intimacy with him. He had a thousand acquaintances, but he accepted no friend. Under the grace and suavity of a very courtly manner he wore the armour of a great reserve.

'At heart you have the taciturnity and the *sauvagerie* of the Armorican beneath all your polished suavity,' said a woman of his world to him once; and he did not contradict her.

Men did not quarrel with him for it: he was a fine swordsman and a dead shot: and women were allured all the more surely to him because they felt that they never really entered his life or took any strong hold on it.

Such as he was he lay now half-awake on the great bed under its amber canopy, and gazed dreamily at the colossal figures of the storied tapestry, where the Tuscan idlers of the Decamerone wore the sombre hues and the stiff and stately garb of Flemish fashion of the sixteenth century.

'I wonder why I tried so hard to live last night! I am not in love with life,' he thought to himself, as he slowly remembered all that had happened, and recalled the face of the lady who had leaned down to him from over the stone parapet in the play of the torchlight and lightnings. And yet life seemed good and worth having as he recalled that boiling dusky swirl of water which had so nearly swallowed him up in its anger.

He was young enough to enjoy; he was blessed with a fine constitution and admirable health, which even his own excesses had not impaired; he had no close ties to the world, but he had a frequent enjoyment of it, which made it welcome to him. The recovery of existence always enhances its savour; and as he lay dreamily recalling the sharp peril he had run, he was simply and honestly glad to be amongst living men.

He remained still when the physician had left and looked around him; in the wide hearth a fire of oak logs was burning; rain was beating against the painted panes of the oriel casements; there was old oak, old silver, old ivory in the furniture of the chamber, and the tapestries were sombre and gorgeous. It was a room of the sixteenth century; but the wine was in jugs of Bacarat glass, and a box of Turkish cigarettes stood beside them, with the Paris and Vienna newspapers. Everything had been thought of that could contribute to his comfort: he wondered if the doctor had thought of all this, or if it was due to the lady. ‘ It is a magnificent hospice,’ he said to himself with a smile, and then he angrily remembered

his rifle, his good English rifle, that was now
sunk for ever with his little boat in the waters
of the Szalrassee. 'Why did she offer me
that outrage?' he said to himself: it went
hard with him to lie under her roof, to touch
her wine and bread. Yet he was aching in
every limb, the bed was easy and spacious, the
warmth and the silence and the aromatic scent
of the burning pine-cones were alluring him to
rest; he dropped off to sleep again, the same
calm sleep of fatigue that had changed into
repose, and nothing woke him till the forenoon
was passed.

'Good heavens! how I am trespassing on
this woman's hospitality!' he thought as he
did awake, angry with himself for having been
lulled into this oblivion; and he began to rise
at once, though he felt his limbs stiff and his
head for the moment light.

'Cannot I get a carriage for S. Johann?
My servant is waiting for me there,' he said to
the youth attending on him, when his bath was
over.

The lad smiled with amusement.

'There are no carriages here but our lady's,
and she will not let you stir this afternoon, my
lord,' he answered in German, as he aided the
stranger to put on his own linen and shooting
breeches, now dry and smoothed out by careful
hands.

'But I have no coat!' said the traveller in discomfiture, remembering that his coat was gone with his rifle and his powder-flask.

'The Herr Professor thought you could perhaps manage with one of these. They were all of Count Gela's, who was a tall man and about your make,' said an older man-servant who had entered, and now showed him several unworn or scarcely worn suits.

'If you could wear one of these, my lord, for this evening, we will send as soon as it is possible for your servant and your clothes to S. Johann; but it is impossible to-day, because a bridge is down over the Burgenbach.'

'You are all of you too good,' said Sabran, as he essayed a coat of black velvet.

Full of his new acquaintance and all his talents, the good man Greswold had hurried away to obey the summons of his ladies, who had desired to see him. He found them in the white room, a grand salon hung with white satin silver-fringed, and stately with white marble friezes and columns, whence it took its name. It was a favourite room with the mistress of the Schloss: at either end of it immense windows, emblazoned and deeply embayed, looked out over the sublime landscape without, of which at this moment every outline was shrouded in the grey veil of an incessantly falling rain.

With humble obeisances Greswold presented the message and the credentials of her guest to Wanda von Szalras; it was the first occasion that he had had of doing so. She read the document signed by the Kaiser with a smile.

'This is the paper which this unhappy gentleman spoke of when I arrested him as a poacher,' she said to her aunt. 'The Marquis de Sabran. The name is familiar to me: I have heard it before.'

'Surely you do not forget the Pontêves-Bargême, the Ducs de Sabran?' said the Princess, with some severity. 'S. Eleazar was a Comte de Sabran!'

'I know! But it is of something nearer to us than S. Eleazar that I am thinking; there was surely some work or another which bore that name, and was much read and quoted.'

'He edited and annotated the great "Mexico,"' said Herr Greswold, as though all were told in that.

' A *savant?* ' murmured the Princess, in some contemptuous chagrin. 'Pray what is the " Mexico " ? '

'The grandest archæological and botanical work, the work of the finest research and most varied learning that has been produced out of Germany,' commenced the Professor, with eagerness, but the Princess arrested him midway in his eloquence.

' The French are all infidels, we know that; but one might have hoped that in one of the old nobility, as his name would imply, some lingering reverence for tradition remained.'

' It is not a subversive, not a philosophic work,' said the Professor, eagerly ; but she silenced him.

' It is a book ! Why should a Marquis de Sabran write a book ? ' said the Princess, with ineffable disdain.

There were all the Fathers for anyone who wanted to read : what need for any other use of printer's type ? So she was accustomed to think and to say when, scandalised, she saw the German, French, and English volumes, of which whole cases were wont to arrive at Hohenszalras for the use of Wanda von Szalras alone : works of philosophy and of science amongst them which had been denounced in the 'Index.'

' Dear mother,' said the Countess Wanda, ' I have read the " Mexico ": it is a grand monument raised to a dead man's memory out of his own labours by one of his own descendants— his only descendant, if I remember aright.'

' Indeed,' said the Princess, unconvinced. ' I know those scientific works by repute ; they always consider the voyage of a germ of. moss, carried on an aerolite through an indefinite space for a billion of ages, a matter much

easier of credence than the " Life of St. Jerome."
I believe they call it sporadic transmission;
they call typhus fever the same.'

' There is nothing of that in the " Mexico ":
it is a very fine work on the archæology and
history of the country, and on its flora.'

'I should have supposed a Marquis de Sabran
a gentleman,' said the Princess, whom no precedent from the many monarchs who have been
guilty of inferior literature could convince that
literature was other than a trade much like
shoemaking: at its best a sort of clerk's quill-
driving, to be equally pitied and censured.

Here Greswold, who valued his post and
knew his place too well to defend either
literature or sporadic germs, timidly ventured
to suggest that the Marquis might be well
known amongst the nobility of western France,
although not of that immense distinction which
finds its chronicle in the Hof-Kalender. The
Princess smiled.

' *Petite noblesse.* You mean petite noblesse,
my good Greswold? But even the petite
noblesse need not write books? '

When, however, the further question arose
of inviting the stranger to come to their dinner-
table, it was the haughtier Princess who advo-
cated the invitation; the mistress of the house
demurred. She thought that all requirements

of courtesy and hospitality would be fulfilled by allowing him to dine in his own apartments.

'We do not know him,' she urged. 'No doubt he may very well be what he says, but it is not easy to refer to an embassy while the rains are making an island of the Tauern! Nay, dear mother, I am not suspicious; but I think, as we are two women alone, we can fulfil all obligations of hospitality towards this gentleman without making him personally acquainted with ourselves.'

'That is really very absurd. It is acting as if Hohenszalras were a *gasthof*,' said the Princess, with petulance. 'It is not so often that we have any relief to the tedium with which you are pleased to surround yourself that we should be required to shut ourselves from any chance break in it. Of course, if you send this person his dinner to his own rooms, he will feel hurt, mortified; he will go away, probably on foot, rather than remain where he is insulted. Breton nobility is not very eminent, but it is very proud; it is provincial, territorial; but every one knows it is ancient, and usually of the most loyal traditions alike to Church and State. I should be the last person to advocate making a friendship, or even an acquaintance, without the fullest inquiry; but when it is a mere question of a politeness for twenty-four hours, which can entail no consequences, then I must confess that I think prejudices should yield before the obligations of courtesy. But of course, my love, decide as you will : you are mistress.'

The Countess Wanda smiled, and did not press her own opposition. She perceived that the mind of her aunt was full of vivid and harmless curiosity.

In the end she suggested that the Princess should represent her, and receive the foreign visitor with all due form and ceremony ; but she herself was still indisposed to admit a person of whose antecedents she had no positive guarantee so suddenly and entirely into her intimacy.

'You are extraordinarily suspicious,' said the elder lady, pettishly. 'If he were a pedlar or a colporteur, you would be willing to talk with him.'

'Pedlars and colporteurs cannot take any social advantage of one's conversation afterwards,' replied her niece. 'We are not usually invaded by men of rank here ; so the precedent may not be perilous. Have your own way, mother mine.'

The Princess demurred, but finally accepted the compromise ; reflecting that if this stranger were to dine alone with her, she would be able to ascertain much more about him than if

Wanda, who had been created void of all natural curiosity, and who would have been capable of living with people twelve months without asking them a single question, would render it possible to do were she present.

Meanwhile, the physician hurried back to his new friend, who had a great and peculiar interest for him as the editor of the 'Mexico,' and offered him, with the permission of the Countess von Szalras, to wile away the chill and gloomy day by an inspection of the Schloss.

Joachim Greswold was a very learned and shrewd man, whom poverty and love of tranquil opportunities of study had induced to bury himself in the heart of the Glöckner mountains. He had already led a long, severe, and blameless life of deep devotion and hard privation, when the post of private physician at Hohenszalras in general, and to the Princess Ottilie in especial, had been procured for him by the interest of Prince Lilienhöhe. He had had many sorrows, trials, and disappointments, which made the simple routine and the entire solitude of his existence here welcome to him. But he was none the less delighted to meet any companion of culture and intelligence to converse with, and in his monotonous and lonely life it was a rare treat to be able to exchange ideas with one fresh from the intellectual movements of the outer world.

The Professor found, not to his surprise since he had read the 'Mexico,' that his elegant *grand seigneur* knew very nearly as much as he did of botany and of comparative anatomy ; that he had travelled nearly all over the world, and travelled to much purpose, and knew many curious things of the flora of the Rio Grande, whilst it appeared that he possessed in his cabinets in Paris a certain variety of orchid that the doctor had always longed to obtain. He was entirely won over when Sabran, to whom the dried flower was very indifferent, promised to send it to him. The French Marquis had not Greswold's absolute love of science ; he had studied every thing that had come to his hand, because he had a high intelligence, and an insatiable appetite for knowledge ; and he had no other kind of devotion to it ; when he had penetrated its mysteries, it lost all interest for him.

At any rate he knew enough to make him an enchanting companion to a learned man who was all alone in his learning, and received little sympathy in it from anyone near him.

'What a grand house to be shut up in the heart of the mountains!' said Sabran, with a sigh. 'I do believe what romance there still is in the world does lie in these forests of Austria, which have all the twilight and the solitude that would suit Merlin or the Sleeping Beauty better than anything we have in France, except, indeed, here and there an old château like Chenonceaux, or Maintenon.'

'The world has not spoilt us as yet,' said the doctor. 'We see few strangers. Our people are full of old faiths, old loyalties, old traditions. They are a sturdy and yet tender people. They are as fearless as their own steinbok, and they are as reverent as saints were in monastic days. Our mountains are as grand as the Swiss ones, but, thank Heaven, they are unspoilt and little known. I tremble when I think they have begun to climb the Gross Glöckner; all the mystery and glory of our glaciers will vanish when they become mere points of ascension. The alpenstock of the tourist is to the everlasting hills what railway metals are to the plains. Thank God! the few railroads we have are hundreds of miles asunder.'

'You are a reactionist, Doctor?'

'I am an old man, and I have learned the value of repose,' said Greswold. 'You know we are called a slow race. It is only the unwise amongst us who have quicksilver in their brains and toes.'

'You have gold in the former, at least,' said Sabran, kindly, ' and I dare say quicksilver is in your feet, too, when there is a charity to be done?'

Herr Joachim, who was simple in the knowledge of mankind, though shrewd in mother-wit, coloured a little with pleasure. How well this stranger understood him!

The day went away imperceptibly and agreeably to the physician and to the stranger in this pleasant rambling talk; whilst the rain poured down in fury on the stone terraces and green lawns without, and the Szalrassee was hidden under a veil of fog.

'Am I not to see her at all?' thought Sabran. He did not like to express his disquietude on that subject to the physician, and he was not sure himself whether he most desired to ride away without meeting the serene eyes of his châtelaine, or to be face to face with her once more.

He stood long before her portrait, done by Carolus Duran; she wore in it a close-fitting gown of white velvet, and held in her hand a great Spanish hat with white plumes; the two hounds were beside her; the attitude had a certain grandeur and gravity in it which were very impressive.

'This was painted last year,' said Greswold,

'at the Princess's request. It is admirably like——'

'It is a noble picture,' said Sabran. 'But what a very proud woman she looks!'

'Blood tells,' said Greswold, 'far more than most people know or admit. It is natural that my Lady, with the blood in her of so many mighty nobles, who had the power of judgment and chastisement over whole provinces, should be sometimes disposed to exercise too despotic a will, to be sometimes contemptuous of the dictates of modern society, which sends the princess and the peasant alike to a law court for sole redress of their wrongs. She is at times irreconcilable with the world as it stands ; she is the representative and descendant in a direct line of arrogant and omnipotent princes. That she combines with that natural arrogance and instinct of dominion a very beautiful pitifulness and even humility is a proof of the chastening influence of religious faith on the nature of women ; we are too apt to forget that, in our haste to destroy the Church. Men might get on perhaps very well without a religion of any kind ; but I tremble to think what their mothers and their mistresses would become.'

They passed the morning in animated discussion, and as it drew to a close, the good doctor did not perceive how adroitly his new acquaintance drew out from him all details of the past and present of Hohenszalras, and of the tastes and habits of its châtelaine, until he knew all that there was to be known of that pure and austere life.

'You may think her grief for her brother Bela's death—for all her brothers' deaths—a morbid sentiment,' said the doctor as he spoke of her. 'But it is not so—no. It is, perhaps, overwrought; but no life can be morbid that is so active in duty, so untiring in charity, so unsparing of itself. Her lands and riches, and all the people dependent on her, are to the Countess Wanda only as so much trust, for which hereafter she will be responsible to Bela and to God. You and I may smile, you and I, who are philosophers, and have settled past dispute that the human life has no more future than the snail-gnawed cabbage, but yet—yet, my dear sir, one cannot deny that there is something exalted in such a conception of duty ; and —of this I am convinced—that on the character of a woman it has a very ennobling influence.'

'No doubt. But has she renounced all her youth ? Does she mean never to go into the world or to marry ? '

'I am quite sure she has made no resolve

of the sort. But I do not think she will ever alter. She has refused many great alliances. Her temperament is serene, almost cold; and her ideal it would be difficult, I imagine, for any mortal man to realise.'

' But when a woman loves——'

'Oh, of course,' said Herr Joachim, rather drily. ' If the aloe flower !——Love does not I think possess any part of the Countess Wanda's thoughts or desires. She fancies it a mere weakness.'

' A woman can scarcely be amiable without that weakness.'

' No. Perhaps she is not precisely what we term amiable. She is rather too far also from human emotions and human needs. The women of the house of Szalras have been mostly very proud, silent, brave, and resolute; great ladies rather than lovable wives. Luitgarde von Szalras held this place with only a few archers and spearmen against Heinrich Jasomergott in the twelfth century, and he raised the siege after five months. "She is not a woman, nor human, she is a *kuttengeier*," he said, as he retreated into his Wiener Wald. All the great monk-vultures and the gyps and the pygargues have been sacred all through the Hohe Tauern since that year.'

' And I was about to shoot a *kuttengeier*—

now I see that my offence was beyond poaching,
it was high treason almost!'

'I heard the story from Otto. He would
have hanged you cheerfully. But I hope,' said
the doctor, with a pang of misgiving, 'that I
have not given you any false impression of my
Lady, as cold and hard and unwomanly. She
is full of tenderness of a high order; she is the
noblest, most truthful, and most generous nature
that I have ever known clothed in human
form, and if she be too proud—well, it is a
stately sin, pardonable in one who has behind
her eleven hundred years of fearless and un-
blemished honour.'

'I am a socialist,' said Sabran, a little
curtly; then added, with a little laugh, 'Though
I believe not in rank, I do believe in race.'

·'*Bon sang ne peut mentir*,' murmured the
old physician; the fair face of Sabran changed
slightly.

'Will you come and look over the house?'
said the Professor, who noticed nothing, and
only thought of propitiating the owner of the
rare orchid. 'There is almost as much to see
as in the Burg at Vienna. Everything has
accumulated here undisturbed for a thousand
years. Hohenszalras has been besieged, but
never deserted or dismantled.

'It is a grand place!' said Sabran, with a

look of impatience. 'It seems intolerable that a woman should possess it all, while I only own a few wind-blown oaks in the wilds of Finisterre.'

'Ah, ah, that is pure socialism!' said the doctor, with a little chuckle. '*Ote-toi, que je m'y mette.* That is genuine Liberalism all the world over.'

'You are no communist yourself, doctor?'

'No,' said Herr Joachim, simply. 'All my studies lead me to the conviction that equality is impossible, and were it possible, it would be hideous. Variety, infinite variety, is the beneficent law of the world's life. Why, in that most perfect of all societies, the beehive, flawless mathematics are found co-existent with impassable social barriers and unalterable social grades.'

Sabran laughed good-humouredly.

'I thought at least the bees enjoyed an undeniable Republic.'

'A Republic with helots, sir, like Sparta. A Republic will always have its helots. But come and wander over the castle. Come first and see the parchments.'

'Where are the ladies?' asked Sabran, wistfully.

'The Princess is at her devotions and taking tisane. I visited her this morning; she thinks

she has a sore throat.   As for our Lady, no one
ever disturbs her or knows what she is doing.
When she wants any of us ordinary folks, we
are summoned.   Sometimes we tremble.   You
know this alone is an immense estate, and then
there is a palace at the capital, and one at
Salzburg, not to speak of the large estates in
Hungary and the mines in Galicia.   All these
our Lady sees after and manages herself.   You
can imagine that her secretary has no easy task,
and that secretary is herself ; for she does not
believe in doing anything well by others.'

'A second Maria Theresa !' said Sabran.

'Not dissimilar, perhaps,' said the doctor,
nettled at the irony of the tone.   'Only where
our great Queen sent thousands out to their
deaths the Countess von Szalras saves many
lives.   There are no mines in the world—I
will make bold to say—where there is so
much comfort and so little peril as those mines
of hers in Stanislaw.   She visited them three
years hence.   But I forget, you are a stranger,
and as you do not share our cultus for the
Grafin, cannot care to hear its Canticles.   Come
to the muniment-room ; you shall see some
strange parchments.'

'Heavens, how it rains !' said Sabran, as
they left his chambers. ' Is that common here ? '

'Very common, indeed ! ' said the doctor,

with a laugh. 'We pass two-thirds of the year between snow and water. But then we have compensation. Where will you see such grass, such forests, such gardens, when the summer sun does shine?'

The Marquis de Sabran charmed him, and as they wandered over the huge castle the physician delightedly displayed his own erudition, and recognised that of his companion. The Hohenszalrasburg was itself like some black-letter record of old South-German history; it was a chronicle written in stone and wood and iron. The brave old house, like a noble person, contained in itself a liberal education, and the stranger whom through an accident it sheltered was educated enough to comprehend and estimate it at its due value. In his passage through it he won the suffrages of the household by his varied knowledge and correct appreciation. In the stables his praises of the various breeds of horses there commended itself by its accuracy to Ulrich, the *stallmeister*, not less than a few difficult shots in the shooting gallery proved his skill to his enemy of the previous day, Otto, the *jägermeister*. Not less did he please Hubert, who was learned in such things, with his cultured admiration of the wonderful old gold and silver plate, the Limoges dishes and bowls, the Vienna and Kronenthal china ; nor less the custodian of the pictures, a collection of Flemish and German masters, with here and there a modern *capolavoro*, hung all by themselves in a little vaulted gallery which led into a much larger one consecrated to tapestries, Flemish, French, and Florentine.

When twilight came, and the greyness of the rain-charged atmosphere deepened into the dark of night, Sabran had made all living things at the castle his firm friends, down to the dogs of the house, save and except the ladies who dwelt in it. Of them he had 'had no glimpse. They kept their own apartments. He began to feel some fresh embarrassment at remaining another night beneath a roof the mistress of which did not deign personally to recognise his presence. A salon hung with tapestries opened out of the bedchamber allotted to him ; he wondered if he were to dine there like a prisoner of state.

He felt an extreme reluctance united to a strong curiosity to meet again the woman who had treated him with such cool authority and indifference as a common poacher in her woods. His cheek tingled still, whenever he thought of the manner in which, at her signal, his hands had been tied, and his rifle taken from him. She was the representative of all that feudal, aristocratic, despotic, dominant spirit of a dead time which he, with his modern, cynical, reckless Parisian Liberalism, most hated, or believed that he hated. She was Austria Felix personified, and he was a man who had always persuaded himself and others that he was a socialist, a Philippe Egalité. And this haughty patrician had mortified him and then had benefited and sheltered him !

He would willingly have gone from under her roof without seeing her, and yet a warm and inquisitive desire impelled him to feel an unreasonable annoyance that the day was going by without his receiving any intimation that he would be allowed to enter her presence, or be expected to make his obeisances to her. When, however, the servants entered to light the many candles in his room, Hubert entered behind them, and expressed the desire of his lady that the Marquis would favour them with his presence : they were about to dine.

Sabran, standing before the mirror, saw himself colour like a boy : he knew not whether he were most annoyed or pleased. He would willingly have ridden away leaving his napoleons for the household, and seeing no more the woman who had made him ridiculous in his own eyes ; yet the remembrance of her haunted him as something strange, imperious, magnetic,

grave, serene, stately; vague memories of a
thousand things he had heard said of her in
embassies and at courts came to his mind; she
had been a mere unknown name to him then; he
had not listened, he had not cared, but now he
remembered all he had heard; curiosity and an
embarrassment wholly foreign to him struggled
together in him. What could he say to a woman
who had first insulted and then protected him?
It would tax all the ingenuity and the tact for
which he was famed. However, he only said
to the major-domo, 'I am much flattered.
Express my profound gratitude to your ladies
for the honour they are so good as to do me.'
Then he made his attire look as well as it
could, and considering that punctuality is due
from guests as well as from monarchs, he said
that he was ready to follow the servant waiting
for him, and did so through the many tapestried
and panelled corridors by which the enormous
house was traversed.

Though light was not spared at the burg
it was only such light as oil and wax could
give the galleries and passages; dim mysterious figures loomed from the rooms and
shadows seemed to stretch away on every
side to vast unknown chambers that might hold
the secrets of a thousand centuries. When he
was ushered into the radiance of the great
white room he felt dazzled and blinded.

He felt his bruise still, and he walked with a
slight lameness from a strain of his left foot, but
this did not detract from the grace and distinction
of his bearing, and the pallor of his handsome
features became them ; and when he advanced
through the opened doors and bent before the
chair and kissed the hands of the Princess
Ottilie she thought to herself, ' What a perfectly beautiful person.   Even Wanda will
have to admit that ! '   Whilst Hubert, going
backward, said to his regiment of under-ser-
vants : ' Look you ! since Count Gela rode out
to his death at the head of the White Hussars,
so grand a man as this stranger has not set foot
in this house.'

He expected to see the Countess Wanda von
Szalras.   Instead, he saw the loveliest little old
lady he had ever seen in his life, clad in a
semi-conventual costume, leaning on a gold-
headed cane, with clouds of fragrant old lace
about her, and a cross of emeralds hung at
her girdle of onyx beads, who saluted him with
the ceremonious grace of that etiquette which
is still the common rule of life amongst the
great nobilities of the north.   He hastened to
respond in the same spirit with an exquisite
deference of manner.

She greeted him with affable and smiling
words, and he devoted himself to her with defer-

ence and gallantry, expressing all his sense of
gratitude for the succour and shelter he received, with a few eloquent and elegant phrases
which said enough and not too much, with a
grace that it is difficult to lend to gratitude
which is generally somewhat halting and un-
couth.

'His name must be in the Hof-Kalendar!'
she thought, as she replied to his protestations
with her prettiest smile which, despite her sacred
calling and her seventy years, was the smile of
a coquette.

'M. le Marquis,' she said, in her tender and
flute-like voice, 'I deserve none of your eloquent thanks. Age is sadly selfish. I did
nothing to rescue you, unless, indeed, Heaven
heard my unworthy prayer!—and this house is
not mine, nor anything in it; the owner of it,
and, therefore, your châtelaine of the moment,
is my grand-niece, the Countess Wanda von
Szalras.'

'That I had your intercession with Heaven,
however indirectly, was far more than I de-
served,' said Sabran, still standing before her.
'For the Countess Wanda, I have been twice in
her power, and she has been very generous.'

'She has done her duty, nothing more,' said
the Princess a little primly and petulantly, if
princesses and petulance can mingle. 'We

should have scarce been Christians if we had
not striven for your life.   As to leaving us this
day it was out of the question.   The storm
continues, the passes are torrents; I fear much
that it will even be impossible for your servant
to come from S. Johann; we could not send to
Matrey even this morning for the post-bag, and
they tell me the bridge is down over the Burgenbach.'

'I have wanted for nothing, and my
Parisian rogue is quite as well .yawning and
smoking his days away at S. Johann,' said Sabran.
'Oh, Madame! how can I ever express to you
all my sense of the profound obligations you
have laid me under, stranger that I am!'

'At least we were bound to atone for the
incivility of the Szalrassee,' said the Princess,
with her pretty smile.   'It is a very horrible
country to live in.   My niece, indeed, thinks it
Arcadia, but an Arcadia subject to the most
violent floods, and imprisoned in snow and frost
for so many months, does not commend itself to
me; no doubt it is very grand and romantic.'

The ideal of the Princess was neither grand
nor romantic : it was life in the little prim, yet
gay north German town in the palace of which
she and all her people had been born; a little
town, with red roofs, green alleys, straight toy-
like streets, clipped trees, stiff soldiers, set in the

midst of a verdant plain ; flat and green, and smooth as a card table.

The new comer interested her; she was quickly won by personal beauty, and he possessed this in a great degree. It was a face unlike any she had ever seen ; it seemed to her to bear mystery with it and melancholy, and she loved both those things ; perhaps because she had never met with either out of the pages of German poets and novelists of France. Those who are united to them in real life find them uneasy bedfellows.

'Perhaps he is some Kronprinz in disguise,' she thought with pleasure ; but then she sadly recollected that she knew every crown prince that there was in Europe. She would have liked to have asked him many questions, but her high-breeding was still stronger than her curiosity ; and a guest could never be interrogated.

Dinner was announced as served.

' My niece, the Countess Wanda,' said the Princess, with a little reluctance visible in her hesitation, 'will dine in her own rooms. She begs you to excuse her ; she is tired from the storm last night.'

' She will not dine with me,' thought Sabran, with the quick intuition natural to him.

' You leave me nothing to regret, Princess,'

he said readily, with a sweet smile, as he offered his arm to this lovely little lady, wrapped in laces fine as cobweb, with her great cross of emeralds pendent from her rosary.

A woman is never too old to be averse to the thought that she can charm; very innocent charming was that of the Princess Ottilie, and she thought with a sigh if she had married—if she had had such a son; yet she was not insensible to the delicate compliment which he paid her in appearing indifferent to the absence of his châtelaine and quite content with her own presence.

Throughout dinner in that great hall, he, sitting on her right hand, amused her, flattered her with that subtlest of all flattery, interest and attention; diverted her with gay stories of worlds unknown to her, and charmed her with his willingness to listen to her lament over the degeneracy of mankind and of manners. After a few words of courtesy as to his hostess's absence he seemed not even to remember that Wanda von Salzras was absent from the head of her table.

'And I have said that she was tired! She who is never more tired than the eagles are! May heaven forgive me the untruth!' thought the Princess more than once during the meal, which was long and magnificent, and at

which her guest ate sparingly and drank but
little.

'You have no appetite?' she said regretfully.

'Pardon me, I have a good one,' he
answered her; 'but I have always been content to eat little and drink less. It is the
secret of health; and my health is all my
riches.'

She looked at him with interest

'I should think your riches in that respect
are inexhaustible?'

He smiled.

'Oh yes! I have never had a day's illness,
except once, long ago in the Mexican swamps,
a marsh fever and a snake-bite.'

'You have travelled much?'

'I have seen most of the known world, and
a little of the unknown,' he answered. 'I am
like Ulysses; only there will be not even a dog
to welcome me when my wanderings are
done.'

'Have you no relatives?'

'None!' he added, with an effort. 'Everyone is dead; dead long ago. I have been long
alone, and I am very well used to it.'

'But you must have troops of friends?'

'Oh!—friends who will win my last napo-
leon at play, or remember me as long as they

meet me every day on the boulevards? Yes,
I have many of that sort, but they are not
worth Ulysses' dog.'

He spoke carelessly, without any regard to
the truth as far as it went, but no study would
have made him more apt to coin words to
attract the sympathy of his listeners.

'He is unfortunate,' she thought. 'How
often beauty brings misfortune. My niece
must certainly see him. I wish he belonged to
the Pontêves-Bargêmes!'

Not to have a name that she knew, one of
those names that fill all Europe as with the
trump of an archangel, was to be as one
maimed or deformed in the eyes of the Princess,
an object for charity, not for intercourse.

'Your title is of Brittany, I think?' she
said a little wistfully, and as he answered something abruptly in the affirmative, she solaced
herself once more with the remembrance that
there was a good deal of *petite noblesse*, honourable enough, though not in the 'Almanac de
Gotha,' which was a great concession from her
prejudices, invented on the spur of the interest
that he excited in her imagination.

'I never saw any person so handsome,' she
thought, as she glanced at his face; while he in
return thought that this silver-haired, soft-
cheeked, lace-enwrapped Holy Mother was *jolie*

à croquer in the language of those boulevards, which had been his nursery and his palestrum. She was so kind to him, she was so gracious and graceful, she chatted with him so frankly and pleasantly, and she took so active an interest in his welfare that he was touched and grateful. He had known many women, many young ones and gay ones; he had never known what the charm of a kindly and serene old age can be like in a woman who has lived with pure thoughts, and will die in hope and in faith; and this lovely old abbess, with her pretty touch of worldliness, was a study to him, new with the novelty of innocence, and of a kind of veneration. And he was careful not to let her perceive his mortification that the Countess von Szalras would not deign to dine in his presence. In truth, he thought of little else, but no trace of irritation or of absence of mind was to be seen in him as he amused the Princess, and discovered with her that they had in common . some friends amongst the nobilities of Saxony, of Wurtemberg, and of Bohemia.

'Come and take your coffee in my own room, the blue-room,' she said to him, and she rose and took his arm. 'We will go through the library; you saw it this morning, I imagine? It is supposed to contain the finest

collection of Black Letter in the empire, or so
we think.'

And she led him through the great halls
and up a few low stairs into a large oval room
lined with oaken bookcases, which held the
manuscripts, missals, and volumes of all dates
which had been originally gathered together by
one of the race who had been also a bishop and
a cardinal.

The library was oak-panelled, and had an
embossed and emblazoned ceiling; silver lamps
of old Italian *trasvorato* work, hung by silver
chains, and shed a subdued clear light; beneath the porphyry sculptures of the hearth a
fire of logs was burning, for the early summer
evening here is chill and damp; there were
many open fireplaces in Hohenszalras, intro-
duced there by a chilly Provençal princess, who
had wedded a Szalras in the seventeenth
century, and who had abolished the huge porcelain stoves in many apartments in favour of
grand carved mantel-pieces, and gilded and-
irons, and sweet smelling simple fires of aromatic woods, such as made glad the sombre hotels
and lonely châteaux of the France of the
Bourbons.

Before this hearth, with the dogs stretched
on the black bearskin rugs, his hostess was
seated; she had dined in a small dining-hall

opening out of the library, and was sitting reading with a shaded light behind her. She rose with astonishment, and, as he fancied, anger upon her face as she saw him enter, and stood in her full height beneath the light of one of the silver hanging lamps. She wore a gown of olive-coloured velvet, with some pale roses fastened amongst the old lace at her breast; she had about her throat several rows of large pearls, which she always wore night and day that they should not change their pure whiteness by disuse; she looked very stately, cold, annoyed, disdainful, as she stood there without speaking.

'It is my niece, the Countess von Szalras,' said the Princess to her companion in some trepidation. 'Wanda, my love, I was not aware you were here; I thought you were in your own octagon room; allow me to make you acquainted with your guest, whom you have already received twice with little ceremony I believe.'

The trifling falsehoods were trippingly but timidly said; the Princess's blue eyes sought consciously her niece's forgiveness with a pathetic appeal, to which Wanda, who loved her tenderly, could not be long obdurate. Had it been any other than Mme. Ottilie who had thus brought by force into .her presence a stranger whom she had marked her desire to avoid, the serene temper of the mistress of the Hohenszalrasburg would not have preserved its equanimity, and she would have quitted her library on the instant, sweeping a grand courtesy which should have been greeting and farewell at once to one too audacious. But the shy entreating appeal of the Princess's regard touched her heart, and the veneration she had borne from childhood to one so holy, and so sacred by years of grace, checked in her any utterance or sign of annoyance.

Sabran, meanwhile, standing by in some hesitation and embarrassment, bowed low with consummate grace, and a timidity not less graceful.

She advanced a step and held her hand out to him.

'I fear I have been inhospitable, sir,' she said to him in his own tongue. 'Are you wholly unhurt? You had a rough greeting from Hohenszalras.'

He took the tip of her fingers on his own and bent over them as humbly as over an empress's.

Well used to the world as he was, to its ceremonies, courts, and etiquettes, he was awed by her as if he were a youth; he lost his ready aptness of language, and his easy manner of adaptability.

'I am but a vagrant, Madame!' he murmured, as he bowed over her hand. 'I have
no right even to your charity!'

For the moment it seemed to her as if he
spoke in bitter and melancholy earnest, and she
looked at him in a passing surprise that changed
into a smile.

'You were a poacher certainly, but that is
forgiven. My aunt has taken you under her
protection; and you had the Kaiser's already:
with such a dual shelter you are safe. Are you
quite recovered?' she said, bending her grave
glance upon him. 'I have to ask your pardon
for my great negligence in not sending one
of my men to guide you over the pass to
Matrey.'

'Nay, if you had done so I should not have
enjoyed the happiness of being your debtor,'
he replied, meeting her close gaze with a
certain sense of confusion most rare with him;
and added a few words of eloquent gratitude,
which she interrupted almost abruptly:

'Pray carry no such burden of imaginary
debt, and have no scruples in staying as long
as you like; we are a mountain refuge, use it
as you would a monastery. In the winter we
have many travellers. We are so entirely in
the heart of the hills that we are bound by
all Christian laws to give a refuge to all who

need it. But how came you on the lake last evening? Could you not read the skies?'

He explained his own folly and hardihood, and added, with a glance at her, 'The offending rifle is in the Szalrassee. It was my haste to quit your dominions that made me venture on to the lake. I had searched in vain for the high road that you had told me of, and I thought if I crossed the lake I should be off your soil.'

'No; for many leagues you would not have been off it,' she answered him. 'Our lands are very large, and, like the Archbishopric of Berchtesgarten, are as high as they are broad. Our hills are very dangerous for strangers, especially until the snows of the passes have all melted. I repented me too late that I did not send a jäger with you as a guide.'

'All is well that ends well,' said the Princess. 'Monsieur is not the worse for his bath in the lake, and we have the novelty of an incident and of a guest, who we will hope in the future will become a friend.'

'Madame, if I dared hope that I should have much to live for!' said the stranger, and the Princess smiled sweetly upon him.

'You must have very much to live for, as it is. Were I a man, and as young as you, and as favoured by nature, I am afraid I should be tempted to live for—myself.'

'And I am most glad when I can escape from so poor a companion,' said he, with a melancholy in the accent and a passing pain that was not assumed.

Before this gentle and gracious old woman in this warm and elegant chamber he felt suddenly that he was a wanderer—perhaps an outcast.

'You need not use the French language with him, Wanda,' interrupted the Princess. 'The Marquis speaks admirable German : it is impossible to speak better.'

'We will speak our own tongue then,' said Wanda, who always regarded her aunt as though she were a petted and rather wayward child. 'Are you quite rested, M. de Sabran? and quite unhurt? I did not dine with you. It must have seemed churlish. But I am very solitary in my habits, and my aunt entertains strangers so much better than I do that I grow more hermitlike every year.'

He smiled ; he thought there was but little of the hermit in this woman's supreme elegance and dignity as she stood beside her hearth with its ruddy, fitful light playing on the great pearls at her throat and burnishing into gold the bronze shadows of her velvet gown.

'The Princess has told me that you are cruel to the world,' he answered her. 'But it is natural with such a kingdom that you seldom care to leave it.'

'It is a kingdom of snow for seven months out of the year,' said the Princess peevishly, 'and a water kingdom the other five. You see what it is to-day, and this is the middle of May!'

'I think one might well forget the rain and every other ill between these four walls,' said the French Marquis, as he glanced around him, and then slowly let his eyes rest on his châtelaine.

'It is a grand library,' she answered him; 'but I must warn you that there is nothing more recent in it than Diderot and Descartes. The cardinal—Hugo von Szalras—who collected it lived in the latter half of last century, and since his day no Szalras has been bookish save myself. The cardinal, however, had all the MSS. and the black letters, or nearly all, ready to his hand; what he added is a vast library of science and history, and he also got together some of the most beautiful missals in the world. Are you curious in such things?'

She rose as she spoke, and unlocked one of the doors of the oak bookcase and brought out an ivory missal carved by the marvellous Prönner of Klagenfurt, with the arms of the Szalras on one side of it and those of a princely German house on the other.

'That was the nuptial missal of Georg von Szalras and Ida Windisgratz in 1501,' she said; 'and these are all the other marriage-hours of our people, if you care to study them; and in that case next to this there is a wonderful Evangelistarium, with miniatures of Angelico's. But I see they tell all their stories to you; I see by the way you touch them that you are a connoisseur.'

'I fear I have studied them chiefly at the sales of the Rue Drouot,' said Sabran, with a smile; but he had a great deal of sound knowledge on all arts and sciences, and a true taste which never led him wrong. With an illuminated chronicle in his hand, or a book of hours on his knee, he conversed easily, discursively, charmingly, of the early scribes and the early masters; of monkish painters and of church libraries; of all the world has lost, and of all aid that art had brought to faith.

He talked well, with graceful and well-chosen language, with picturesque illustration, with a memory that never was at fault for name or date, or apt quotation; he spoke fluent and eloquent German, in which there was scarcely any trace of foreign accent; and he disclosed without effort the resources of a cultured and even learned mind.

The antagonism she had felt against the poacher of her woods melted away as she listened and replied to him; there was a melody in his voice and a charm in his manner that it was not easy to resist; and with the pale lights from the Italian lamp which swung near upon the fairness of his face she reluctantly owned that her aunt had been right: he was singularly handsome, with that uncommon and grand cast of beauty which in these days is rarer than it was in the times of Vandyck and of Velasquez—for manners and moods leave their trace on the features, and this age is not great.

The Princess in her easy-chair, for once not sleeping after dinner, listened to her and thought to herself, 'She is angry with me; but how much better it is to talk with a living being than to pass the evening over a philosophical treatise, or the accounts of her schools, or her stables!'

Sabran having conquered the momentary reluctance and embarrassment which had overcome him in the presence of the woman to whom he owed both an outrage and a rescue, endeavoured, with all the skill he possessed, to interest and beguile her attention. He knew

that she was a great lady, a proud woman, a
recluse, and a student, and a person averse to
homage and flattery of every kind ; he met her
on the common ground of art and learning,
and could prove himself her equal at all times,
even occasionally her master.　When he fancied
she had enough of such serious themes he spoke
of music.　There was a new opera then out at
Paris, of which the theme was as yet scarcely
known.　He looked round the library and said
to her :

'Were there an organ here or a piano I
could give you some idea of the motive ; I can
recall most of it.'

'There are both in my own room.　It
is near here,' she said to him.　'Will you
come ?'

Then she led the way across the gallery,
which alone separated the library from that
octagon room which was so essentially her
own where all were hers. The Princess accompanied her : content as a child is who has put a
light to a slow match that leads it knows not
whither.　'She must approve of him, or she
would not take him there,' thought the wise
Princess.

'Go and play to us,' said Wanda von
Szalras, as her guest entered the sacred room.
'I am sure you are a great musician ; you

speak of music as we only speak of what we love.'

'What do you love?' he wondered mutely, as he sat down before the grand piano and struck a few chords. He sat down and played without prelude one of the most tender and most grave of Schubert's sonatas. It was subtle, delicate, difficult to interpret, but he gave it with consummate truth of touch and feeling. He had always loved German music best. He played on and on, dreamily, with a perfection of skill that was matched by his tenderness of interpretation.

'You are a great artist,' said his hostess, as he paused.

He rose and approached her.

'Alas! no, I am only an amateur,' he answered her. 'To be an artist one must needs have immense faith in one's art and in oneself: I have no faith in anything. An artist steers straight to one goal; I drift.'

'You have drifted to wise purpose——' You must have studied much?'

'In my youth. Not since. An artist! Ah! how I envy artists! They believe; they aspire; even if they never attain, they are happy, happy in their very torment, and through it, like lovers.'

'But your talent——'

'Ah, Madame, it is only talent; it is nothing else.　The *feu sacré* is wanting.'

She looked at him with some curiosity.

'Perhaps the habit of the world has put out that fire : it often does.　But if even it be only talent, what a beautiful talent it is !　To carry all that store of melody safe in your memory—— it is like having sunlight and moonlight ever at command.'

Lizst had more than once summoned the spirits of Heaven to his call there in that same room in Hohenszalras ; and since his touch no one had ever made the dumb notes speak as this stranger could do, and the subdued power of his voice added to the melody he evoked.　The light of the lamps filled with silvery shadows the twilight of the chamber ; the hues of the tapestries, of the ivories, of the gold and silver work, of the paintings, of the embroideries, made a rich chiaro-oscuro of colour ; the pine cones and the dried thyme burning on the hearth shed an aromatic smell on the air ; there were large baskets and vases full of hothouse roses and white lilies from the gardens ; she sat by the hearth, left in shadow. except where the twilight caught the gleam of her pearls and the shine of her eyes ; she listened, the jewels on her hand glancing like little stars as she slowly waved to and fro a feather screen in rhythm with what he sang or played : so might Mary Stuart have looked, listening to Rizzio or Ronsard. 'She is a queen !' he thought, and he sang—

' Si j'étais Roi ! '

'Go on !' she said, as he paused ; he had thrown eloquence and passion into the song.

'Shall I not tire you ?'

'That is only a phrase ! Save when Liszt passes by here I never hear such music as yours.'

He obeyed her, and played and sang many and very different things.

At last he rose a little abruptly.

Two hours had gone by since they had entered the octagon chamber.

'It would be commonplace to thank you,' she murmured with a little hesitation. 'You have a great gift ; one of all gifts the most generous to others.'

He made a gesture of repudiation, and walked across to a spinet of the fifteenth century, inlaid with curious devices by Martin Pacher of Brauneck, and having a painting of his in its lid.

'What a beautiful old box,' he said, as he touched it. 'Has it any sound, I wonder ? If one be disposed to be sad, surely of all sad things an old spinet is the saddest ! To

think of the hands that have touched, of
the children that have danced to it, of the
tender old ballads that have been sung to the
notes that to us seem so hoarse and so
faulty! All the musicians dead, dead so long
ago, and the old spinet still answering when
anyone calls! Shall I sing you a madrigal
to it?'

Very tenderly, very lightly, he touched the
ivory keys of the painted toy of the ladies so
long dead and gone, and he sang in a minor
key the sweet, sad, quaint poem :—

Où sont les neiges d'antan ?

That ballad of fair women echoed softly
through the stillness of the chamber, touched
with the sobbing notes of the spinet, even as
it might have been in the days of its writer :

Où sont les neiges d'antan ?

The chords of the old music-box seemed to
sigh and tremble with remembrance. Where
were they, all the beautiful dead women, all
the fair imperious queens, all the loved, and all
the lovers? Where were they? The snow had
fallen through so many white winters since that
song was sung—so many! so many!

The last words thrilled sadly and sweetly
through the silence.

He rose and bowed very low.

'I have trespassed too long on your patience, madame; I have the honour to wish you good-night.'

Wanda von Szalras was not a woman quickly touched to any emotion, but her eyelids were heavy with a mist of unshed tears, as she raised them and looked up from the fire, letting drop on her lap the screen of plumes.

'If there be a Lorelei in our lake, no wonder from envy she tried to drown you,' she said, with a smile that cost her a little effort. 'Good-night, sir; should you wish to leave us in the morning, Hubert will see you reach S. Johann safely and as quickly as can be.'

'Your goodness overwhelms me,' he murmured. 'I can never hope to show my gratitude——'

'There is nothing to be grateful for,' she said quickly. 'And if there were, you would have repaid it: you have made a spinet, silent for centuries, speak, and speak to our hearts. Good-night, sir; may you have good rest and a fair journey!'

When he had bowed himself out, and the tapestry of the door had closed behind him, she rose and looked at a clock.

'It is actually twelve!'

'Acknowledge at least that he has made

the evening pass well!' said the Princess, with
a little petulance and much triumph.

'He has made it pass admirably,' said her
niece. 'At the same time, dear aunt, I think it
would have been perhaps better if you had not
made a friend of a stranger.'

'Why?' said the Princess with some asperity.

'Because I think we can fulfil all the duties
of hospitality without doing so, and we know
nothing of this gentleman.'

'He is certainly a gentleman,' said the
Princess, with not less asperity. 'It seems to
me, my dear Wanda, that you are for once in
your life—if you will pardon me the expression
—ill-natured.'

The Countess Wanda smiled a little.

'I cannot imagine myself ill-natured; but
I may be so. One never knows oneself.'

'And ungrateful,' added the Princess.
'When, I should like to know, have you
for years reached twelve o'clock at night without being conscious of it?'

'Oh, he sang beautifully, and he played
superbly,' said her niece, still with the same
smile, balancing her ostrich-feathers. 'But let
him go on his way to-morrow; you and I cannot entertain strange men, even though they
give us music like Rubenstein's.'

'If Egon were here ——'

'Oh, poor Egon! I think he would not like your friend at all. They both want to shoot eagles——'

'Perhaps he would not like him for another reason,' said the Princess, with a look of mystery. 'Egon could never make the spinet speak.'

'No; but who knows? Perhaps he can take better care of his own soul because he cannot lend one to a spinet!'

'You are perverse, Wanda!'

'Perverse, inhospitable, and ill-natured? I fear I shall carry a heavy burden of sins to Father Ferdinand in the morning!'

'I wish you would not send horses to S. Johann in the morning. We never have anything to amuse us in this solemn solitary place.'

'Dear aunt, one would think you were very indiscreet.'

'I wish you were more so!' said the pretty old lady with impatience, and then her hand made a sign over the cross of emeralds, for she knew that she had uttered an unholy wish. She kissed her niece with repentant tenderness, and went to her own apartments.

Wanda von Szalras, left alone in her chamber, stood awhile thoughtfully beside the fire; then she moved away and touched the yellow ivory of the spinet keys.

'Why could he make them speak,' she said to herself, 'when everyone else always failed?'

CHAPTER IV.

SABRAN, as he undressed himself and laid himself down under the great gold-fringed canopy of the stately bed, thought: 'Was I only a clever comedian to-night, or did my eyes really grow wet as I sang that old song and see her face through a mist as if she and I had met in the old centuries long ago?'

He stood and looked a moment at his own reflection in the great mirror with the wax candles burning in its sconces. He was very pale.

Où sont les neiges d'antan ?

The burden of it ran through his mind.

Almost it seemed to him long ago—long ago—she had been his lady and he her knight, and she had stooped to him, and he had died for her.   Then he laughed a little harshly.

' I grow that best of all actors,' he thought, ' an actor who believes in himself!'

Then he turned from the mirror and stretched himself on the great bed, with its carved warriors at its foot and its golden crown at its head, and its heavy amber tissues shining in the shadows.   He was a sound sleeper at all times.   He had slept peacefully on a wreck, in a hurricane, in a lonely hut on the Andes, as after a night of play in Paris, in Vienna, in Monaco.   He had a nerve of steel, and that perfect natural constitution which even excess and dissipation cannot easily impair.   But this night, under the roof of Hohenszalras, in the guest-chamber of Hohenszalras, he could not summon sleep at his will, and he lay long wide awake and restless, watching the firelight play on the figures upon the tapestried walls, where the lords and ladies of Tuscan Boccaccio and their sinful loves were portrayed in stately and sombre guise, and German costumes of the days of Maximilian.

Où sont les neiges d'antan ?

The line of the old romaunt ran through his brain, and when towards dawn he did at length fall asleep it was not of Hohenszalras that he dreamed, but of wide white steppes, of a great ice-fed rolling river, of monotonous pine woods, with the gilded domes of a half eastern city rising beyond them in the pale blue air of a northern twilight.

With the early morning he awoke, resolute to get away be the weather what it would. As it chanced, the skies were heavy still, but no rain fell; the sun was faintly struggling through the great black masses of cloud; the roads might be dangerous, but they were not impassable; the bridge over the Bürgenbach might be broken, but at least Matrey could be reached, if it were not possible to go on farther to Taxenbach or S. Johann im Wald. High north, where far away stretched the wild marshes and stony swamps of the Pinzgau (the Pinzgau so beautiful, where in its hilly district the grand Salzach rolls on its impetuous way beneath deep shade of fir-clad hills, tracks desolate as a desert of sand or stone), the sky was overcast, and of an angry tawny colour that brooded ill for the fall of night. But the skies were momentarily clear, and he desired to rid of his presence the hospitable roof beneath which he was but an alien and unbidden.

He proposed to leave on foot, but of this neither Greswold nor the major-domo would hear : they declared that such an indignity would dishonour the Hohenszalrasburg for evermore. Guests there were masters. 'Bidden guests, perhaps,' said Sabran, reluctantly yielding to be sped on his way by a pair of the strong Hungarian horses that he had seen and admired in their stalls. He did not venture to disturb the ladies of the castle by a request for a farewell audience at the early hour at which it was necessary he should depart if he wished to try to reach a railway the same evening, but he left two notes for them, couched in that graceful compliment of which his Parisian culture made him an admirable master, and took a warm adieu of the good physician, with a promise not to forget the orchid of the Spiritù Santo. Then he breakfasted hastily, and left the tapestried chamber in which he had dreamed of the Nibelungen Queen.

At the door he drew a ring of great value from his finger and passed it to Hubert, but the old man, thanking him, protested he dared not take it.

'Old as I am in her service,' he said, 'the Countess would dismiss me in an hour if I accepted any gifts from a guest.'

'Your lady is very severe,' said Sabran. 'It is happy for her she has servitors who subscribe to feudalism. If she were in Paris——'

'We are bound to obey,' said the old man, simply. 'The Countess deals with us most generously and justly. We are bound, in return, to render her obedience.'

'All the antique virtues have indeed found refuge here!' said Sabran; but he left the ring behind him lying on a table in the Rittersäal.

Four instead of two vigorous and half-broke horses from the Magyar plains bore him away in a light travelling carriage towards the Virgenthal; the household, with Herr Joachim at their head, watching with regret the travelling carriage wind up amongst the woods and disappear on the farther side of the lake. He himself looked back with a pang of envy and regret at the stately pile towering towards the clouds, with its deep red banner streaming out on the wind that blew from the northern plains.

'Happy woman!' he thought; 'happy—thrice happy—to possess such dominion, such riches, and such ancestry! If I had had them I would have had the world under my foot as well!'

It was with a sense of pain that he saw the great house disappear behind its screen of mantling woods, as his horses climbed the hilly path beyond, higher and higher at every step, until all that he saw of Hohenszalras was a strip of the green lake—green as an arum leaf—

lying far down below, bearing on its waters the grey willows of the Holy Isle.

'When I am very old and weary I will come and die there,' he thought, with a touch of that melancholy which all his irony and cynicism could not dispel from his natural temper. There were moments when he felt that he was but a lonely and homeless wanderer on the face of the earth, and this was one of those moments, as, alone, he went upon his way along the perilous path, cut along the face of precipitous rocks, passing over rough bridges that spanned deep defiles and darkening ravines, clinging to the side of a mountain as a swallow's nest clings to the wall of a house, and running high on swaying galleries above dizzy depths, where nameless torrents plunged with noise and foam into impenetrable chasms. The road had been made in the fifteenth century by the Szalras lords themselves, and the engineering of it was bold and vigorous though rude, and kept in sound repair, though not much changed.

He had left a small roll of paper lying beside the ring in the knight's hall. Hubert took them both to his mistress when, a few hours later, he was admitted to her presence. Opening the paper she saw a roll of a hundred napoleons, and on the paper was written, 'There can be

no poor where the Countess von Szalras rules.
Let these be spent in masses for the dead.'

'What a delicate and graceful sentiment,'
said the Princess Ottilie, with vivacity and
emotion.

'It is prettily expressed and gracefully
thought of,' her niece admitted.

'Charmingly—admirably!' said the Princess, with a much warmer accent. 'There is
delicate gratitude there, as well as a proper
feeling towards a merciful God.'

'Perhaps,' said her niece, with a little smile,
'the money was won at play, in giving some-
one else what they call a *culotte*; what would
you say then, dear aunt? Would it be puri-
fied by entering the service of the Church?'

'I do not know why you are satirical,' said
the Princess; 'and I cannot tell either how you
can bring yourself to use Parisian bad words.'

'I will send these to the Bishop,' said
Wanda, rolling up the gold. 'Alas! alas!
there are always poor. As for the ring, Hubert,
give it to Herr Greswold, and he will trans-
mit it to this gentleman's address in Paris, as
though it had been left behind by accident.
You were so right not to take it; but my dear
people are always faithful.'

These few words were dearer and more precious to the honest old man than all the jewels

in the world could ever have become. But the
offer of it and the gift of the gold for the
Church's use had confirmed the high opinion in
which he and the whole household of Hohenszalras held the departed guest.

'Allow at least that this evening will be
much duller than last!' said the Princess, with
much irritation.

'Your friend played admirably,' said Wanda
von Szalras, as she sat at her embroidery frame.

'You speak as if he were an itinerant
pianist! What is your dislike to your fellow-
creatures, when they are of your own rank,
based upon? If he had been a carpet-dealer
from the Defreggerthal, as I said before, you
would have bidden him stay a month.'

'Dearest aunt, be reasonable. How was
it possible to keep here on a visit a French
Marquis of whom we know absolutely nothing,
except from himself?'

'I never knew you were prudish!'

'I never knew either that I was,' said the
Countess Wanda, with her serene temper unruffled. 'I quite admit your new friend has
many attractive qualities—on the surface at any
rate; but if it were possible for me to be angry
with you, I should be so for bringing him as you
did into the library last night.'

'You would never have known your spinet

could speak if I had not. You are very un-grateful, and I should not be in the least sur-prised to find that he was a Crown Prince or a Grand Duke travelling incognito.'

'We know them all, I fear.'

'It is strange he should not have his name in the Hof-Kalender, beside the Sabran-Pon-têves!' insisted the Princess. 'He looks *prince du sang*, if ever anyone did; so——'

'There is good blood outside your Hof Kalender, dear mother mine.'

'Certainly,' said the Princess, 'he must surely be a branch of that family, though it would be more satisfactory if one found his record there. One can never know too much or too certainly of a person whom one admits to friendship.'

'Friendship is a very strong word,' said Wanda von Szalras, with a smile. 'This gentle-man has only made a hostelry of Hohenszalras for a day or two, and even that was made against his will. But as you are so interested in him, *meine Liebe*, read this little record I have found.'

She gave the Princess an old leather-bound volume of memoirs, written and published at Lausanne, by an obscure noble in his exile, in the year 1798. She had opened the book at one of the pages that narrated the fates of

many nobles of Brittany, relatives or comrades
of the writer.

'And foremost amongst these,' said this
little book, 'do I ever and unceasingly regret
the loss of my beloved cousin and friend, Yvon
Marquis de Sabran-Romaris. So beloved was
he in his own province that even the Con-
vention was afraid to touch him, and being
poor, despite his high descent, as his father
had ruined his fortunes in play and splendour
at the court of Louis XV., he thought to escape
the general proscription, and dwell peaceably
on his rock-bound shores with his young children. But the blood madness of the time so
grew upon the nation that even the love of his
peasantry and his own poverty could not defend
him, and one black, bitter day an armed mob
from Vannes came over the heath, burning all
they saw of ricks, or homesteads, or châteaux,
or cots, that they might warm themselves by
those leaping fires; and so they came on at last,
yelling, and drunk, and furious, with torches
flaming and pikes blood-stained, up through
the gates of Romaris. Sabran went out to
meet them, leading his eldest son by the hand,
a child of eight years old. "What seek ye?"
he said to them: "I am as poor as the poorest
of you, and consciously have done no living
creature wrong. What do you come for here?"

The calm courage of him, and the glance of his eyes, which were very beautiful and proud, quelled the disordered, mouthing, blood-drunk multitude in a manner, and moved them to a sort of reverence, so that the leader of them, stepping forth, said roughly, " Citizen, we come to slit your throat and burn your house ; but if you will curse God and the King, and cry ' Long live the sovereign people ! ' we will leave you alone, for you have been the friend of the poor. Come, say it !—come, shout it with both lungs !—it is not much to ask." Sabran put his little boy behind him with a tender gesture, then kissed the hilt of his sword, which he held unsheathed in his hand : " I sorrow for the people," he said, " since they are misguided and mad. But I believe in my God and I love my King, and even so shall my children do after me ; " and the words were scarce out of his mouth before a score of pikes ran him through the body, and the torches were tossed into his house, and he and his perished like so many gallant gentlemen of the time, a prey to the blind fury of an ingrate mob.'

The Princess Ottilie's tender eyes moistened as she read, and she closed the volume reverently, as though it were a sacred thing.

' I thank you for sending me such a history,' she said. ' It does one's soul good in these sad, bitter days of spiritless selfishness and utter lack of all impersonal devotion. This gentleman must, then, be a descendant of the child named in this narrative?'

'The story says that he and his perished,' replied her niece. 'But I suppose that child, or some other younger one, escaped the fire and the massacre. If ever we see him again, we will ask him. Such a tradition is as good as a page in the Almanac de Gotha.'

'It is,' accented the Princess. 'Where did you find it?'

'I read those memoirs when I was a child, with so many others of that time,' answered the Countess Wanda. 'When I heard the name of your new friend it seemed familiar to me, and thinking over it, I remembered these Breton narratives.'

'At least you need not have been afraid to dine with him!' said the Princess Ottilie, who could never resist having the last word, though she felt that the retort was a little ungenerous, and perhaps undeserved.

Meantime Sabran went on his way through the green valley under the shadow of the Klein and the Kristallwand, with the ice of the great Schaltten Gletscher descending like a huge frozen torrent. When he reached the last stage before Matrey he dismissed his postillions with a gratuity as large as the money remaining in his belt would permit, and insisted on taking his way on foot over the remaining miles. Baggage he had none, and he had not even the weight of his knapsack and rifle. The men remonstrated with him, for they were afraid of their lady's anger if they returned when they were still half a German mile off their destination. But he was determined, and sent them backwards, whilst they could yet reach home by daylight. The path to Matrey passed across pastures and tracts of stony ground; he took a little goatherd with him as a guide, being unwilling to run the risk of a second misadventure, and pressed on his way without delay.

The sun had come forth from out a watery world of cloud and mist, which shrouded from sight all the domes and peaks and walls of ice of the mountain region in which he was once more a wanderer. But when the mists had lifted, and the sun was shining, it was beautiful exceedingly: all the grasses were full of the countless wild flowers of the late Austrian spring; the swollen brooks were blue with mouse-ear, and the pastures with gentian; clumps of daffodils blossomed in all the mossy nooks, and hyacinths purpled the pine-woods. On the upper slopes the rain-fog still hung heavily, but the sun-rays pierced it here and there, and the white vaporous atmosphere was full of fantastic suggestions and weird half-seen shapes, as pine-trees loomed out of the mist or a vast black mass of rock towered above the clouds. A love of nature, of out-of-door movement, of healthful exercise and sports, resisted in him the enervating influences of the Paris life which he had led. He had always left the gay world at intervals for the simple and rude pleasures of the mountaineer and the hunter. There was an impulse towards that forest freedom which at times mastered him, and made the routine of worldly dissipation and diversion wholly intolerable to him. It was what his fair critic of Paris had called his barbarism, which broke up out of the artificial restraints and habits imposed by the world.

His wakeful night had made him fanciful, and his departure from Hohenszalras had made him regretful; for he, on his way back to Paris and all his habits and associates and pleasures, looking around him on the calm white mountain-sides, and penetrated by the pure, austere mountain silence, suddenly felt an intense desire to stay amidst that stillness and that solitude, and rest here in the green heart of the Tauern.

'Who knows but one might see her again?' he thought, as the sound of the fall of the Gschlossbach came on his ear from the distance.

That stately figure seated by the great wood fire, with the light on her velvet skirts, and the pearls at her throat, and the hounds lying couched beside her, was always before his memory and his vision.

And he paid and dismissed his goatherd at the humble door of the Zum Rautter in Windisch-Matrey, and that evening began discussing with Christ Rangediner and Egger, the guides there, the ascent of the Kahralpe and the Lasörling, and the pass to Krimml, over the ice crests of the Venediger group.

A mountaineer who had dwelt beneath the shadow of Orizaba was not common in the heart of the Tauern, and the men made much of their new comrade, not the less because the gold pieces rattled in his pouch, and the hunting-watch he carried had jewels at its back.

'If anyone had told me that in the Mois de Marie I should bury myself under an Austrian glacier!' he thought, with some wonder at his own decision, for he was one of those foster-sons of Paris to whom *parisine* is an habitual and necessary intoxication.

But there comes a time when even parisine, like chloral, ceases to have power to charm; in a vague way he had often felt the folly and the hollowness of the life that turned night into day, made the green cloth of the gaming-table the sole field of battle, and offered as all form of love the purchased smile of the *belle petite*. A sense of repose and of freshness, like the breath of a cool morning blowing on tired eyes, came to him as he sat in the grey twilight amidst the green landscape, with the night coming down upon the eternal snows above, whilst the honest, simple souls around him talked of hill perils and mountaineers' adventures, and all the exploits of a hardy life; and in the stillness, when their voices ceased, there was no sound but the sound of water up above amidst the woods, tumbling and rippling in a hundred unseen brooks and falls.

'If they had let me alone,' he thought, 'I should have been a hunter all my days; a guide, perhaps, like this Christ and this Egger here. An honest man, at least——'.

His heart was heavy and his conscience ill at ease. The grand, serene glance of Wanda von Szalras seemed to have reached his soul and called up in him unavailing regrets, pangs of doubt long dormant, vague remorse long put to sleep with the opiate of the world-taught cynicism, which had become his second nature. The most impenetrable cynicism will yield and melt, and seem but a poor armour, when it is brought amidst the solemnity and solitude of the high hills.

CHAPTER V.

A FEW days later there arrived by post the 'Spiritù Santo' of Mexico, addressed to the Professor Joachim Greswold.

If he had received the order of the Saint Esprit he would not have been more honoured, more enchanted; and he was deeply touched by the remembrance of him testified by the gift whose donor he supposed was back in the gay world of men, not knowing the spell which the snow mountains of the Tauern had cast on a worldly soul. When he was admitted to the presence of the Princess Ottilie to consult with her on her various ailments, she conversed with him of this passer-by who had so fascinated her fancy, and she even went so far as to permit him to bring her the great

volumes of the 'Mexico' out of the library, and
point her out those chapters which he considered most likely to interest her.

'It is the work of a true Catholic and gentleman,' she said with satisfaction, and perused
with special commendation the passages which
treated of the noble conduct of the Catholic
priesthood in those regions, their frequent
martyrdom and their devoted self-negation.
When she had thoroughly identified their late
guest with the editor of these goodly and
blameless volumes, she was content to declare
that better credentials no man could bear.   Indeed she talked so continually of this single
point of interest in her monotonous routine of
life, that her niece said to her, with a jest that
was more than half earnest, 'Dearest mother,
almost you make me regret that this gentleman
did not break his neck over the Engelhorn, or
sink with his rifle in the Szalrassee.'

'The spinet would never have spoken,' said
the Princess; 'and I am surprised that a
Christian woman can say such things, even in
joke!'

The weather cleared, the sun shone, the
gardens began to grow gorgeous, and great
parterres of roses glowed between the emerald of
the velvet lawns : an Austrian garden has not a
long life, but it has a very brilliant one.   All

on a sudden, as the rains ceased, every alley, group, and terrace were filled with every variety of blossom, and the flora of Africa and India was planted out side by side with the gentians and the alpine roses natural to the soil. All the northern coniferæ spread the deep green of their branches above the turf, and the larch, the birch, the beech, and the oak were massed in clusters, or spread away in long avenues—deep defiles of foliage through which the water of the lake far down below glistened like a jewel.

'If your friend had been a fortnight later he would have seen Hohenszalras in all its beauty,' said its mistress once to the Princess Ottilie. 'It has two seasons of perfection : one its mid-summer flowering, and the other when all the world is frozen round it.'

The Princess shivered in retrospect and in anticipation. She hated winter. 'I should never live through another winter,' she said with a sigh.

'Then you shall not be tried by one ; we will go elsewhere,' said Wanda, to whom the ice-bound world, the absolute silence, the sense of the sleigh flying over the hard snow, the perfect purity of the rarefied air of night and day, made up the most welcome season of the year.

'I suppose it is dull for you,' she added,

indulgently. ' I have so many occupations in the winter; a pair of skates and a sleigh are to me of all forms of motion the most delightful. But you, shut up in your blue-room, do no doubt find our winter hard and long.'

'I hybernate, I do not live,' said the Princess, pettishly. 'It is not even as if the house were full.'

'With ill-assorted guests whose cumbersome weariness one would have to try all day long to dissipate! Oh, my dear aunt, of all wearisome *corvées* the world holds there is nothing so bad as a house party—even when Egon is here to lead the cotillion and the hunting.'

'You are very inhospitable!'

'That is the third time lately you have made that charge against me. I begin to fear that I must deserve it.'

'You deserve it, certainly. Oh, you are hospitable to the poor. You set pedlars, or mule-drivers, or travelling clockmakers, by the dozen round your hall fires, and you would feed a pilgrimage all the winter long. But to your own order, to your own society, you are inhospitable. In your mother's time the Schloss had two hundred guests for the autumn parties, and then the winter season, from Carnival to Easter, was always spent in the capital.'

' She liked that, I suppose.'

' Of course she liked it; everyone ought to like it at what was her age then, and what is yours now.'

' I like this,' said the Countess Wanda, to change the subject, as the servants set a little Japanese tea-table and two arm-chairs of gilt osier-work under one of the Siberian pines, whose boughs spread tent-like over the grass, on which the dogs were already stretched in anticipation of sugar and cakes.

From this lawn there were seen only the old keep of the burg and the turrets and towers of the rest of the building; ivy clambered over one-half of the great stone pile, that had been raised with hewn rock in the ninth century; and some arolla pines grew about it. A low terrace, with low broad steps, separated it from the gardens. A balustrade of stone, ivy-mantled, protected the gardens from the rocks; while these plunged in a perpendicular descent of a hundred feet into the lake. Some black yews and oaks, very large and old, grew against the low stone pillars. It was a favourite spot with the mistress of Hohenszalras; it looked westward, and beyond the masses of the vast forests there shone the snow summit of the Venediger and the fantastic peaks of the Klein and Kristallwand, whilst on a still day there could be heard a low sound which she, familiar with it, knew came from the thunder of the subterranean torrents filling the Szalrassee.

'Oh, it is very nice,' said the Princess, a little deprecatingly. 'And of course I at my years want nothing better than a gilt chair in the sunshine. But then there is so very little sunshine! The chair must generally stand by the stove! And I confess that I think it would be fitter for your years and your rank if these chairs were multiplied by ten or twenty, and if there were some pretty people laughing and talking and playing games in those great gardens.'

'It is glorious weather now,' said her niece, who would not assent and did not desire to dispute.

'Yes,' interrupted the Princess. 'But it will rain to-morrow. You know we never have two fine days together.'

'We will take it while we have it, and be thankful,' said Wanda, with a good-humour that refused to be ruffled. 'Here is Hubert coming out to us. What can he want? He looks very startled and alarmed.'

The old major-domo's face was indeed gravely troubled, as he bowed before his lady.

'Pardon me the intrusion, my Countess,' he said hurriedly. 'But I thought it right to inform you myself that a lad has come over from Steiner's Inn to say that the foreign gentleman who was here fifteen days ago has had an accident on the Umbal glacier. It seems he stayed on in Matrey for sake of the climbing and the shooting. I do not make out from the boy what the accident was, but the Umbal is very dangerous at this season. The gentleman lies now at Pregratten. You know, my ladies, what a very wretched place that is.'

'I suppose they have come for the Herr Professor?' said Wanda, vaguely disturbed, while the Princess very sorrowfully was putting a score of irrelevant questions which Hubert could not answer.

'No doubt he has no doctor there, and these people send for that reason,' said Wanda, interrupting with an apology for the useless interrogations. 'Get horses ready directly, and send for Greswold at once wherever he may be. But it is a long bad way to Pregratten; I do not see how he can return under twenty-four hours.'

'Let him stay two nights, if he be wanted,' said the Princess, to whom she spoke. She had always insisted that the physician should never be an hour out of Hohenszalras whilst she was in it.

'Your friend has been trying to shoot a

kuttengeier again, I suppose,' said her niece, with a smile. ' He is very adventurous.'

' And you are very heartless.'

Wanda did not deny the charge ; but she went into the house, saw the doctor, and requested him to take everything with him of linen, wines, food, or cordials that might possibly be wanted.

' And stay as long as you are required,' she added, ' and send mules over to us for anything you wish for. Do not think of us. If my dear aunt should ail anything I can dispatch a messenger to you, or call a physician from Salzburg.'

Herr Joachim said a very few words, thanked her gratefully, and took his departure behind two sure-footed mountain cobs that could climb almost like chamois.

' I think one of the Fathers should have gone too,' said Mme. Ottilie, regretfully.

' I hope he is not *in extremis*,' said her niece. ' And I fear if he were he would hardly care for spiritual assistance.'

' You are so prejudiced against him, Wanda ! '

' I do not think I am ever prejudiced,' said the Countess von Szalras.

' That is so like a prejudiced person ! ' said the Princess, triumphantly.

For twenty-four hours they heard nothing from Pregratten, which is in itself a miserable little hamlet lying amidst some of the grandest scenes that the earth holds : towards evening the next day a lad of the village came on a mule and brought a letter to his ladies from the Herr Professor, who wrote that the accident had been due, as usual, to the gentleman's own carelessness, and to the fact of the snow being melted by the midsummer sun until it was a thin crust over a deep crevasse. He had found his patient suffering from severe contusions, high fever, lethargy, and neuralgic pains, but he did not as yet consider there were seriously dangerous symptoms. He begged permission to remain, and requested certain things to be sent to him from his medicine-chests and the kitchens.

The boy slept at Hohenszalras that night, and in the morning returned over the hills to Pregratten with all the doctor had asked for. Wanda selected the medicines herself, and sent also some fruit and wine for which he did not ask : the Princess sent a bone of S. Ottilie in an ivory case and the assurance of her constant prayers. She was sincerely anxious and troubled. 'Such a charming person, and so handsome,' she said again and again. 'I suppose the priest of Pregratten is with him,'

Her niece did not remind her that her physician did not greatly love any priests whatever, though on that subject he was always discreetly mute at Hohenszalras.

For the next ten days Greswold stayed at Pregratten, and the Princess bore his absence, since it was to serve a person who had had the good fortune to fascinate her, and whom also she chose to uphold because her niece was, as she considered, unjust to him. Moreover, life at the burg was very dull to the Princess, whatever it might be to its châtelaine, who had so much interest in its farms, its schools, its mountains, and its villages : an interest which to her great-aunt seemed quite out of place, as all those questions, she considered, should belong to the priesthood and the stewards, who ought not to be disturbed in their direction, the one of spiritual and the other of agricultural matters. This break in the monotony of her time was agreeable to her—of the bulletins from Pregratten, of the dispatch of all that was wanted, of the additional pleasure of complaining that she was deprived of her doctor's counsels, and also of feeling at the same time that in enduring this deprivation she was doing a charitable and self-denying action. She further insisted on sending out to Steiner's Inn, greatly to his own discomfort, her own confessor.

'Nobles of Brittany have always deep religious feeling,' she said to her niece; 'and Father Ferdinand has such skill and persuasion with the dying.'

'But no one is dying,' said Wanda, a little impatiently.

'That is more than any human being can tell,' said the Princess, piously. 'At all events, Father Ferdinand always uses every occasion judiciously and well.'

Father Ferdinand, however, was not very comfortable in Pregratten, and soon returned, much jolted and worn by the transit on a hill pony. He was reserved about his visitation, and told his patroness sadly that he had been unable to effect much spiritual good, but that the stranger was certainly recovering from his hurts, and had the ivory case of S. Ottilie on his pillow; he had seemed averse, however, to confession, and therefore, of course, there had been no possibility for administration of the Sacrament.

The Princess was inclined to set this rebelliousness down to the fault of the physician, and determined to talk seriously to Greswold on spiritual belief as soon as he should return.

'If he be not orthodox we cannot keep him,' she said severely.

'He is orthodox, dear aunt,' said Wanda

von Szalras, with a smile. 'He adores the wonders of every tiny blossom that blows, and every little moss that clothes the rocks.'

'What a profane, almost sacrilegious answer!' said the Princess. 'I never should have imagined that *you* would have jested on sacred themes.'

'I did not intend a jest. I was never more serious. A life like our old Professor's is a perpetual prayer.'

'Your great-aunt Walburga belonged to the Perpetual Adoration,' rejoined the Princess, who only heard the last word but one. 'The order was very severe. I always think it too great a strain on finite human powers. She was betrothed to the Margraf Paul, but he was killed at Austerlitz, and she took refuge in a life of devotion. I always used to think that you would change Hohenszalras into a sacred foundation; but now I am afraid. You are a deeply religious woman, Wanda—at least I have always thought so—but you read too much German and French philosophy, and I fear it takes something from your fervour, from your entirety of devotion. You have a certain liberty of expression that alarms me at times.'

'I think it is a poor faith that dares not examine its adversaries' charges,' said her niece, quietly. 'You would have faith blindfolded,

They call me a bigot at the Court, however.
So you see it is hard to please all.'

'Bigot is not a word for a Christian and
Catholic sovereign to employ,' said the Princess,
severely. 'Her Majesty must know that there
can never be too great an excess in faith and
service.'

On the eleventh day Greswold returned
over the hills and was admitted to immediate
audience with his ladies.

'Herr von Sabran is well enough for me to
leave him,' he said, after his first very humble
salutations. 'But if your excellencies permit
it would be desirable for me to return there in
a day or two. Yes, my ladies, he is lying at
Steiner's Inn in Pregratten, a poor place enough,
but your goodness supplied much that was
lacking in comfort. He can be moved before
long. . There was never any great danger, but
it was a very bad accident. He is a good
mountaineer it seems, and he had been climbing
a vast deal in the Venediger group; that
morning he meant to cross the Umbal glacier
to the Ahrenthal, and he refused to take a
guide, so Isaiah Steiner tells me.'

'But I thought he left here to go to Paris?'

'He did so, my Countess,' answered the
doctor. 'But it seems he loves the mountains,
and their spell fell on him. When he sent back

your postillions he went on foot to Matrey, and there he remained; he thought the weather advanced enough to make climbing safe; but it is a dangerous pastime so early in summer, though Christ from Matrey, who came over to see him, tells me he is of the first form as a mountaineer. He reached the Clarahutte safely, and broke his fast there; crossing the Umbal the ice gave way, and he fell into a deep crevasse. He would be a dead man if a hunter on the Welitz side had not seen him disappear and given the alarm at the hut. With ropes and men enough they contrived to haul him up, after some hours, from a great depth. These accidents are very common, and he has to thank his own folly in going out on to the glacier un-accompanied. Of course he was insensible, con-tused, and in high fever when I reached there: the surgeon they had called from Lienz was an ignorant, who would soon have sent him for ever to as great a deep as the crevasse. He is very grateful to you both, my ladies, and would be more so were he not so angry with himself that it makes him sullen with the world. Men of his kind bear isolation and confinement ill. Steiner's is a dull place: there is nothing to hear but the tolling of the church bell and the fret of the Isel waters.'

'That means, my friend, that you want him

moved as soon as he can bear it?' said Wanda.
'I think he cannot very well come here. We
know nothing of him. But there is no reason
why you should not bring him to the Lake
Monastery. There is a good guest-chamber
(the Archbishop stayed there once), and he could
have your constant care there, and from here
every comfort.'

'Why should he not be brought to this
house?' interrupted Mdme. Ottilie; 'there are
fifty men in it already——'

'Servants and priests, no strangers. Beside,
this gentleman will be much more at his ease
on the Holy Isle, where he can recompense
the monks at his pleasure; he would feel infinitely annoyed to be further burdened with a
hospitality he never asked!'

'Of course it is as you please!' said the
Princess, a little irritably.

'Dear aunt! when he is on the island you
can send him all the luxuries and all the holy
books you may think good for him. Go over
to the monks if you will be so kind, Herr
Joachim, and prepare them for a sick guest;
and as for transport and all the rest of the
assistance you may need, use the horses and
the household as you see fit. I give you carte
blanche. I know your wisdom and your pru-
dence and your charity.'

The physician again returned to Pregratten, where he found his patient fretting with restless impatience at his enforced imprisonment. He had a difficulty in persuading Sabran to go back to that Szalrassee which had cost him so dear; but when he was assured that he could pay the monks what he chose for their hospitality, he at last consented to be taken to the island.

'I shall see her again,' he thought, with a little anger at himself. The mountain spirits had their own way of granting wishes, but they had granted his.

On the Holy Isle of the Szalrassee there was a small Dominican congregation, never more than twelve, of men chiefly peasant-born, and at this time all advanced in years. The monastery was a low, grey pile, almost hidden beneath the great willows and larches of the isle, but rich within from many centuries of gifts in art from the piety of the lords of Szaravola. It had two guest-chambers for male visitors, which were lofty and hung with tapestry, and which looked down the lake towards the north and west, to where beyond the length of water there rose the mighty forest hills washed by the Salzach and the Ache, backed by the distant Rhœtian Alps.

The island was almost in the centre of

the lake, and, at a distance of three miles, the rocks, on which the castle stood, faced it across the water that rippled around it and splashed its trees and banks. It was a refuge chosen in wild and rough times when repose was precious, and no spot on earth was ever calmer, quieter, more secluded than this where the fishermen never landed without asking a blessing of those who dwelt there, and nothing divided the hours except the bells that called to prayer or frugal food. The green willows and the green waters met and blended and covered up this house of peace as a warbler's nest is hidden in the reeds. A stranger resting-place had never befallen the world-tossed, restless, imperious, and dissatisfied spirit of the man who was brought there by careful hands lying on a litter, on a raft, one gorgeous evening of a summer's day—one month after he had lifted his rifle to bring down the *kuttengeier* in the woods of Wanda von Szalras.

'Almost thou makest me believe,' he murmured, when he lay and looked upward at the cross that shone against the evening skies, while the raft glided slowly over the water, and from the walled retreat upon the isle there came the low sound of the monks chanting their evensong.

They laid him down on a low, broad bed

opposite a window of three bays, which let him look from his couch along the shining length of the Szalrassee towards the great burg, where it frowned upon its wooded cliffs with the stone brows of many mountains towering behind it, and behind them the glaciers of the Glöckner and its lesser comrades.

The sun had just then set. There was a lingering glow upon the water, a slender moon had risen above a distant chain of pine-clothed hills, the slow, soft twilight of the German Alps was bathing the grandeur of the scene with tenderest, faintest colours and mists ethereal. The Ave Maria was ringing from the chapel, and presently the deep bells of the monastery chimed a Laus Deus.

'Do you believe in fate?' said Sabran abruptly to his companion Greswold.

The old physician gave a little gesture of doubt.

'Sometimes there seems something stronger than ourselves and our will, but maybe it is only our own weakness that has risen up and stands in another shape like a giant before us, as our shadow will do on a glacier in certain seasons and states of the atmosphere.'

'Perhaps that is all,' said Sabran. But he laid his head back on his pillow with a deep breath that had in it an equal share of contentment and regret, and lay still, looking eastward, while the peaceful night came down upon land and water unbroken by any sound except that of a gentle wind stirring amidst the willows or the plunge of an otter in the lake.

That deep stillness was strange to him who had lived so long in all the gayest cities of the world; but it was welcome: it seemed like a silent blessing: his life seemed to stand still while holy men prayed for him and the ramparts of the mountains shut out the mad and headlong world.

With these fancies he fell asleep and dreamed of pathless steppes, which in the winter snows were so vast and vague, stretching away, away, away to the frozen sea and the ice that no suns can melt, and ceaseless silence, where sleep is death.

In the monastic quiet of the isle he soon recovered sufficient strength to leave his bed and move about slowly, though he was still stiff and sprained from the fall on the Umbal; he could take his dinner in the refectory, could get out and sit under the great willows of the bank, and could touch their organ as the monks never had heard it played.

It was a monotonous and perfectly simple life; but either because his health was not yet strong, or because he had been surfeited

with excitement, it was not disagreeable or
irksome to him; he bore it with a serenity
and cheerfulness which the monks attributed
to religious patience, and Herr Joachim to
philosophy. It was not one nor the other: it
was partly from such willingness as an over-
taxed racer feels to lie down in the repose of
the stall for a while to recruit his courage and
speed: it was partly due to the certainty which
he felt that now, sooner or later, he must
see face to face once more the woman who had
forbade him to shoot the vulture.

The face which had looked on him in the
pale sunlight of the pine-woods, and made him
think of the Nibelungen queen, had been always
present to his thoughts, even during the semi-
stupor of sedative-lulled rest in his dull chamber
by the lonely Isel stream.

From this guest-room, where he passed his
convalescence, the wide casements all day long
showed him the towers and turrets, the metal
roofs, the pinnacles and spires of her mighty
home, backed by its solemn neighbours of the
glacier and the alps, and girdled with the
sombre green of the great forests. Once or
twice he thought as he looked at it and saw
the noon sun make its countless oriels sparkle
like diamonds, or the starlight change its stones
and marbles into dream-like edifices meet for

Arthur's own Avilion, once or twice he thought to himself, 'If I owned Hohenszalras, and she Romaris, I would write to her and say : " A moment is enough for love to be born." '

But Romaris was his—those aged oaks, torn by sea-winds and splashed with Atlantic spray, were all he had ; and she was mistress here.

When a young man made his first appearance in the society of Paris who was called Réné Philippe Xavier, Marquis de Sabran-Romaris, his personal appearance, which was singularly attractive, his manners, which were of extreme distinction, and his talents, which were great, made him at once successful in its highest society. He had a romantic history.

The son of that Marquis de Sabran who had fallen under the pikes of the mob of Carrier had been taken in secret out of the country by a faithful servant, smuggled on board a *chasse-marée*, which had carried him to an outward-bound sailing ship destined for the seaboard of America. The chaplain was devoted, the servant faithful. The boy was brought up well at a Jesuit college in Mexico, and placed in full possession, when he reached manhood, of his family papers and of such remnants of the family jewels as had been brought away with him. His identity as his father's only living son, and the sole representative of the Sabrans of

Romaris, was fully established and confirmed before the French Consulate of the city. Instead of returning to his country, as his Jesuit tutors advised and desired, the youth, when he left college, gave the reins to a spirit of adventure and a passion for archæology and natural history. He was possessed beyond all with the desire to penetrate the mystery of the buried cities, and he had conceived a strong attachment to the flowery and romantic land of Guatemozin and of Montezuma. He plunged, therefore, into the interior of that country, and, half as a Jesuit lay-missionary, and half as an archæological explorer, let all his best years slip away under the twilight shadows of the virgin forests, and amidst the flowering wilderness of the banks of the great rivers, making endless notes upon the ancient and natural history of these solitudes, and gathering together an interminable store of tradition from the Indians and the half-breeds with whom he grew familiar. He went further and further away from the cities, and let longer and longer intervals elapse without his old friends and teachers hearing anything of him. All that was known of him was that he had married a beautiful Mexican woman, who was said to have in her the blood of the old royal race, and that he lived far from the steps of white men in the depths of the hills whence the Pacific was in sight.   Once he went to the capital for the purpose of registering and baptizing his son by his Mexican wife.   After that he was lost sight of by those who cared for him, and it was only known that he was compiling a history of those lost nations whose temples and tombs, amidst the wilderness, had so powerfully attracted his interest as a boy.   A quarter of a century passed ; his old friends died away one by one, nobody remained in the country who remembered or asked for him.   The West is wide, and wild, and silent ; endless wars and revolutions changed the surface of the country and the thoughts of men ; the scholarly Marquis de Sabran, who only cared for a hieroglyphic, or an orchid, or a piece of archaic sculpture, passed away from the memories of the white men whose fellow student he had been.   The land was soaked in blood, the treasures were given up to adventurers ; the chiefs that each reigned their little hour, slew, and robbed, and burned, and fell in their turn shot like vultures or stabbed like sheep ; and no one in that murderous *tohu-bohu* had either time or patience to give to the thought of a student of perished altars and of swamp-flora.   The college, even, where the Jesuits had sheltered him, had been sacked and set on fire, and the old men and

the young men butchered indiscriminately.
When six-and-twenty years later he returned
to the capital to register the birth of his
grandson there was no one who remembered
his name.   Another quarter of a century passed
by, and when his young representative left the
Western world for Paris he received a tender
and ardent welcome from men and women to
whom his name was still a talisman, and found
a cordial recognition from that old nobility
whose pride is so cautious and impregnable in
its isolation and reserve.   Everyone knew that
the young Marquis de Sabran was the legitimate
representative of the old race that had made its
nest on the rocks with the sea birds through a
dozen centuries : that he had but little wealth
was rather to his credit than against it.

When he gave to the world, in his grandfather's name, the result of all those long years
of study and of solitude in the heart of the
Mexican forests, he carried out the task as only
a scientific scholar could have done it, and the
vast undigested mass of record, tradition, and
observation which the elder man had collected
together in his many years of observation and
abstraction were edited and arranged with so
much skill that their mere preparation placed
their young compiler in the front frank of culture.   That he disclaimed all merit of his own,

affirming that he had simply put together into shape all the scattered memoranda of the elder scholar, did not detract from the learning or from the value of his annotations. The volumes became the first authority on the ancient history and the natural history of a strange country, of which alike the past and the present were of rare interest, and their production made his name known where neither rank nor grace would have taken it. To those who congratulated him on the execution of so complicated and learned a work, he only replied: 'It is·no merit of mine: all the learning is his. In giving it to the world I do but pay my debt to him, and I am but a mere instrument of his as the printing-press is that prints it.'

This modesty, this affectionate loyalty in a young man whose attributes seemed rather to lie on the side of arrogance, of disdainfulness, and of coldness, attracted to him the regard of many persons to whom the mere idler, which he soon became, would have been utterly indifferent. He chose, as such persons thought, most unfortunately, to let his intellectual powers lie in abeyance, but he had shown that he possessed them. No one without large stores of learning and a great variety of attainments could have edited and annotated as he had done the manuscripts bequeathed to him by the Marquis

Xavier as his most precious legacy. ·He might have occupied a prominent place in the world of science ; but he was too indolent or too sceptical even of natural facts, or too swayed towards the pleasures of manhood, to care for continued consecration of his life to studies of which he was early a master, and it was the only serious work that he ever carried out or seemed likely ever to attempt. Gradually these severe studies were left further and further behind him ; but they had given him a certain place that no future carelessness could entirely forfeit. He grew to prefer to hear a *bluette d'amateur* praised at the Mirliton, to be more flattered when his presence was prayed for at a *première* of the Française; but it had carried his name wherever, in remote corners of the earth, two or three wise men were gathered together.

He had no possessions in France to entail any obligations upon him. The single tower of the manoir which the flames had left untouched, and an acre or two of barren shore, were all which the documents of the Sabrans enabled him to claim. The people of the department were indeed ready to adore him for the sake of the name he bore ; but he had the true Parisian's impatience of the province, and the hamlet of Romaris but rarely saw his face. The sombre seaboard; with its primitive people, its wintry storms, its monotonous country, its sad, hard, pious ways of life, had nothing to attract a man who loved the gaslights of the Champs-Elysées. Women loved him for that union of coldness and of romance which always most allures them, and men felt a certain charm of unused power in him which, coupled with his great courage and his skill at all games, fascinated them often against their judgment. He was a much weaker man than they thought him, but none of either sex ever discovered it. Perhaps he was also a better man than he himself believed. As he dwelt in the calm of this religious community his sins seemed to him many and beyond the reach of pardon.

Yet even with remorse, and a sense of shame in the background, this tranquil life did him good. The simple fare, the absence of excitement, the silent lake-dwelling where no sound came, except that of the bells or the organ, or the voices of fishermen on the waters, the 'early to bed and early to rise,' which were the daily laws of the monastic life—these soothed, refreshed, and ennobled his life.

CHAPTER VI.

THE days drifted by; the little boat crossed thrice a day from castle to monastery, bringing the physician, bringing books, food, fruit, wine; the rain came often, sheets of white water sweeping over the lake, and blotting the burg and the hills and the forests from sight; the sunshine came more rarely, but when it came it lit up the amphitheatre of the Glöckner group to a supreme splendour, of solemn darkness of massed pines, of snow-peaks shrouded in the clouds. So the month wore away; he was in no haste to recover entirely; he could pay the monks for his maintenance, and so felt free to stay, not being allowed to know that his food came from the castle as his books did. The simple priests were conquered and captivated

by him ; he played grand Sistine masses for
them, and canticles which he had listened to in
Nôtre Dame. Herr Joachim marvelled to see
him so passive and easily satisfied ; for he perceived that his patient could not be by nature
either very tranquil or quickly content ; but
the doctor thought that perhaps the severe
nervous shock of the descent on the Umbal
might have shakened and weakened him, and
knew that the pure Alpine air, the harmless
pursuits, and the early hours were the best
tonics and restoratives in the pharmacy of
Nature. Therefore he could consistently en-
courage him to stay, as his own wishes moved
him to do ; for to the professor the companionship and discussion of a scholarly and cultivated
man were rarities, and he had conceived an
affectionate interest in one whose life he had
in some measure saved ; for without skilled
care the crevasse of the Iselthal might have
been fatal to a mountaineer who had successfully climbed the highest peaks of the Andes.

‘ No doubt if I passed a year here,’ thought
Sabran, ‘ I should rebel and grow sick with
longing for the old unrest, the old tumult,
the old intoxication—no doubt ; but just now
it is very welcome : it makes me comprehend
why De Rancy created La Trappe, why so
many soldiers and princes and riotous livers

were glad to go out into a Paraclete amongst
the hills with S. Bruno or S. Bernard.'

He said something of the sort to Herr
Joachim, who nodded consent; but added:
'Only they took a great belief with them, and
a great penitence, the recluses of that time;
in ours men mistake satiety for sorrow, and
so when their tired vices have had time to
grow again, like nettles that have been gnawed
to the root but can spring up with fresh power
to sting, then, as their penitence was nothing
but fatigue, they get quickly impatient to go out
and become beasts again. All the difference
between our times and S. Bruno's lies there;
they believed in sin, we do not. I say, " we,"
I mean the voluptuaries and idlers of your
world.'

'Perhaps not,' answered Sabran, a little
gloomily. 'But we do believe in dishonour.'

'Do you?' said the doctor, with some
irony. 'Oh, I suppose you do. You may
seduce Gretchen: you must not forsake Faus-
tine; you must not lie to a man: you may lie
to a woman. You must not steal: you may
beggar your friend at baccara. I confess I
have never understood the confusion of your
unwritten laws on ethics and etiquette.'

Sabran laughed, but he did not take up the
argument; and the doctor thought that he

seemed becoming a little morose; since his escape from the tedium of confinement at Pregratten, confinement intolerable to a man of strength and spirit, he had always found his patient of great equability of temper, and of a good-humour and docility that had seemed as charming as they were invariable.

When he was recovered enough to make movement and change harmless to him, there came to him a note in the fine and miniature writing of the Princess Ottilie, bidding him come over to the castle at his pleasure, and especially inviting him, in her niece's name, to the noon-day breakfast at the castle on the following day, if his strength allowed.

He sat a quarter of an hour or more with the note on his knee, looking out at the light green willow foliage as it drooped above the deeper green of the lake.

'Our ladies are not used to refusals,' said the doctor, seeing his hesitation.

'I should be a churl to refuse,' said Sabran, with some little effort, which the doctor attributed to a remembered mortification, and so hastened to say:

'You are resentful still that the Countess Wanda took your rifle away? Surely she has made amends?'

'I was not thinking of that. She was per-

fectly right. She only treated me too well.
She placed her house and her household at my
disposition with a hospitality quite Spanish. I
owe her too much ever to be able to express
my sense of it.'

'Then you will come and tell her so?'

'I can do no less.'

Princess Ottilie and the mistress of Hohenszalras had had a discussion before that note of
invitation was sent; a discussion which had
ended as usual in the stronger reasoner giving
way to the whim and will of the weaker.

'Why should we not be kind to him?' the
Princess had urged; 'he is a gentleman. You
know I took the precaution to write to Kaulnitz; Kaulnitz's answer is clear enough: and
to Frohsdorf, from which it was equally satisfactory. I wrote also to the Comte de la
Barée; his reply was everything which could
be desired.'

'No doubt,' her niece had answered for the
twentieth time; 'but I think we have already
done enough for Christianity and hospitality;
we need not offer him our personal friendship;
as there is no master in this house he will not
expect to be invited to it. We will wish him
God-speed when he is fully restored and is
going away.'

'You are really too prudish!' said the-

Princess, very angrily. 'I should be the last person to counsel an imprudence, a failure in due caution, in correct reserve and hesitation; but for you to pretend that a Countess von Szalras cannot venture to invite a person to her own residence because that person is of the opposite sex——'

'That is not the question; the root of the matter is that he is a chance acquaintance made quite informally; we should have been cruel if we had done less than we have done, but there can be no need that we should do more.'

'I can ask more about him of Kaulnitz,' said Madame Ottilie.

Kaulnitz was one of her innumerable cousins, and was then minister in Paris.

'Why should you?' said her niece. 'Do you think either that it is quite honourable to make inquiries unknown to people? It always savours to me too much of the Third Section.'

'You are so exaggerated in all your scruples; you prefer to be suspicious of a person in silence than to ask a few questions,' said the Princess. 'But surely when two ambassadors and the Kaiser guarantee his position you may be content.'

The answer she had received from Kaulnitz

had indeed only moderately satisfied her.
It said that there was nothing known to the
detriment of the Marquis de Sabran; that
he had never been accused of anything unfit-
ting his rank and name; but that he was a
viveur, and was said to be very successful at
play; he was not known to have any debts,
but he was believed to be poor and of pre-
carious fortunes. On the whole the Princess
had decided to keep the answer to herself; she
had remembered with irritation that her niece
had suggested baccara as the source of the
hundred gold pieces.

'I never intended to convey that ambassadors would disown him or the Kaiser either,
whose signature is in his pocket-book. Only,'
said Wanda, 'as you and I are all alone, surely
it will be as well to leave this gentleman to
the monks and to Greswold. That is all I
mean.'

'It is a perfectly unnecessary scruple, and
not at all like one of your race. The Szalras
have always been hospitable and headstrong.'

'I hope I am the first—I have done my
best for M. de Sabran; as for being headstrong
—surely that is not a sweet or wise quality that
you should lament my loss of it?'

'You need not quarrel with me,' said the

Princess, pettishly. 'You have a terrible habit of contradiction, Wanda: and you never give up your opinion.'

The mistress of Hohenszalras smiled, and sighed a little.

'Dear mother, we will do anything that amuses you.'

So the note was sent.

The Princess had been always eager for such glimpses of the moving world as had been allowed to her by any accidental change. Her temperament would have led her to find happiness in the frivolous froth and fume of a worldly existence; she delighted in gossip, in innocent gaiety, in curiosity, in wonder; all her early years had been passed under repression and constraint, and now in her old age she was as eager as a child for any plaything, as inquisitive as a marmoset, as animated as a squirrel. Her mother had been a daughter of a great French family of the south, and much of the vivacity and sportive malice and quick temper of the Gallic blood was in her still, beneath the primness and the placidity that had become her habit, from long years passed in a little German court and in a stately semi-religious order.

This stranger whom chance had brought to them was to her idea a precious and providential source of excitement : already a hundred romances had suggested themselves to her fertile mind ; already a hundred impossibilities had suggested themselves to her as probable. She did not in the least believe that accident had brought him there. She imagined that he had wandered there for the sake of seeing the mistress of Hohenszalras, who had for so long been unseen by the world, but whose personal graces and great fortune had remained in the memories of many. To the romantic fancy of the Princess, which had never been blunted by contact with harsh facts, nothing seemed prettier or more probable than that the French marquis, when arrested as a poacher, had been upon a pilgrimage of poetic adventure. It should not be her fault, she resolved, if the wounded knight had to go away in sorrow and silence, without the castle gates being swung open once at least.

'After all, if she would only take an interest in anything human,' she thought, ' instead of always horses and mountains, and philosophical treatises and councils, and calculations with the stewards ! She ought not to live and die alone. They made me vow to do so, and perhaps it was for the best, but I would never say to anyone—Do likewise.'

And then the Princess felt the warm tears

on her own cheeks, thinking of herself as she had been at seventeen, pacing up and down the stiff straight alley of clipped trees at Lilienhöhe with a bright young soldier who had fallen in a duel ere he was twenty. It was all so long ago, so long ago, and she was a true submissive daughter of her princely house, and of her Holy Church ; yet she knew that it was not meet for a woman to live and die without a man's heart to beat by her own, without a child's hands to close her glazing eyes.

And Wanda von Szalras wished so to live and so to die! Only one magician could change her. Why should he not come?

So on the morrow the little boat that had brought the physician to him so often took him over the two miles of water to the landing stairs at the foot of the castle rock. In a little while he stood in the presence of his châtelaine.

He was a man who never in his life had been confused, unnerved, or at a loss for words ; yet now he felt as a boy might have done, as a rustic might ; he had a mist before his eyes, his heart beat quickly, he grew very pale.

She thought he was still suffering, and looked at him with interest.

'I am afraid that we did wrong to tempt

you from the monastery,' she said, in her grave melodious voice; and she stretched out her hand to him with a look of sympathy. 'I am afraid you are still suffering and weak, are you not?'

He bent low as he touched it.

'How can I thank you?' he murmured. 'You have treated a vagrant like a king!'

'You were a munificent vagrant to our chapel and our poor,' she replied with a smile. 'And what have we done for you? Nothing more than is our commonest duty, far removed from cities or even villages, as we are. Are you really recovered? I may tell you now that there was a moment when Herr Greswold was alarmed for you.'

The Princess Ottilie entered at that moment and welcomed him with more effusion and congratulation. They breakfasted in a chamber called the Saxe room, an oval room lined throughout with lacquered white wood, in the Louis Seize style; the panels were painted in Watteau-like designs; it had been decorated by a French artist in the middle of the eighteenth century, and with its hangings of flowered white satin, and its collection of Meissen china figures, and its great window, which looked over a small garden with velvet grass plots and huge yews, was the place of all others to make an early morning meal most agreeable, whether in summer when the casements were open to the old-fashioned roses that climbed about them, or in winter when on the open hearth great oak logs burned beneath the carved white wood mantelpiece, gay with its plaques of Saxe and its garlands of foliage. The little oval table bore a service of old Meissen, with tiny Watteau figures painted on a ground of palest rose. Watteau figures of the same royal china upheld great shells filled with the late violets of the woods of Hohenszalras.

'What an enchanting little room!' said Sabran, glancing round it, and appreciating with the eyes of a connoisseur the Lancret designs, the Riesiner cabinets, and the old china. He was as well versed in the art and lore of the Beau Siècle as Arsene Houssaye or the Goncourts; he talked now of the epoch with skill and grace, with that accuracy of knowledge and that fineness of criticism which had made his observations and his approval treasured and sought for by the artists and the art patrons of Paris.

The day was grey and mild; the casements were open; the fresh, pure fragrance of the forests came in through the aromatic warmth of the chamber; the little gay shepherds and shepherdesses seemed to breathe and laugh.

'This room was a caprice of an ancestress of mine, who was of your country, and was, I am afraid, very wretched here,' said Wanda von Szalras. 'She brought her taste from Marly and Versailles. It is not the finest or the purest taste, but it has a grace and elegance of its own that is very charming, as a change.'

'It is a madrigal in porcelain,' he said, looking around him. 'I am glad that the *alouette gauloise* has sung here beside the dread and majestic Austrian vulture.'

'The *alouette gauloise* always sings in Aunt Ottilie's heart; it is what keeps her so young always. I assure you she is a great deal younger than I am,' said his châtelaine, resting a glance of tender affection on the pretty figure of the Princess caressing her Spitz dog Bijou.

She herself, with her great pearls about her throat, and a gown of white serge, looked a stately and almost severe figure beside the dainty picturesque prettiness of the elder lady and the fantastic gaiety and gilding of the porcelain and the paintings. He felt a certain awe of her, a certain hesitation before her, which the habits of the world enabled him to conceal, but which moved him with a sense of timidity, novel and almost painful.

'One ought to be Dorat and Marmontel to be worthy of such a repast,' he said, as he seated himself between his hostesses.

'Neither Dorat nor Marmontel would have enjoyed your very terrible adventure,' said the Princess, reflecting with satisfaction that it was herself who had saved this charming and chivalrous life, since, at her own risk and loss, she had sent her physicians, alike of body and of soul, to wrestle for him with death by his sick bed at Pregratten.

'Wanda would never have sent anyone to him,' thought the Princess: 'she is so unaccountably indifferent to any human life higher than her peasantry.'

'Adventures are to the adventurous,' quoted Sabran.

'Yes,' said the Princess; 'but the pity is that the adventurous are too often the questionable——'

'Perhaps that is saying too much,' said Wanda; 'but it is certain that the more solid qualities do not often lead into a career of excitement. It has been always conceded—with a sigh—that duty is dull.'

'I think adventure is like calamity: some people are born to it,' he added, 'and such cannot escape from it. Loyola may cover his head with a cowl: he cannot become obscure. Eugene may make himself an abbé: he cannot escape his horoscope cast in the House of Mars.'

'What a fatalist you are!'

'Do you think we ever escape our fate? Alexander slew all whom he suspected, but he did not for that die in his bed of old age.'

'That merely proves that crime is no buckler.'

Sabran was silent.

'My life has been very adventurous,' he said lightly, after a pause; 'but I have only regarded that as another name for misfortune. The picturesque is not the prosperous; all beggars look well on canvas, whilst Carolus Duran himself can make nothing of a portrait of Dives, *roulant carrosse* through his fifty millions.'

He had not his usual strength; his loins had had a wrench in the crashing fall from the Umbal which they had not wholly recovered, despite the wise medicaments of Greswold.

He moved with some difficulty, and, not to weary him, she remained after breakfast in the Watteau room, making him recline at length in a long chair beside one of the windows. She was touched by the weakness of a man evidently so strong and daring by nature, and she regretted the rough and inhospitable handling which he had experienced from her beloved hills and waters. She, who spoke to no one all the year through except her stewards and her priests, did not fail to be sensible of the pleasure she derived from the cultured and sympathetic companionship of a brilliant and talented mind.

'Ah! if Egon had only talent like that!' she thought, with a sigh of remembrance. Her cousin was a gallant nobleman and soldier, but of literature he had no knowledge; for art he had a consummate indifference; and the only eloquence he could command was a brief address to his troopers, which would be answered by an *Eljén*! ringing loud and long, like steel smiting upon iron.

Sabran could at all times talk well.

He had the gift of facile and eloquent words, and he had also what most attracted the sympathies of his hostess, a genuine and healthful love of the mountains and forests. All his life in Paris had not eradicated from his character a deep love for Nature in her wildest and her stormiest moods. They conversed long and with mutual pleasure of the country around them, of which she knew every ravine and torrent, and of whose bold and sombre beauty he was honestly enamoured.

The noon had deepened into afternoon, and the chimes of the clock-tower were sounding four when he rose to take his leave, and go on his way across the green brilliancy of the tumbling water to his quiet home with the Dominican brethren. He had still the languor and fatigue about him of recent illness, and he moved slowly and with considerable weakness. She said to him in parting, with unaffected kindness, 'Come across to us whenever you like; we are concerned to think that one of our own glaciers should have treated you so cruelly. I am often out riding far and wide, but my aunt will always be pleased to receive you.'

'I am the debtor of the Umbal ice,' he said, in a low voice. 'But for that happy fall I should have gone on my way to my old senseless life without ever having known true rest as I know it yonder. Will you be offended, too, if I say that I stayed at Matrey with a vague, faint, unfounded hope that your mountains might be merciful, and let me——'

'Shoot a *kuttengeier?*' she said quickly, as though not desiring to hear his sentence finished. 'You might shoot one easily sitting at a window in the monastery, and watching till the vultures flew across the lake; but you will remember you are on parole. I am sure you will be faithful.'

Long, long afterwards she remembered that he shrank a little at the word, and that a flush of colour went over his face.

'I will,' he said simply; 'and it was not the *kuttengeier* for which I desired to be allowed to revisit Hohenszalras.'

'Well, if the monks starve you or weary you, you can remember that we are here, and you must not give their organ quite all the music that you bear so wonderfully in your mind and hands.'

'I will play to you all day, if you will only allow me.'

'Next time you come—to-morrow, if you like.'

He went away, lying listlessly in the little boat, for he was still far from strong; but life seemed to him very sweet and serene as the evening light spread over the broad, bright water, and the water birds rose and scattered before the plunge of the oars.

Had the sovereign mistress of Hohenszalras ever said before to any other living friend— to-morrow? Yet he was too clever a man to be vain ; and he did not misinterpret the calm kindness of her invitation.

He went thither again the next day, though he left them early, for he had a sensitive fear of wearying with his presence ladies to whom he owed so much.

But the Princess urged his speedy return, and the châtelaine of Szaravola said once more, with that grave smile which was rather in the eyes than on the lips, 'We shall always be happy to see you when you are inclined to cross the lake.'

He was a great adept at painting, and he made several broad, bold sketches of the landscapes visible from the lake; he was famous for many a drawing *brossé dans le vrai,* which hung at his favourite club the Mirliton ; he could paint, more finely and delicately also, on ivory, on satin, on leather. He sent for some fans and screens from Vienna, and did in *gouache* upon them exquisite birds, foliage, flowers, legends of saints, which were beautiful enough to be not unworthy a place in those rooms of the burg where the Penicauds, the Fragonards, the Pettitôts, were represented by much of their most perfect work.

He passed his mornings in labour of this sort ; at noonday or in the afternoon he rowed across to Hohenszalras, and loitered for an hour or two in the gardens or the library. Little by little they became so accustomed to his coming that it would have seemed strange if more than a day had gone by without the little striped blue boat gliding from the Holy Isle to the castle stairs. He never stayed very long; not so long as the Princess desired.

'Never in my life have I spent weeks so harmlessly!' he said once with a smile to the doctor; then he gave a quick sigh and turned away, for he thought to himself in a sudden repentance that these innocent and blameless days were perhaps but the prelude to one of the greatest sins of a not sinless life.

He came to be looked for quite naturally at the noonday breakfast in the pretty Saxe chamber. He would spend hours playing on the chapel organ, or on the piano in the octagon room which Liszt had chosen. The grand and dreamy music rolled out over the green lake towards the green hills, and Wanda would look often at the marble figure of her brother on his tomb, lying like the statue of the young Gaston de Foix, and think to herself, 'If only Bela were listening, too!'

Sometimes she was startled when she remembered into what continual intimacy she had admitted a man of whom she had no real knowledge.

The Princess, indeed, had said to her, ‘I did ask Kaulnitz: Kaulnitz knows him quite well;’ but that was hardly enough to satisfy a woman as reserved in her friendships, and as habituated to the observance of a severe etiquette, as was the châtelaine of Hohenszalras. Every day almost she said to herself that she would not see him when he came, or, if she saw him, would show him, by greater chilliness of manner, that it was time he quitted the island. But when he did come, if he did not see her he went to the chapel and played a mass, a requiem, an anthem, a sonata; and Beethoven, Palestrina, Schumann, Wagner, Berlioz, surely allured her from her solitude, and she would come on to the terrace and listen to the waves of melody rolling out through the cool sunless air, through the open door of the place where her beloved dead rested. Then, as a matter of course, he stayed, and after the noonday meal sometimes he rode with her in the forests, or drove the Princess in her pony chair, or received permission to bear his châtelaine company in her mountain walks. They were seldom alone, but they were much together.

‘It is much better for her than solitude,’ thought the Princess. ‘It is not likely that she will ever care anything for him: she is so cold; but if she did, there would be no great harm done. He is of old blood, and she has wealth enough to need no more. Of course any one of our great princes would be better; but, then, as she will never take any one of them——'

And the Princess, who was completely fascinated by the deferential homage to her of Sabran, and the pleasure he honestly found in her society, would do all she could, in her innocent and delicate way, to give her favourite the opportunities he desired of intercourse with the mistress of Hohenszalras. She wanted to see again the life that she had seen in other days at the Schloss; grand parties for the hunting season and the summer season, royal and noble people in the guest-chambers, great gatherings for the chase on the *rond-point* in the woods, covers for fifty laid at the table in the banqueting-hall, and besides—besides, thought the childless and loving old woman—little children with long fair curls and gay voices wakening the echoes in the Rittersäal with their sports and pastimes.

It was noble and austere, no doubt, this life led by Wanda von Szalras amidst the mountains in the Tauern, but it was lonely and monotonous to the Princess, who still loved a certain movement, gossip, and diversion as she liked to nibble a *nougat* and sip her chocolate

foaming under its thick cream.　It seemed to
her that even to suffer a little would be better
for her niece than this unvarying solitude, this
eternal calm.　That she should have mourned
for her brother was most natural, but this
perpetual seclusion was an exaggeration of
regret.

If the presence of Sabran reconciled her
with the world, with life as it was, and induced
her to return to the court and to those pleasures
natural to her rank and to her years, it would
be well done, thought the Princess; and as for
him—if he carried away a broken heart it
would be a great pity, but persons who like to
move others as puppets cannot concern themselves with the accidental injury of one of their
toys; and Mdme. Ottilie was too content with
her success of the moment to look much
beyond it.

'The charm of being here is to me precisely
what I daresay makes it tiresome to you,' the
mistress of Hohenszalras said to him one day,
'I mean its isolation.　One can entirely forget
that beyond those mountains there is a world
fussing, fuming, brewing its storms in saucers,
and inventing a quantity of increased unwhole-
someness, in noise and stench, which it calls a
higher civilisation.　No! I would never have
a telegraph wire brought here from Matrey.

There is nothing I ever particularly care to
know about. If there were anyone I loved
who was away from me it would be different.
But there is no one. There are people I like,
of course——'

'But political events?' he suggested.

'They do not attract me. They are ignoble.
They are for the most part contemptibly ill-
managed, and to think that after so many
thousands of years humanity has not really
progressed beyond the wild beasts' method of
settling disputes——'

'There is so much of the wild beast in it.
With such an opinion of political life why
do you counsel me to seek it?'

'You are a man. There is nothing else for
a man who has talent, and who is—who is as
you are, *désœuvré*. Intellectual work would be
better, but you do not care for it, it seems.
Since your " Mexico "——'

'The " Mexico " was no work of mine.'

'Oh yes, pardon me: I have read it. All
your notes, all your addenda, show how the
learning of the editor was even superior to that
of the original author.'

'No; all that I could do was to simplify his
immense erudition and arrange it. I never
loved the work; do not accredit me with so
much industry: but it was a debt that I paid,

and paid easily too, for the materials lay all to
my hand, if in disorder.'

'The Marquis Xavier must at least have
infused his own love of archæology and science
into you?'

'I can scarcely say even so much. I have
a facility at acquiring knowledge, which is not
a very high quality. Things come easily to me.
I fear if Herr Joachim examined me he would
find my science shallow.'

'You have so many talents that perhaps
you are like one of your own Mexican forests;
one luxuriance kills another.'

'Had I had fewer I might have been more
useful in my generation,' he said, with a certain
sincerity of regret.

'You would have been much less interesting,' she thought to herself, as she said aloud,
'There are the horses coming up to the steps:
will you ride with me? And do not be ungrateful for your good gifts. Talent is a *Schlüs-
selblume* that opens to all hidden treasures.'

'Why are you not in the Chamber?' she had
said a little before to him. 'You are eloquent;
you have an ancestry that binds you to do
your best for France.'

'I have no convictions,' he had said, with a
flush on his face. 'It is a sad thing to confess.'

'It is; but if you have nothing better to substitute for them you might be content to abide by those of your fathers.'

He had been silent.

'Besides,' she had added, 'patriotism is not an opinion, it is an instinct.'

'With good men. I am not one of them.'

'Go into public life,' she had repeated. 'Convictions will come to you in an active career, as the muscles develop in the gymnasium.'

'I am indolent,' he had demurred, 'and I have desultory habits.'

'You may break yourself of these. There must be much in which you could interest yourself. Begin with the fishing interests of the coast that belongs to you.'

'Honestly, I care for nothing except for myself. You will say it is base.'

'I am afraid it is natural.'

He but seldom spoke of his early life. When he did so it was with reluctance, as if it gave him pain. His father he had never known; of his grandfather, the Marquis Xavier, as he usually called him, he spoke with extreme and reverent tenderness, but with little reticence. The grave old man, in the stateliness and simplicity of his solitary life, had been to his youthful imagination a solemn and sacred figure.

'His was the noblest life I have ever

known,' he said once, with an emotion in the accent of the words which she had never heard in his voice before, and which gave her a passing impression of a regret in him that was almost remorse.

It might be, she reflected, the remorse of a man who, in his careless youth, had been less heedful of the value of an affection and the greatness of a character which, as he grew older and wiser, he learned to appreciate when it was too late. He related willingly how the old man had trusted him to carry out into the light of the world the fruits of his life of research, and with what pleasure he had seen the instant and universal recognition of the labours of the brain and the hand that were dust. But of his own life in the West he said little; he referred his skill in riding to the wild horses of the pampas, and his botanical and scientific knowledge to the studies which the solitudes of the sierras had made him turn to as relaxation and occupation; but of himself he said little, nothing, unless the conversation so turned upon his life there that it was impossible for him to avoid those reminiscences which were evidently little agreeable to him. Perhaps she thought some youthful passion, some unwise love, had made those flowering swamps and sombre plains painful in memory to him. There

might be other graves than that of the
Marquis Xavier beneath the plumes of pampas
grass. Perhaps, also, to a man of the world, a
man of mere pleasure as he had become, that
studious and lonesome youth of his already
had drifted so far away that, seen in distance,
it seemed dim and unreal as any dream.

'How happy you are to have so many
admirable gifts!' said Wanda to him one day,
when he had offered her a fan that he had
painted on ivory. He had a facile skill at most
of the arts, and had acquired accuracy and
technique lounging through the painting-rooms
of Paris. The fan was an exquisite trifle, and
bore on one side her monogram and the arms
of her house, and on the other mountain
flowers and birds, rendered with the delicacy
of a miniaturist.

'What is the use of a mere amateur?' he
said, with indifference. 'When one has lived
amongst artists one learns heartily to despise
oneself for daring to flirt with those sacred
sisters the Muses.'

'Why? And, after all, when one has such
perfect talent as yours, the definition of
amateur and artist seems a very arbitrary and
meaningless one. If you needed to make your
fame and fortune by painting faces you could
do so. You do not need. Does that make the

fan the less precious? The more, I think, since
gold cannot buy it.'

'You are too kind to me. The world would
not be as much so if I really wanted its
suffrages.'

'You cannot tell that. I think you have that
facility which is the first note of genius. It is
true all your wonderful talents seem the more
wonderful to me because I have none myself.
I feel art, but I have no power over it; and
as for what are called accomplishments I have
none. I could, perhaps, beat you in the shooting gallery, and I will try some day if you like,
and I can ride—well, like my Kaiserin—
but accomplishments I have none.'

'Surely you were yesterday reading Plato
in his own text?'

'I learnt Greek and Latin with my brother.
You cannot call that an accomplishment. The
ladies of the old time often knew the learned
tongues, though they were greater at tapestry
or distilling and at the ordering of their household. In a solitary place like this it is needful
to know so many useful things. I can shoe
my horse and harness a sleigh; I can tell every
useful herb and flower in the woods; I know
well what to do in frostbite or accidents; if I
were lost in the hills I could make my way by
the stars; I can milk a cow, and can row any

boat, and I can climb with crampons; I am a mountaineer. Do not be so surprised. I do all that I have the children taught in my schools. But in a salon I am useless and stupid; the last new lady whose lord has been decorated because he sold something wholesale or cheated successfully at the Bourse would, I assure you, eclipse me easily in the talents of the drawing-room.'

Sabran looked at her and laughed outright. A compliment would have seemed ridiculous before this beautiful patrician, with her serene dignity, her instinctive grace, her unconscious hauteur, her entire possession of all those attributes which are the best heirlooms of a great nobility. To protest against her words would have been like an insult to this daughter of knights and princes, to whom half the sovereigns of modern Europe would have seemed but parvenus, the accidental mushroom growth of the decay in the contest of nations.

His laughter amused her, though it was, perhaps, the most discreet and delicate of compliments. She was not offended by it as she would have been with any spoken flattery.

' After all, do not think me modest in what I have said,' she pursued. '*Talents de société* are but slight things at the best, and in our day need not even have either wit or culture: a

good travesty at a costume-ball, a startling
gown on a racecourse, a series of adventures
more or less true, a trick of laughing often and
laughing long—any one of these is enough for
renown in your Paris. In Vienna we do more
homage to tradition still; our Court life has
still something of the grace of the minuet.'

'Yet even in Vienna you refuse——'

'To spend my time? Why not? The
ceremonies of a Court are wearisome to me;
my duties lie here; and for the mirth and pomp
of society I have had no heart since the grief
that you know of fell upon me.'

It was the first time that she had ever
spoken of her brother's loss to him: he bowed
very low in silent sympathy.

'Who would not envy his death, since it
has brought such remembrance!' he said in a
low tone, after some moments.

'Ah, if only we could be sure that un-
ceasing regret consoles the dead!' she said,
with an emotion that softened and dimmed all
her beauty. Then, as if ashamed or repentant
of having shown her feeling for Bela to a
stranger, she turned to him and said more
distantly:

'Would it entertain you to see my little
scholars? I will take you to the schoolhouses
if you like.'

He could only eagerly accept the offer: he felt his heart beat and his eyes lighten as she spoke. He knew that such a condescension in her was a mark of friendship, a sign of familiar intimacy.

'It is but a mile or so through the woods. We will walk there,' she said, as she took her tall cane from its rack and called to Neva and Donau, where they lay on the terrace without.

He fancied that the vague mistrust of him, the vague prejudice against him of which he had been sensible in her, were passing away from her mind; but still he doubted—doubted bitterly—whether she would ever give him any other thought than that due to a passing and indifferent acquaintance. That she admired his intelligence and that she pitied his loneliness he saw; but there seemed to him that never, never, never, would he break down in his own favour that impalpable but impassable barrier due, half to her pride, half to her reserve, and absolutely to her indifference, which separated Wanda von Szalras from the rest of mankind.

If she had any weakness or foible it was the children's schools on the estates in the High Tauern and elsewhere. They had been founded on a scheme of Bela's and her own,

when they had been very young, and the
world to them a lovely day without end.
Their too elaborate theories had been of
necessity curtailed, but the schools had been
established on the basis of their early dreams,
and were unlike any others that existed. She
had read much and deeply, and had thought
out all she had read, and as she enjoyed that
happy power of realising and embodying her
own theories which most theorists are denied,
she had founded the schools of the High
Tauern in absolute opposition to all that the
school-boards of her generation have decreed
as desirable. And in every one of her villages
she had her schools on this principle, and they
throve, and the children with them. Many of
these could not read a printed page, but all of
them could read the shepherd's weather-glass
in sky and flower; all of them knew the worm
that was harmful to the crops, the beetle that
was harmless in the grass; all knew a tree by
a leaf, a bird by a feather, an insect by a
grub.

Modern teaching makes a multitude of
gabblers. She did not think it necessary for the
little goatherds, and dairymaids, and foresters,
and charcoal-burners, and sennerinn, and car-
penters, and cobblers, to study the exact
sciences or draw casts from the antique. She

was of opinion, with Pope, that ' a little learning is a dangerous thing,' and that a smattering
of it will easily make a man morose and discontented, whilst it takes a very deep and even
lifelong devotion to it to teach a man content
with his lot. Genius, she thought, is too rare
a thing to make it necessary to construct
village schools for it, and whenever or wherever
it comes upon earth it will surely be its own
master.

She did not believe in culture for little
peasants who have to work for their daily
bread at the plough-tail or with the reaping-
hook. She knew that a mere glimpse of a
Canaan of art and learning is cruelty to those
who never can enter into and never even can
have leisure to merely gaze on it. She thought
that a vast amount of useful knowledge is consigned to oblivion whilst children are taught to
waste their time in picking up the crumbs of
a great indigestible loaf of artificial learning.
She had her scholars taught their ' A B C,'
and that was all. Those who wished to write
were taught, but writing was not enforced.
What they were made to learn was the name
and use of every plant in their own country ;
the habits and ways of all animals ; how to
cook plain food well, and make good bread ;
how to brew simples from the herbs of their

fields and woods, and how to discern the
coming weather from the aspect of the skies,
the shutting-up of certain blossoms, and the
time of day from those 'poor men's watches,'
the opening flowers.   In all countries there is
a great deal of useful household and out-of-
door lore that is fast being choked out of existence under books and globes, and which, unless
it passes by word of mouth from generation to
generation, is quickly and irrevocably lost.
All this lore she had cherished by her school-
children.   Her boys were taught in addition
any useful trade they liked—boot-making,
crampon-making, horse-shoeing, wheel-making,
or carpentry.   This trade was made a pastime
to each.   The little maidens learned to sew,
to cook, to spin, to card, to keep fowls and
sheep and cattle in good health, and to know
all poisonous plants and berries by sight.

'I think it is what is wanted,' she said.
'A little peasant child does not need to be
able to talk of the corolla and the spathe,
but he does want to recognise at a glance
the flower that will give him healing and the
berries that will give him death.   His sister
does not in the least require to know why a
kettle boils, but she does need to know when
a warm bath will be good for a sick baby or
when hurtful.   We want a new generation

to be helpful, to have eyes, and to know the beauty of silence. I do not mind much whether my children read or not. The labourer that reads turns Socialist, because his brain cannot digest the hard mass of wonderful facts he encounters. But I believe every one of my little peasants, being wrecked like Crusoe, would prove as handy as he.'

She was fond of her scholars and proud of them, and they were never afraid of her. They knew well it was the great lady who filled all their sacks the night of Santa Claus—even those of the naughty children, because, as she said, childhood was so short that she thought it cruel to give it any disappointments.

The walk to the schoolhouse lay through the woods to the south of the castle; woods of larch and beech and walnut and the graceful Siberian pine, with deep mosses and thick fern-brakes beneath them, and ever and again a watercourse tumbling through their greenery to fall into the Szalrassee below.

'I always fancy I can hear here the echo of the great Krimler torrents,' she said to him as they passed through the trees. 'No doubt it *is* fancy, and the sound is only from our own falls. But the peasants' tradition is, you may know, that our lake is the water of the Krimler come to us underground from the Pinzgau.

Do you know our Sahara of the North ?   It is
monotonous and barren enough, and yet with
its vast solitudes of marsh and stones, its flocks
of wild fowl, its reedy wastes, its countless
streams, it is grand in its own way.   And then
in the heart of it there are the thunder and
the boiling fury of Krimml!   You will smile
because I am an enthusiast for my country,
you who have seen Orinoco and Chimborazo;
but even you will own that the old Duchy of
Austria, the old Archbishopric of Salzburg, the
old Countship of Tirol, have some beauty and
glory in them.   Here is the schoolhouse.   Now
you shall see what I think needful for the
peasant of the future.   Perhaps you will condemn me as a true Austrian: that is, as a
Reactionist.'

The schoolhouse was a châlet, or rather a
collection of châlets, set one against another
on a green pasture belted by pine woods,
above which the snows of the distant Venediger
were gleaming amidst the clouds.   There was
a loud hum of childish voices rising through
the open lattice, and these did not cease as they
entered the foremost house.

'Do not be surprised that they take no
notice of our entrance,' she said to him.   'I
have taught them not to do so unless I bid
them.   If they left off their tasks I could

never tell how they did them; and is not
the truest respect shown in obedience ? '

'They are as well disciplined as soldiers,'
he said with a smile, as twenty curly heads
bent over desks were lifted for a moment to
instantly go down again.

'Surely discipline is next to health,' added
Wanda. 'If the child do not learn it early he
must suffer fearfully when he reaches manhood,
since all men, even princes, have to obey some
time or other, and the majority of men are not
princes, but are soldiers, clerks, porters, guides,
labourers, tradesmen, what not; certainly something subject to law if not to a master. How
many lives have been lost because a man failed
to understand the meaning of immediate and
unquestioning obedience! Soldiers are shot for
want of it, yet children are not to be taught it !'

Whilst she spoke not a child looked up or
left off his lesson: the teacher, a white-haired
old man, went on with his recitation.

'Your teachers are not priests?' he said in
some surprise.

'No,' she answered; 'I am a faithful
daughter of the Church, as you know; but
every priest is perforce a specialist, if I may
be forgiven the profanity, and the teacher of
children should be of perfectly open, simple
and unbiassed mind; the priest's can never be

that. Besides, his teaching is apart. The love and fear of God are themes too vast and too intimate to be mingled with the pains of the alphabet and the multiplication tables. There alone I agree with your French Radicals, though from a very different reason to theirs. Now in this part of the schools you see the children are learning from books. These children have wished to read, and are taught to do so; but I do not enforce though I recommend it. You think that very barbarous? Oh! reflect for a moment how much more glorious was the world, was literature itself, before printing was invented. Sometimes I think it was a book, not a fruit, that Satan gave. You smile incredulously. Well, no doubt to a Parisian it seems absurd. How should you understand what is wanted in the heart of these hills? Come and see the other houses.'

In the next which they entered there was a group of small sturdy boys, very sunburnt and rough and bright, who were seated in a row listening with rapt attention to a teacher who was talking to them of birds and their uses and ways; there were prints of birds and birds'-nests, and the teacher was making them understand why and how a bird flew.

'That is the natural history school,' she said; 'one day it is birds, another animals, another insects, that they are told about. Those are all little foresters born. They will go about their woods with eyes that see, and with tenderness for all creation.'

In the next school Herr Joachim himself, who took no notice of their entrance, was giving a simple little lecture on the useful herbs and the edible tubers, the way to know them and to turn them to profit. There were several girls listening here.

'Those girls will not poison their people at home with a false cryptogram,' said Wanda, as they passed on to another place, where a lesson on farriery and the treatment of cattle was going on, and another where a teacher was instructing a mixed group of boys and little maidens in the lore of the forests, of the grasses, of the various causes that kill a tree in its prime, of the insects that dwell in them, and of the different soils that they needed. In another chamber there was a spinning-class and a sewing-class under a kindly-faced old dame; and in yet another there were music-classes, some playing on the zither, and others singing part-songs and glees with baby voices.

'Now you have seen all I have to show you,' said Wanda. 'In these two other châlets are the workshops, where the boys learn any trade they choose, and the girls are also taught to make a shoe or a jacket. My children would not pass examinations in cities, certainly; but they are being fitted in the best way they can for their future life, which will pass either in these mountains and forests, as I hope, or in the armies of the Emperor, and the humble work-a-day ways of poor folks everywhere. If there be a Grillparzer or a Kaulbach amongst them, the education is large and simple enough to let the originality he has been born with develop itself; if, as is far more likely, they are all made of ordinary human stuff, then the teaching they receive is such as to make them contented, pious, honest, and useful working people. At least that is what I strive for; and this is certain, that the children come some of them a German mile and more with joy and willingness to their schools, and that this at least they take away with them into their future life—the sense of duty as a supreme rein over all instincts, and mercifulness towards every living thing that God has given us.'

She had spoken with unusual animation, and with an earnestness that brought warmth over her cheek and moisture into her eyes.

Sabran looked at her timidly; then as timidly he touched the tips of her fingers, and raised them to his lips.

'You are a noble woman,' he said very

low ; a sense of his own utter unworthiness overwhelmed him and held him mute.

She glanced at him in some surprise, vaguely tinged with displeasure.

'There are schools on every estate,' she said, a little angrily and disconnectedly. 'These are modelled on my own whim ; that is all. The world would say I ought to teach these little peasants the science that dissects its own sources, and the philosophies that resolve all creation into an egg. But I follow ancient ways enough to think the country life the best, the healthiest, the sweetest : it is for this that they are born, and to this I train them. If we had more naturalists we should have fewer Communists.'

'Yes, Audubon would scarcely have been a regicide, or Humboldt a Camorrist,' he answered her, regaining his self-possession. ' No doubt a love of nature is a triple armour against self-love. How can I say how right I think your system with these children ? You seem not to believe me. There is only one thing in which I differ with you ; you think the "eyes that see" bring content. Surely not! surely not ! '

'It depends on what they see,' she said meditatively. ' When they are wide open in the woods and fields, when they have been taught to see how the tree-bee forms her cell and the mole his fortress, how the warbler builds his nest for his love and the water-spider makes his little raft, how the leaf comes forth from the hard stem and the fungi from the rank mould, then I think that sight is content —content in the simple life of the woodland place, and in such delighted wonder that the heart of its own accord goes up in peace and praise to the Creator. The printed page may teach envy, desire, covetousness, hatred, but the Book of Nature teaches resignation, hope, willingness to labour and live, submission to die. The world has gone further and further from peace since larger and larger have grown its cities and its shepherd kings are no more.'

He was silent.

Her voice moved him like sweet remembered music; yet in his own remembrance what were there? Only 'envy, desire, covetousness, hatred,' the unlovely shapes that were to her as emblems of the powers of evil. His reason was with her, and his emotions were with her also, but memory was busy in him, and in it he saw 'as in a glass darkly,' all his passionate, cold, embittered youth, all his warped, irresolute, useless, and untrue manhood.

'Do not think,' she added, unconscious of

the pain that she had caused him, 'that I undervalue the blessing of great books; but I do think that, to recognise the beauty of literature, as much culture and comprehension are needed as to understand Leonardo's painting, or the structure of Wagner's music. Those who read well are as rare as those who love well. The curse of our age is superficial knowledge; it is a *cryptogram* of the rankest sort, and I will not let my scholars touch it. Do you not think it is better for a country child to know what flowers are poisonous for her cattle, and what herbs are useful in her neighbours' fever, than to be able to spell through a Jesuit's newspaper, or suck evil from a Communist's pamphlet? You will not have your horse well shod if the smith be thinking of Bakounine while he hammers the iron.'

'I have held the views of Bakounine myself,' said Sabran, with hesitation. 'I do not know what you will think of me. I have even been tempted to be an anarchist, a Nihilist.'

'You speak in the past tense. You must have abandoned those views? You are received at Frohsdorf?'

'They have, perhaps, abandoned me. My life has been idle, sinful often. I have liked luxury, and have not denied myself folly. I recognised the absurdity of such a man as I was joining in any movement of seriousness and self-negation, so I threw away my political persuasions, as one throws off a knapsack when tired of a journey on foot.'

'That was not very conscientious, surely?'

'No, madame. It is perhaps, however, better than helping to adjust the contradictions of the world with dynamite. And I cannot even claim that they were persuasions; I fear they were mere personal impatience with narrow fortunes and useless ambitions.'

'I cannot pardon anyone of an old nobility turning Republican; it is like a son insulting the tombs of his fathers!' she said, with emphasis; then, fearing she had reproved him too strongly, she added, with a smile, 'And yet I also could almost join the anarchists when I see the enormous wealth of baseborn speculators and Hebrew capitalists in such bitter contrast with the hunger of the poor, who starve all over the world in winter like birds frozen on the snow. Oh, do not suppose that, though I am an Austrian, I cannot see that feudalism is doomed. We are still feudal here, but then in so much we are still as we were in crusading days. The nobles have been, almost everywhere except here, ousted by capitalists, and the capitalists will in turn be devoured by the democracy. *Les loups se mangeront entre eux.* You see,

though I may be prejudiced, I am not blind.
But you, as a Breton, should think feudalism a
loss, as I do.'

'In those days, Barbe Bleue or Gilles de
Retz were the nearest neighbours of Romaris,'
he said, with a smile. ' Yet if feudalism could be
sure of such chatêlaines as the Countess von
Szalras, I would wish it back to-morrow.'

'That is very prettily put for a Socialist.
But you cannot be a Socialist. You are received
at Frohsdorf. Bretons are always royal; they
are born with the *cultus* of God and the
King.'

He laughed a little, not quite easily.

'Paris is a witch's caldron, in which all
cultes are melted down, and evaporate in a
steam of disillusion and mockery; into the caldron we have long flung, alas! cross and crown,
actual and allegoric. I am not a Breton; I
am that idle creation of modern life, a *boulevardier.*'

'But do you never visit Romaris?'

'Why should I? There is nothing but a
few sea-tormented oaks, endless sands, endless
marshes, and a dark dirty village jammed
among rocks, and reeking with the smell of
the oil and the fish.'

'Then I would go and make the village
clean and the marshes healthy, were I you.

There must be something of interest in any people who remain natural in their ways and dwell beside a sea. Is Romaris not prosperous?'

'Prosperous! God and man have forgotten it ever since the world began, I should say. It is on a bay, so treacherous that it is called the Pool of Death. The *landes* separate it by leagues from any town. All it has to live on is the fishing. It is dull as a grave, harried by every storm, unutterably horrible.'

' Well, I would not forsake its horrors were I a son of Romaris,' she said softly; then, as she perceived that some association made the name and memory of the old Armorican village painful to him, she blew the whistle she always used, and at the summons the eldest pupil of the school, a handsome boy of fourteen, came out and stood bareheaded before her.

' Hansl, ask the teachers to grant you all an hour's frolic, that you may amuse this gentleman,' she said to him. 'And, Hansl, take care that you do your best, all of you, in dancing, wrestling, and singing, and above all with the zither, for the honour of the empire.'

The lad, with a face of sunshine, bowed low and ran into the school-houses.

' It is almost their hour for rest, or I would not have disturbed them,' she said to him.

' They come here at sunrise; bring their bread
and meat, and milk is given them; they dis-
perse according to season, a little before sunset.
They have two hours' rest at different times,
but it is hardly wanted, for their labours interest them, and their classes are varied.'

Soon the children all trooped out, made their
bow or curtsey reverently, but without shyness,
and began with song and national airs played on
the zither or the 'jumping wood.' Their singing
and music were tender, ardent, and yet perfectly
precise. There was no false note or slurred
passage. Then they danced the merry national
dances that make gay the long nights in the
snow-covered châlets in many a mountain
village which even the mountain letter-carrier,
on his climbing irons, cannot reach for months
together when all the highlands are ice. They
ended their dances with the Hungarian czardas,
into which they threw all the vigour of their
healthful young limbs and happy hearts.

' My cousin Egon taught them the czardas;
have you ever seen the Magyar nobles in the
madness of that dance? '

' Your cousin Egon? Do you mean Prince
Vàsàrhely? '

' Yes. Do you know him? '

' I have seen him.'

His face grew paler as he spoke. He

ceased to watch with interest the figures of the jumping children in their picturesque national dress, as they whirled and shouted in the sunshine on the green turf, with the woods and the rocks towering beyond them.

When the czardas was ended, the girls sat down on the sward to rest, and the boys began their leaping, running, and stone-heaving, with their favourite wrestling at the close.

'They are as strong as chamois,' she said to him. 'There is no need here to have a gymnasium. Their mountains teach them climbing, and every Sunday on their village green their fathers make them wrestle and shoot at marks. The favourite sport here is one I will not countenance—the finger-hooking. If I gave the word any two of those little fellows would hook their middle fingers together and pull till a joint broke.'

The boys were duly commended for their skill, and Sabran would have thrown them a shower of florin notes had she allowed it. Then she bade them sing as a farewell the Kaiser's Hymn.

The grand melody rolled out on the fresh clear Alpine air in voices as fresh and as clear, that went upward and upward towards the zenith like the carol of the larks.

'I would fain be the Emperor to have that

prayer sung so for me,' said Sabran, with truth, as the glad young voices dropped down into silence—the intense silence of the earth where the glaciers reign.

'He heard them last year, and he was pleased,' she said, as the children raised a loud 'Hoch!' made their reverence once more at a sign of dismissal from her, and vanished in a proud and happy crowd into the school-houses.

'Do you never praise them or reward them?' he asked in surprise.

'Santa Claus rewards them. As for praise, they know when I smile that all is well.'

'But surely they have shown very unusual musical talent?'

'They sing well because they are well taught. But they are not any of them going to become singers. Those zithers and part-songs will all serve to enliven the long nights of the farmhouse or the summer solitude of the cattle-hut. We do not cultivate music one-half enough among the peasantry. It lightens labour; it purifies and strengthens the home-life; it sweetens black-bread. Do you re-member that happy picture of Jordaens' " Where the old sing, the young chirp," where the old grandfather and grandmother, and the baby in its mother's arms, and the hale five-

year-old boy, and the rough servant, are all
joining in the same melody, while the goat
crops the vine-leaves off the table? I should
like to see every cottage interior like that when
the work was done. I would hang up an
etching from Jordaens where you would hang
up, perhaps, the programme of Proudhon.'

Then she walked back with him through
the green sun-gleaming woods.

'I hope that I teach them content,' she continued. 'It is the lesson most neglected in our
day. "*Niemand will ein Schuster seyn; Jeder-
man ein Dichter.*" It is true we are very
happy in our surroundings. A mountaineer's is
such a beautiful life; so simple, healthful, hardy,
and fine; always face to face with nature. I
try to teach them what an inestimable joy that
alone is. I do not altogether believe in the
prosaic views of rural life. It is true that the
peasant digging his trench sees the clod, not
the sky; but then when he does lift his head
the sky is there, not the roof, not the ceiling.
That is so much in itself. And here the sky is
an everlasting grandeur: clouds and domes of
snow are blent together. When the stars are
out above the glaciers how serene the night is,
how majestic! even the humblest creature feels
lifted up into that eternal greatness. Then you
think of the home-life in the long winters as

dreary ; but it is not so. Over away there, at Lahn, and other places on the Hallstadtersee, they do not see the sun for five months ; the wall of rock behind them shuts them from all light of day ; but they live together, they dance, they work. The young men recite poems, and the old men tell tales of the mountains and the French war, and they sing the homely songs of the *Schnaderhupfeln.* Then when winter passes, when the sun comes again up over the wall of rocks, when they go out into the light once more, what happiness it is ! One old man said to me, " It is like being born again ! " and another said, " Where it is always warm and light I doubt they forget to thank God for the sunshine ; " and quite a young child said, all of his own accord, " The primroses live in the dusk all the winter, like us, and then when the sun comes up we and they run out together, and the Mother of Christ has set the waters and the little birds laughing." I would rather have the winter of Lahn than the winter of Belleville.'

'But they do go away from their mountains a good deal ?   One meets them——'

'My own people never do, but from the valleys around they go—yes, sometimes ; but then they always come back. The Defereggenthal men, over yonder where you see those

ice summits, constantly go elsewhere on reach-
ing manhood ; but as soon as they have made
a little money they return to dwell at home
for the remainder of their days.   I think
living amidst the great mountains creates a
restfulness, a steadfastness in the character.   If
Paris were set amidst Alps you would have had
Lamartine, you would not have had Rochefort.'

When she spoke thus of her own country,
of her own people, all her coldness vanished,
her eyes grew full of light, her reserve was
broken up into animation.   They were what
she truly loved, what touched her affections
and her sympathies.

When he heard her speak thus, he thought
if any man should succeed in arousing in her
the love and the loyalty that she gave her
Austrian Alps, what treasures he would win,
into what a kingdom he would enter!   And
then something that was perhaps higher than
vanity and deeper than egotism stirring in him
whispered, ' If any, why not you ? '

Herr Joachim had at a message from her
joined them.   He talked of the flowers around
them and of the culture and flora of Mexico.
Sabran answered him with apparent interest,
and with that knowledge which he had always
the presence of mind to recall at need, but his
heart was heavy and his mind absent.

She had spoken to him of Romaris, and he had once known Egon Vàsàrhely.

Those two facts overshadowed the sweetness and sunshine of the day ; yet he knew very well that he should have been prepared for both.

The Princess Ottilie, seated in her gilt wickerwork chair under the great yew on the south side of the house, saw them approach with pleasure.

'Come and have a cup of tea,' she said to them. 'But, my beloved Wanda, you should not let the doctor walk beside you. Oh, I saw him in the distance; of course he left you before you joined *me*. He is a worthy man, a most worthy man; but so is Hubert, and you do not walk with Hubert and converse with him about flowers.'

'Are you so inexorable as to social grades, madame?' murmured Sabran, as he took his cup from her still pretty hand.

'Most certainly!' said the Princess, with a little, a very little, asperity. 'The world was much happier when distinctions and divisions were impassable. There are no sumptuary laws now. What is the consequence? That your bourgeoise ruins her husband in wearing gowns fit only for a duchess, and your prince imagines it makes him popular to look precisely like a cabman or a bailiff.'

'And even in the matter of utility,' said Sabran, who always agreed with her, 'those sumptuary laws had much in their favour. If one look through the chronicles and miniatures, say of the thirteenth and fourteenth centuries, how much more sensible for the change of seasons and the ease of work seems the costume of the working people? The *cotte hardie* was a thousand times more comfortable and more becoming than anything we have. If we could dress once more as all did under Louis Treize gentle and simple would alike benefit.'

'What a charmingly intelligent person he is!' thought the Princess, as she remarked that in Austria they were happier than the rest of the world: there were peasant costumes still there.

Wanda left them a little later to confer with one of her land stewards. Sabran remained seated by the Princess, in whom he felt that he possessed a friend.

'What did you think of those schools?' said Frau Ottilie. 'Oh, of course you admire and approve; you must admire and approve when they are the hobby of a beautiful woman, who is also your hostess.'

'Does that mean, Princess, that you do not?'

'No doubt the schools are excellent,' replied the Princess, in a tone which condemned them as ridiculous. 'But for my own part I prefer those things left to the Church, of which they constitute alike the privilege and the province. I cannot see either why a peasant child requires to know how a tree grows; that a merciful Providence placed it there is all he can need to be told, and that he should be able to cut it down without cutting off his own fingers is all the science that can possibly be necessary to him. However, Wanda thinks otherwise, and she is mistress here.'

'But the schools surely are eminently practical ones?'

'Practical! Is it practical to weave a romance as long as "Pamela" about the changes of a chrysalis? I fail to see it. That a grub is a destructive creature is all that any one needs to know; there is nothing practical in making it the heroine of an interminable metempsychosis. But all those ideas of Wanda's have a taint of that modern poison which her mind, though it is so strong in many things, has not been strong enough to resist. She does not believe in the efficacy of our holy relics (such as that which I sent you, and which wrought your cure), but she does believe in the fables that naturalists invent about weeds and beetles, and she finds a Kosmos in a puddle!'

'You are very severe, Princess.'

'I dislike inconsistency, and my niece is inconsistent, though she imagines that perfect consistency is the staple of her character.'

'Nay, madame, surely her character is the most evenly balanced, the most harmonious, and consequently the most perfect that is possible to humanity.'

The Princess looked at him with a keen little glance.

'You admire her very much? Are you sure you understand her?'

'I should not dare to say that, but I dare to hope it. Her nature seems to me serene and transparent as fine sunlight.'

'So it is; but she has faults, I can assure you,' said the Princess, with her curious union of shrewdness and simplicity. 'My niece is a perfectly good woman, so far as goodness is possible to finite nature; she is the best woman I have ever known out of the cloister. But then there is this to be said—she has never been tempted. True, she might be tempted to be arrogant, despotic, tyrannical; and she is not so. But that is not precisely the temptation to try her. She is mild and merciful out of her very pride; but her character would be sure destruction of her pride were such a thing possible. You think she is not proud because she is so gentle? You might as well say that Her Májesty is not Empress because she washes the feet of the twelve poor men! Wanda is the best woman that I know, but she is also the proudest.'

'The Countess has never loved anyone?' said Sabran, who grew paler as he heard.

'Terrestrial love—no. It has not touched her. But it would not alter her, believe me. Some women lose themselves in their affections; she would not. She would always remain the mistress of it, and it would be a love like her character. Of that I am sure.'

Sabran was silent; he was discouraged.

'I think the boldest man would always be held at a distance from her,' he said, after a pause. 'I think none would ever acquire dominion over her life.'

'That is exactly what I have said,' replied the Princess. 'Your phrase is differently worded, but it comes to the same thing.'

'It would depend very much——'

'On what?'

'On how much she loved, and perhaps a little on how much she was loved.'

'Not at all,' said the Princess, decidedly; 'you cannot get more out of a nature than there is in it, and there is no sort of passion in the nature of my niece.'

He was silent again.

'She was admirably educated,' added the Princess, hastily, conscious of a remark not strictly becoming in herself; 'and her rare temperament is serene, well balanced, void of all excess. Heaven has mercifully eliminated from her almost all mortal errors.'

'By pride
Angels have fallen ere thy time!'

suggested Sabran.

'Angels, perhaps,' said the Princess, drily. 'But for women it is an admirable preservative, second only to piety.'

He went home sculling himself across the lake, now perfectly calm beneath the rose and gold of a midsummer sunset. His heart was heavy, and a dull fear seemed to beat at his conscience like a child suddenly awaking who knocks at a long-closed door. Still, as a crime allures men who contemplate it by the fascination of its weird power, so the sin he desired to commit held him with its unholy beguilement, and almost it looked holy to him because it wore the guise of Wanda von Szalras.

He was not insensible to the charm of this interchange of thought. He had had many passions in which his senses alone had been enlisted. There was a more delicate attraction in the gradual and numberless steps by which, only slowly and with patience, could he win any way into her regard. She had for him the puissance that the almost unattainable has for all humanity. When he could feel that he had awakened any sympathy in her, his pride was more flattered than it could have been by the most complete subjection of any other woman. He had looked on all women with the chill, amorous cynicism of the Parisian psychology, as *l'éternel féminin,* at best as ' *la forme perverse, vaporeuse, langoureuse, souple comme les roseaux, blanche comme les lis, incapable de se mouvoir pendant les deux tiers du jour—sans équilibre, sans but, sans équateur, donnant son corps en pâture à sa tête.'* He had had no other ideal; no other conception. This psychology, like some other sciences, brutalises as it equalises. In the woman who had risen up before him in the night of storm upon the Szalrassee he had recognised with his intelligence a woman who made his philosophy at fault, who aroused something beyond his mere instincts, who was not to be classified with the Lias, or the Cesarines, or the Jane de Simeroses, who had been in his love, as in his literature, the various types of the *éternel féminin.* The simplicity and the dignity of her life astonished and convinced him; he began to understand that where he had imagined he had studied the universe in his knowledge of women, he had in reality only seen two phases of it—the hothouse and the ditch. It is a common error to take the forced flower and the slime weed, and think that there is nothing between or beyond the two.

He had the convictions of his school that all women were at heart coquettes or hypocrites, consciously or unconsciously. Wanda von Szalras routed all his theories. Before her candour, her directness and gravity of thought, her serene indifference to all forms of compliment, all his doctrines and all his experiences were useless. She inspired him with reverential and hopeless admiration, which was mingled with an angry astonishment, and something of the bitterness of envy. Sometimes, as he sat and watched the green water of the lake tumble and roll beneath a north wind's wrath under a cloudy sky which hid the snows of the Glöckner range, he remembered a horrible story that had once fascinated him of Malatesta of Rimini slaying the princess that would have none of his love, striking his sword across her white throat in the dusky evening time, and casting her body upon the silken curtains of her wicked litter. Almost he could have found it in him to do such a crime—almost.

Only he thought that at one look of her eyes his sword would have dropped upon the dust.

Her personal beauty had inspired him with a sudden passion, but her character checked it with the sense of fear which it imposed on him; fear of those high and blameless instincts which were an integral part of her nature, fear of that frank, unswerving truth which was the paramount law of her life. As he rode with her, walked with her, conversed with her in the long, light summer hours, he saw more and more of the purity and nobility of her temper, but he saw or thought he saw also an inexorable pride and a sternness in judgment which made him believe that she would be utterly unforgiving to weakness or to sin.

She remained the Nibelungen Queen to him, clothed in flawless armour and aloof from men.

He lingered on at the Holy Isle, finding a fresh charm each day in this simple and peaceful existence, filled with the dreams of a woman unlike every other he had known. He knew that it could not last, but he was unwilling to end it himself. To rise to the sound of the monks' matins, to pass his forenoons in art or open-air exercise, to be sure that some hour or another before sunset he would meet her, either in her home or abroad in the woods; to go early to bed, seeing, as he lay, the pile of the great burg looming high above the water, like the citadel of the Sleeping Beauty—all this, together making up an existence so monotonous, harmless, and calm that a few months before he would have deemed it impossible to endure it, was soothing, alluring, and beguiling to him. He had told no one where he was; his letters might lie and accumulate by the hundred in his rooms in Paris for aught that he cared; he had no creditors, for he had been always scrupulously careful to avoid all debt, and he had no friend for whose existence he cared a straw. There were those who cared for him, indeed, but these seldom trouble any man very greatly.

In the last week of August, however, a letter found its way to him ; it was written in a very bad hand, on paper gorgeous with gold and silver. It was signed ' Cochonette.'

It contained a torrent of reproaches made in the broadest language that the slang of the hour furnished, and every third word was misspelt. How the writer had tracked him she did not say. He tore the letter up and threw the pieces into the water flowing beneath his window. Had he ever passionately desired and triumphed in the possession of that woman? It seemed wonderful to him now. She was an

idol of Paris; a creature with the voice of a
lark and the laugh of a child, with a lovely,
mutinous face, and eyes that could speak without words. As a pierrot, as a mousquetaire, as a
little prince, as a fairy king of operetta, she had
no rival in the eyes of Paris. She blazed with
jewels when she played a peasant, and she
wore the costliest costume of Felix's devising
when she sung her triplets as a soubrette. She
had been constant to no one for three months,
and she had been constant to him for three
years, or, at the least, had made him believe so;
and she wrote to him now furiously, reproach-
fully, entreatingly—fierce reproaches and en-
treaties, all misspelt.

The letter which he threw into the lake
brought all the memories of his old life before him; it was like the flavour of absinthe
after drinking spring water. It was a life
which had had its successes, a life, as the world
called it, of pleasure; and it seemed utterly
senseless to him now as he tore up the note of
Cochonette, and looked down the water to
where the towers and spires and battlements of
Hohenszalras soared upward in the mists. He
shook himself as though to shake off the
memory of an unpleasant dream as he went
out, descended the landing steps, drew his boat
from under the willows and sculled himself

across towards the water-stairs of the Schloss. In a quarter of an hour he was playing the themes of the ' Gotterdammerung,' whilst his châtelaine sat at her spinning-wheel a few yards from him.

' Good heavens! can she and Cochonette belong to the same human race ? ' he thought, as whilst he played his glance wandered to that patrician figure seated in the light from the oriel window, with the white hound leaning against her velvet skirts, and her jewelled fingers plying the distaff and disentangling the flax.

After the noonday breakfast the sun shone, the mists lifted from the water, the clouds drifted from the lower mountains, only leaving the snow-capped head of the Glöckner enveloped in them.

' I am going to ride ; will you come ? ' said Wanda von Szalras to him. He assented with ardour, and a hunter, Siegfried, the mount which was always given to him, was led round under the great terrace, in company with her Arab riding-horse Ali. They rode far through the forests and out on the one level road there was, which swept round the south side of the lake ; a road, turf-bordered, over-hung with huge trees, closed in with a dewy veil of greenery, across which ever and anon some flash of falling water or some shimmer of glacier or of snow crest shone through the dense leafage. They rode too fast for conversation, both the horses racing like greyhounds ; but as they returned, towards the close of the afternoon, they slackened their pace in pity to the steaming heaving flanks beneath their saddles, and then they could hear each other's voices.

' What a lovely life it is here ! ' he said, with a sigh. ' The world will seem very vulgar and noisy to me after it.'

' You would soon tire, and wish for the world,' she answered him.

' No,' he said quickly ; ' I have been two months on the Holy Isle, and I have not known weariness for a moment.'

' That is because it is still summer. If you were here in the winter you would bemoan your imprisonment, like my aunt Ottilie. Even the post sometimes fails us.'

' I should not lament the post,' he replied, thinking of the letter he had cast into the lake. ' My old life seems to me insanity, fever, disease, beside these past two months I have spent with the monks.'

' You can take the vows,' she suggested with a smile. He smiled too.

' Nay : I should not dare to so insult our mother Church. One must not empty ashes into a reliquary.'

'Your life is not ashes yet.'

He was silent. He could not say to her what he would have said could he have laid his heart bare.

'When you go away,' she pursued, 're-member my words. Choose some career; make yourself some aim in life; do not fold your talents in a napkin—in a napkin that lies on the supper table at Bignon's. That idle, aimless life is very attractive, I dare say, in its way, but it must grow wearisome and unsatisfactory as years roll on. The men of my house have never been content with it; they have always been soldiers, statesmen, something or other beside mere nobles.'

'But they have had a great position.'

'Men make their own position; they cannot make a name (at least, not to my thinking). You have that good fortune; you have a great name; you only need, pardon me, to make your manner of life worthy of it.'

He grew pale as she spoke.

'Cannot make a name?' he said, with forced gaiety. 'Surely in these days the beggar rides on horseback in all the ministries and half the nobilities!'

A great contempt passed over her face. 'You mean that Hans, Pierre, or Richard becomes a count, an excellency, or an earl?

What does that change?   It alters the handle;
it does not alter the saucepan.   No one can be
ennobled.   Blood is blood; nobility can only
be inherited; it cannot be conferred by all the
heralds in the world.   The very meaning and
essence of nobility are descent, inherited traditions, instincts, habits, and memories—all that
is meant by *noblesse oblige.*'

' Would you allow,' thought her companion,
' would you allow the same nobility to Falcon-
bridge as to Plantagenet ? '

But he dared not name the bar sinister to
this daughter of princes.

Siegfried started and reared : his rider did
not reply, being absorbed in calming him.

' What frightened him ? ' she asked.

' A hawk flew by,' said Sabran.

' A hawk, flying low enough for a horse to
see it?   It must be wounded.'

He did not answer, and they quickened
their pace, as the sun sunk behind the glaciers
of the west.

When he returned to the monastery the
evening had closed in ; the lantern was lit at
his boat's prow.   Dinner was prepared for him,
but he ate little.   Later the moon rose ; golden
and round as a bowl.   It was a beautiful spectacle as it gave its light to the amphitheatre of
the mountains, to the rippling surface of the

lake, to the stately, irregular lines of the castle backed by the blackness of its woods. He sat long by the open window lost in thought, pondering on the great race which had ruled there. *L'honneur parle: il suffit,* had been their law, and she who represented them held a creed no less stern and pure than theirs. Her words spoken in their ride were like a weight of ice on his heart. Never to her, never, could he confess the errors of his past. He was a man bold to temerity, but he was not bold enough to risk the contempt of Wanda von Szalras. He had never much heeded right or wrong, or much believed in such ethical distinctions, only adhering to the conventional honour and good breeding of the world, but before her his moral sense awakened.

' The Marquis Xavier would bid me go from here,' he thought to himself, as the night wore on and he heard the footfall of the monks passing down the passages to their midnight orisons.

' After all these years in the *pourriture* of Paris, have I such a thing as conscience left? ' he asked his own thoughts, bitterly. The moon passed behind a cloud and darkness fell over the lake and hid the great pile of the Hohenszalrasburg from his sight. He closed the casement and turned away. ' Farewell ! ' he said, to the vanished castle.

'Will you think of me sometimes, dear Princess, when I am far away?' said Sabran abruptly the next morning to his best friend, who looked up startled.

' Away?   Are you going away?'

' Yes,' said Sabran, abruptly; ' and you, I think, madame, who have been so good to me, can guess easily why.'

' You love my niece?'

He inclined his head in silence.

'It is very natural,' said the Princess, faintly.   ' Wanda is a beautiful woman; many men have loved her; they might as well have loved that glacier yonder.'

' It is not that,' said Sabran, hastily.   ' It is my own poverty——'

The Princess looked at him keenly.

' Do you think her not cold?'

' She who can so love a brother would surely love her lover not less, did she stoop to one,' he replied evasively.   ' At least I think so; I ought not to presume to judge.'

' And you care for her?'   The glance her eyes gave him added as plainly as words could have done, 'It is not only her wealth, her position?   Are you sure?'

He coloured very much as he answered quickly: ' Were she beggared to-morrow, you would see.'

'It is a pity,' murmured the Princess. He did not ask her what she regretted ; he knew her sympathy was with him.

They were both mute. The Princess pushed the end of her cane thoughtfully into the velvet turf. She hesitated some moments, then said in a low voice : ' Were I you I would stay.'

'Do not tempt me ! I have stayed too long as it is. What can she think of me ? '

'She does not think about your reasons ; she is too proud a woman to be vain. In a measure you have won her friendship. Perhaps—I do not know, I have no grounds to say so—but perhaps in time you might win more.'

She looked at him as she concluded. He grew exceedingly pale.

He stooped over her chair, and spoke very low :

'It is just because that appears possible that I go. Do not misunderstand me, I am not a coxcomb; *je ne me pose pas en vainqueur.* But I have no place here, since I have no equality with her from which to be able to say, " I love you ! " Absence alone can say it for me without offence as without hope.'

The Princess was silent. She was thinking

of the maxim, ' *L'absence éteint les petites passions et allume les grandes.*'   Which was his?

'You have been so good to me,' he murmured caressingly, 'so benevolent, so merciful, I dare to ask of you a greater kindness yet. Will you explain for me to the Countess von Szalras that I am called away suddenly, and make my excuses and my farewell? It will save me much fruitless pain.'

'And if it give her pain?'

'I cannot suppose that, and I should not dare to hope it.'

'I have no reason to suppose it either, but I think you are *de guerre las* before the battle is decided.'

'There is no battle possible for me.   There is only a quite certain dishonour.'

His face was dark and weary. He spoke low and with effort. She glanced at him, and felt the vague awe with which strong unintelligible emotion always filled her.

'You must judge the question for yourself,' she said with a little hesitation. 'I will express what you wish to my niece if you really desire it.'

'You are always so good to me,' he murmured, with some agitation, and he bent down before her and reverently kissed her little white hands.

'God be with you, sir,' she said, with tears in her own tender eyes.

'You have been so good to me,' he murmured; 'the purest hours of my worthless life have been spent at Hohenszalras. Here only have I known what peace and holiness can mean. Give me your blessing ere I go.'

In another moment he had bowed himself from her presence, and the Princess sat mute and motionless in the sun. When she looked up at the great feudal pile of the Schloss which towered above her, it was with reproach and aversion to that stone emblem of the great possessions of its châtelaine.

'If she were a humbler woman,' she thought, 'how much happier she would be! What a pity it all is—what a pity! Of course he is right; of course he can do nothing else. If he did do anything else the world would condemn him, and even she very likely would despise him—but it is such a pity! If only she could have a woman's natural life about her—— This life is not good. It is very well while she is young, but when she shall be no longer young?'

And the tender heart of the old gentlewoman ached for a sorrow not her own; and could she have given him a duchy to make him able to declare his love, she would have done so at all costs.

CHAPTER VII.

THE sun was setting when the Countess Wanda returned from her distant ride. She dismounted at the foot of the terrace-steps and ascended them slowly, with Donau and Neva behind her, both tired and breathless.

'You are safe home, my love?' said the Princess, turning her head towards the steps.

'Yes, dear mother mine; you always, I know, think that Death gets up on the saddle. Is anything amiss? You looked troubled.'

'I have a message for you,' said the Princess with a sigh, and she gave Sabran's.

Wanda von Szalras heard in silence. She showed neither surprise nor regret.

The Princess waited a little.

'Well,' she said, at length, 'well, you do not even ask me why he goes!'

'You say he has been called away,' her niece answered. 'Surely that is reason enough.'

'You have no heart, Wanda.'

'I do not understand you,' said the Countess von Szalras, very coldly.

'Do you mean to say you have not seen that he loved you?'

The face of Wanda grew colder still.

'Did he instruct you to say this also?'

'No, no,' said the Princess, hurriedly, perceiving her error. 'He only bade me say that he was called away and must leave at once, and begged you to accept through me his adieus and the expression of his gratitude. But it is very certain that he does love you, and that because he is too poor and too proud to say so he goes.'

'You must weave your little romance!' said her niece, with some impatience, striking the gilt wicker table with her riding-whip. 'I prefer to think that M. de Sabran is, very naturally, gone back to the world to which he belongs. My only wonder has been that he has borne so long with the solitudes of the Szalrassee.'

'If you were not the most sincere woman in the world, I should believe you were endeavouring to deceive me. As it is,' said the

Princess, with some temper, ' I can only suppose that you deceive yourself.'

' Have you any tea there ? ' said her niece,
laying aside her gauntlets and her whip, and
casting some cakes to the two hounds.

She had very plainly and resolutely closed
the subject almost before it was fairly opened.
The Princess, a little intimidated and keenly
disappointed, did not venture to renew it.

When, the next morning, questioning Hubert, the Princess found that indeed her favourite
had left the island monastery at dawn, the
landscape of the Hohe Tauern seemed to her
more monotonous and melancholy than it had
ever done, and the days more tedious and
dull.

' You will miss the music, at least,' she said,
with asperity, to her niece. ' I suppose you
will give him as much regret as you have done
at times to the Abbé Liszt ? '

' I shall miss the music, certainly,' said the
Countess Wanda, calmly. ' Our poor Kapell-
meister is very indifferent. If he were not so
old that it would be cruel to displace him, I
would take another from the Conservatorium.'

The Princess was irritated and even in-
censed at the reply, but she let it pass. Sabran's
name was mentioned no more between them
for many days.

No one knew whither he had gone, and no tidings came of him to Hohenszalras.

One day a foreign journal, amongst the many news-sheets that came by post there, contained his name: 'The Marquis de Sabran broke the bank at Monte Carlo yesterday,' was all that it said in its news of the Riviera.

'A winner at a *tripot*, what a hero for you, mother mine!' she said with some bitterness, handing the paper to the Princess. She was surprised at the disgust and impatience which she felt herself. What could it concern her?

That day as she rode slowly through the grass drives of her forests, she thought with pain of her companion of a few weeks, who so late had ridden over these very paths beside her, the dogs racing before them, the wild flowers scenting the air, the pale sunshine falling down across the glossy necks of their horses.

'He ought to do better things than break a bank at a gaming-place,' she thought with regret. 'With such natural gifts of body and mind, it is a sin—a sin against himself and others—to waste his years in those base and trivial follies. When he was here he seemed to feel so keenly the charm of Nature, the beauty of repose, the possibility of noble effort.'

She let the reins droop on her mare's throat and paced slowly over the moss and the grass; though she was all alone—for in her own forests she would not be accompanied even by a groom —-the colour came into her face as she remembered many things, many words, many looks, which confirmed the assertion Madame Ottilie had made to her.

'That may very well be,' she thought; ' but if it be, I think my memory might have restrained him from becoming the hero of a gambling apotheosis.'

And she was astonished at herself to find how much regret mingled with her disgust, and how much her disgust was intensified by a sentiment of personal offence.

When she reached home it was twilight, and she was told that her cousin Prince Egon Vàsàrhely had arrived. She would have been perfectly glad to see him, if she had been perfectly sure that he would have accepted quietly the reply she had sent to his letter received on the night of the great storm. As it was she met him in the blue-room before the Princess Ottilie, and nothing could be said on that subject.

Prince Egon, though still young, had already a glorious past behind him. He came of a race of warriors, and the Vàsàrhely Hussars had been famous since the days of Maria Theresa. The command of that brilliant regiment was hereditary, and he had led them in repeated charges into the French lines and the Prussian lines with such headlong and dauntless gallantry that he had been called the 'Wild Boar of Taròc' throughout the army. His hussars were the most splendid cavalry that ever shook their bridles in the sunlight on the wide Magyar plains. Their uniform remained the same as in the days of Aspern, and he was prodigal of gold, and embroidery, and rich furs, and trappings, with that martial coquetry which has been characteristic of so many great soldiers from Scylla to Michael Skobeleff.

With his regiment in the field, and without it in many adventures in the wilder parts of the Austrian Empire and on the Turkish border, he had become a synonym for heroism throughout the Imperial army, whilst in his manner and mode of life no more magnificent noble ever came from the dim romantic solitudes of Hungary to the court and the capital. He had great personal beauty; he had unrivalled traditions of valour; and he had a character as generous as it was daring: but he failed to awaken more than a sisterly attachment in the heart of his cousin. She had been so used to see him with her brothers that he seemed as near to her as they had been. She loved him tenderly, but with no sort of passion. She wondered that he should care for her in that sense, and grew sometimes impatient of his reiterated prayers.

'There are so many women who would listen to him and adore him,' she said. 'Why must he come to me?'

Before Bela's death, and before she became her own mistress, she had always urged that her own sisterly affection for Egon made any thought of marriage with him out of the question.

'I am fond of him as I was of Gela and Victor,' she said often to those who pressed the alliance upon her; 'but that is not love. I will not marry a man whom I do not love.'

When she became absolutely her own mistress he was for some time silent, fearing to importune her, or to seem mercenary. She had become by Bela's death one of the greatest alliances in Europe. But at length, confident that his own position exempted him from any possible appearance of covetousness, he gently reminded her of her father's and her brother's wishes; but to no effect. She gave him the same answer. 'You are sure of my affection, but I will not do you so bad a service as to become your wife. I have no love for you.' From that he had no power to move or change her. He had made her many appeals in his

frequent visits to Hohenszalras, but none with
any success in inducing her to depart from the
frank and placid regard of close relationship.
She liked him well, and held him in high
esteem; but this was not love; nor, had she
consented to call it love, would it ever have
contented the impetuous, ardent, and passionate
spirit of Egon Vàsàrhely.

They could not be lovers, but they still
remained friends, partly through consanguinity,
partly because he could bear to see her thus so
long as no other was nearer to her than he. They
greeted each other now cordially and simply, and
talked of the many cares and duties and interests that sprang up daily in the administration of such vast properties as theirs.

Prince Vàsàrhely, though a brilliant soldier
and magnificent noble, was simple in his tastes,
and occupied himself largely with the welfare
of his people.

The Princess yawned discreetly behind her
fan many times during this conversation, to her
utterly uninteresting, upon villages, vines, har-
vests, bridges swept away by floods, stewards
just and unjust, and the tolls and general
navigation of the Danube. Quite tired of all
these details and discussion of subjects which
she considered ought to be abandoned to the
men of business, she said suddenly, in a pause:

'Egon, did you ever know a very charming person, the Marquis de Sabran?'

Vàsàrhely reflected a moment.

'No,' he answered slowly. 'I have no recollection of such a name.'

'I thought you might have met him in Paris.'

'I am so rarely in Paris; since my father's death I have scarcely passed a month there. Who is he?'

'A stranger whose acquaintance we made through his being cast adrift here in a storm,' said the Countess Wanda, with some impatience. 'My dear aunt is devoted to him, because he has painted her a St. Ottilie on a screen, with the skill of Meissonnier. Since he left us he has become celebrated: he has broken the bank at Monte Carlo.'

Egon Vàsàrhely looked at her quickly.

'It seems to anger you? Did this stranger stay here any time?'

'Sometime, yes; he had a bad accident on the Venediger. Herr Greswold brought him to our island to pass his convalescence with the monks. From the monks to Monte Carlo!— it is at least a leap requiring some elasticity in moral gymnastics.'

She spoke with some irritation, which did not escape the ear of her cousin. He said merely himself:

‘ Did you receive him, knowing nothing about him ? ’

‘ We certainly did.   It was an imprudence ; but if he paint like Meissonnier, he plays like Liszt : who was to resist such a combination of gifts ? ’

‘ You say that very contemptuously, Wanda,’ said the Prince.

‘ I am not contemptuous of the talent ; I am of the possessor of it, who comprehends his own powers so little that he breaks the bank at Monaco.’

‘ I envy him at least his power to anger you,’ said Egon Vàsàrhely.

‘ I am angered to see anything wasted,’ she answered, conscious of the impatience she had shown.   ‘ I was very angry with Otto’s little daughter yesterday ; she had gathered a huge bundle of cowslips and thrown it down in the sun ; it was ingratitude to God who made them. This friend of my aunt’s does worse ; he changes his cowslip into monkshood.’

‘ Is he indeed such a favourite of yours, dear mother ? ’ said Vàsàrhely.

The Princess answered petulantly :

‘ Certainly, a charming person.   And our cousin Kaulnitz knows him well.   Wanda for once talks foolishly.   Gambling is, it is true, a great sin at all times, but I do not know that it

is worse at public tables than it is in your clubs.
I myself am, of course, ignorant of these
matters; but I have heard that privately, at
cards, whole fortunes have been lost in a night,
scribbled away with a pencil on a scrap of
paper.'

'To lose a fortune is better than to win one,'
said her niece, as she rose from the head of her
table.

When the Princess slept in her blue-room
Egon Vàsàrhely approached his cousin, where
she sat at her embroidery frame.

'This stranger has the power to make you
angry,' he said sadly. 'I have not even
that.'

'Dear Egon,' she said tenderly, 'you have
done nothing in your life that I could despise.
Why should you be discontented at that?'

'Would you care if I did?'

'Certainly; I should be very sorry if my
noble cousin did anything that could belie his
chivalry; but why should we suppose impossibilities?'

'Suppose we were not cousins, would you
love me then?'

'How can I tell? This is mere non-
sense——'

'No; it is all my life. You know, Wanda,
that I have loved you, only you, ever since I

saw you as I came back from France—a child,
but such a beautiful child, with your hair
braided with pearls, and a dress all stiff with
gold, and your lap full of red roses.'

'Oh, I remember,' she said hastily. 'There
was a child's costume ball at the Hof; I called
myself Elizabeth of Thuringia, and Bela, my
own Bela, was my little Louis of Hungary. Oh,
Egon, why will you speak of those times?'

'Because surely they make a kind of tie
between us? They——'

'They do make one that will last all our
lives, unless you strain it to bear a weight it is
not made to bear. Dear Egon, you are very
dear to me, but not dear *so*. As my cousin,
my gallant, kind, and loyal cousin, you are
very precious to me; but, Egon, if you could
force me to be your wife I should not be indifferent to you, I should hate you!'

He grew white under his olive skin. He
shrank a little, as if he suffered some sharp
physical pain.

'Hate me!' he echoed in a stupor of surprise and suffering.

'I believe I should. I *could* hate. It is a
frightful thing to say. Dear Egon, look elsewhere; find some other amongst the many lovely
women that you see; do not waste your brilliant life on me. I shall never say otherwise

'than I say to-night, and you will compel me to lose the most trusted friend I have.'

He was still very pale. He breathed heavily. There was a mist over his handsome dark eyes, which were cast down. 'Until you love any other, I shall never abandon hope.'

'That is unwise. I shall probably love no one all my life long; I have told you so often.'

'All say so until love finds them out. I will not trouble you; I will be your cousin, your friend, rather than be nothing to you. But it is hard.'

'Why think of me so? Your career has so much brilliancy, so many charms, so many interests——'

'You do not know what it is to love. I talk to you in an unknown tongue, and you have no pity, because you do not understand.'

She did not answer. Over her thoughts passed the memory of the spinet whose music she had said he could not touch and waken.

He remained a week at Hohenszalras, but he did not again speak to her of his own sufferings. He was a proud man, though humble to her.

With a sort of contrition she noticed for the first time that he wearied her; that when he spoke of his departure she was glad. He was a fine soldier, a keen hunter, rather than a man of talents. The life he loved best was his life at home in his great castles, amidst the immense plains and the primeval forests of Hungary and the lonely fastnesses of the Karpathians, or scouring a field of battle with his splendid troopers behind him, all of them his kith and kin, or men of his own soil, whom he ruled with a firm, high hand, in a generous despotism.

When he was with her she missed all the graceful tact, the subtle meanings, the varied suggestions and allusions that had made the companionship of Sabran so welcome to her. Egon Vàsàrhely was no scholar, no thinker, no satirist; he was only brave and generous, as lions are, and, vaguely, a poet without words, from the wild solitudes he loved, and the romance that lies in the nature of the Magyar. 'He knows nothing!' she thought, impatiently recalling the stores of most various and recondite knowledge with which her late companion had played so carelessly and with such ease. It seemed to her that never in her life had she weighed her cousin in scales so severe and found him so uttterly wanting.

And yet how many others she knew would have found their ideal in that gallant gentleman, with his prowess, and his hardihood, and his gallantry in war, and his winsome temper, so full of fire to men, so full of chivalry for women! When Prince Egon, in his glittering dress, all fur and gold and velvet, passed up the ball-room at the Burg in Vienna, no other man in all that magnificent assembly was so watched, so admired, so sighed for: and he was her cousin, and he only wearied her!

As he was leaving, he paused a moment after bidding her farewell, and after some moments of silence, said in a low voice:

'Dear, I will not trouble you again until you summon me. Perhaps that will be many years; but whether we meet or not, time will make no change in me. I am your servant ever.'

Then he bowed over her hand once more, once more saluted her, and in a moment or two the quick trot of the horses that bore him away woke the echoes of the green hills.

She looked out of the huge arched entrance door down the green defile that led to the outer world, and felt a pang of self-reproach, of self-condemnation.

'If one could force oneself to love by any pilgrimage or penance,' she thought, 'there are none I would not take upon me to be able to love Egon.'

As she stood thoughtfully there on the

doorway of her great castle, the sweet linnet-like voice of the Princess Ottilie came on her ear. It said, a little shrilly: 'You are always looking for a four-leaved shamrock. In that sort of search life slips away unperceived; one is very soon left alone with one's dead leaves.'

Wanda von Szalras turned and smiled.

'I am not afraid of being left alone,' she said. 'I shall have my people and my forests always.'

Then, apprehensive lest she should have seemed thankless and cold of heart, she turned caressingly to Madame Ottilie.

'Nay, I could not bear to lose you, my sweet fairy godmother. Think me neither forgetful nor ungrateful.'

'You could never be one or the other to me. But I shall not live, like a fairy godmother, for ever. Before I die I would fain see you content like others with the shamrocks as nature has made them.'

'I think there are few people as content as I am,' said the Countess Wanda, and said the truth.

'You are content with yourself, not with others. You will pardon me if I say there is a great difference between the two,' replied the Princess Ottilie, with a little smile that was almost sarcastic on her pretty small features,

'You mean that I have a great deal of vanity and no sympathy?'

'You have a great deal of pride,' said the Princess, discreetly, as she began to take her customary noontide walk up and down the terrace, her tall cane tapping the stones and her little dog running before her, whilst a hood of point-lace and a sunshade of satin kept the wind from her pretty white hair and the sun from her eyes, that were still blue as the acres of mouse-ear that grew by the lake.

CHAPTER VIII.

THE summer glided away and became autumn, and the Countess Wanda refused obstinately to fill Hohenszalras with house-parties. In vain her aunt spoke of the Lynau, the Windischgrätz, the Hohenlöhe, and the other great families who were their relatives or their friends. In vain she referred continually to the fact that every Schloss in Austria and all adjacent countries was filling with guests at this season, and the woods around it resounding with the hunter's horn and the hound's bay. In vain did she recapitulate the glories of Hohenszalras in an earlier time, and hint that the mistress of so vast a domain owed some duties to society.

Wanda von Szalras opposed to all these suggestions and declarations that indifference

which would have seemed obstinacy had it been
less mild. As for the hunting parties, she
avowed with truth that although a daughter
of mighty hunters, she herself regarded all
pastimes founded on cruelty with aversion and
contempt; the bears and the boars, the wild
deer and the mountain chamois, might dwell
undisturbed for the whole of their lives so far
as she was concerned. When a bear came down
and ate off the heads of an acre or two of wheat,
she recompensed .the peasant who had suffered
the loss, but she would not have her *jägermeister* track the poor beast. The *jägermeister*
sighed as Madame Ottilie did for the bygone
times when a score of princes and nobles had
ridden out on a wolf-chase, or hundreds of
peasants had threshed the woods to drive the
big game towards the Kaiser's rifle; but for
poachers his place would have been a sinecure
and his days a weariness. His mistress was not
to be persuaded. She .preferred her forests left
to their unbroken peace, their stillness filled with
the sounds of rushing waters and the calls of
birds.

The weeks glided on one after one with
the even measured pace of monotonous and
unruffled time; her hours were never unoccu-
pied, for her duties were constant and numerous.

She would go and visit the sennerinn in their

loftiest cattle-huts, and would descend an ice-slope with the swiftness and security of a practised mountaineer. In her childhood she and Bela had gone almost everywhere the chamois went, and she came of a race which, joined to high courage, had the hereditary habits of a great endurance. In the throne room of Vienna, with her great pearls about her, that had once been sent by a Sultan to a Szalras who fought with Wenceslaus, she was the stateliest and proudest lady of the greatest aristocracy of the world ; but on her own mountain sides she was as dauntless as an ibis, as sure-footed as a goat, and would sit in the alpine cabins and drink a draught of milk and break a crust of rye-bread as willingly as though she were a sennerinn herself ; so she would take the oars and row herself unaided down the lake, so she would saddle her horse and ride it over the wildest country, so she would drive her sledge over many a German mile of snow, and even in the teeth of a north wind blowing straight from the Russian plains and the Arctic seas.

'Fear nothing!' had been said again and again to her in her childhood, and she had learned that her race transmitted to and imposed its courage no less on its daughters than on its sons. Cato would have admired this mountain brood, even though its mountain lair

was more luxurious than he would have deemed
was wise.

She knew thoroughly what all her rights,
titles, and possessions were. She was never
vague or uncertain as to any of her affairs,
and it would have been impossible to deceive
or to cheat her. No one tried to do so, for her
lawyers were men of old-fashioned ways and
high repute, and for centuries the vast properties of the Counts von Szalras had been
administered wisely and honestly in the same
advocates' offices, which were close underneath
the Calvarienburg in the good city of Salzburg.
Her trustees were her uncle Cardinal Vàsàrhely
and her great-uncle Prince George of Lilienhöhe ; they were old men, both devoted to her,
and both fully conscious that her intelligence
was much abler and keener than their own. All
these vast possessions gave her an infinite variety
of occupation and of interests, and she neglected
none of them. Still, all the properties and duties
in the world will not suffice to fill up the heart
and mind of a woman of four-and-twenty years of
age, who enjoys the perfection of bodily health
and of physical beauty. The most spiritual
and the most dutiful of characters cannot
altogether resist the impulses of nature. There
were times when she now began to think that
her life was somewhat empty and passionless.

But a certain sense of their monotony had begun for the first time to come upon her; a certain vague dissatisfaction stirred in her now and then. The discontent of Sabran seemed to have left a shadow of itself upon her. For the first time she seemed to be listening, as it were, to her life and to find a great silence in it; there was no echo in it of voices she loved.

Why had she never perceived it before? Why did she become conscious of it now? She asked herself this impatiently as the slight but bitter flavour of dissatisfaction touched her, and the days for once seemed—now and then—over long.

She loved her people and her forests and her mountains, and she had always thought that they would be sufficient for her, and she had honestly told the Princess that of solitude she was not afraid; and yet a certain sense that her life was cold and in a measure empty had of late crept upon her. She wondered angrily why a vague and intangible melancholy stole on her at times, which was different from the sorrow which still weighed on her for her brother's death. Now and then she looked at the old painted box of the spinet, and thought of the player who had awakened its dumb strings; but she did not suspect for a moment that it was in any sense his companionship which,

now that it was lost, made the even familiar
tenor of her time appear monotonous and without much interest. In the long evenings, whilst
the Princess slumbered and she herself sat
alone watching the twilight give way to the
night over the broad and solemn landscape, she
felt a lassitude which did not trouble her in
the open air, in the daylight, or when she was
busied indoors over the reports and requirements of her estates. Unacknowledged, indeed,
unknown to her, she missed the coming of the
little boat from the Holy Isle, and missed the
prayer and praise of the great tone-poets rolling
to her ear from the organ within. If anyone
had told her that her late guest had possessed
any such power to make her days look grey and
pass tediously she would have denied it, and
been quite sincere in her denial. But as he had
called out the long mute music from the spinet,
so he had touched, if only faintly, certain chords
in her nature that until then had been dumb.

'I am not like you, my dear Olga,' she wrote
to her relative, the Countess Brancka. 'I am
not easily amused. That *course effrénée* of the
great world carries you honestly away with it ;
all those incessant balls, those endless visits,
those interminable conferences on your toilettes,
that continual circling of human butterflies
round you, those perpetual courtships of half a

score of young men; it all diverts you. You
are never tired of it; you cannot understand any
life outside its pale. All your days, whether
they pass in Paris or Petersburg, at Trouville,
at Biarritz, or at Vienna or Scheveningen, are
modelled on the same lines; you must have
excitement as you have your cup of chocolate
when you wake. What I envy you is that the
excitement excites you. When I was amidst it
I was not excited; I was seldom even diverted.
See the misfortune that it is to be born with a
grave nature! I am as serious as Marcus An-
toninus. You will say that it comes of having
learned Latin and Greek. I do not think so;
I fear I was born unamusable. I only truly
care about horses and trees, and they are both
grave things, though a horse can be playful
enough sometimes when he is allowed to forget
his servitude. Your friends, the famous tailors,
send me admirably-chosen costumes which please
that sense in me which Titians and Vandycks
do (I do not mean to be profane); but I only
put them on as the monks do their frocks.
Perhaps I am very unworthy of them; at least,
I cannot talk toilette as you can with ardour a
whole morning and every whole morning of
your life. You will think I am laughing at
you; indeed I am not. I envy your faculty of
sitting, as I am sure you are sitting now, in a

straw chair on the shore, with a group of *boule-vardiers* around you, and a crowd making a double hedge to look at you when it is your pleasure to pace the planks. My language is involved. I do not envy you the faculty of doing it, of course ; I could do it myself to-morrow. I envy you the faculty of finding amusement in doing it, and finding flattery in the double hedge.'

A few days afterwards the Countess Brancka wrote back in reply :

' The world is like wine ; *ça se mousse et ça monte.* There are heads it does not affect; there are palates that do not like it, yours amongst them. But there is so much too in habit. Living alone amidst your mountains you have lost all taste for the *brouhaha* of society, which grows noisier, it must be said, every year. Yes, we are noisy : we have lost our dignity. You alone keep yours, you are the châtelaine of the middle ages. Perceforest or Parsifal should come riding to your gates of granite. By the way, I hear you have been entertaining one of our *boulevardiers.* Réné de Sabran is charming, and the handsomest man in Paris ; but he is not Parsifal or Perceforest. Between ourselves, he has an indifferent repu-tation, but perhaps he has repented on your Holy Isle. They say he is changed ; that he has quarrelled with Cochonette, and that he is about to be made deputy for his department, whose representative has just died. Pardon me for naming Cochonett ; it is part of our decadence that we laugh about all these naughty things and naughty people who are, after all, not so very much worse than we are ourselves. But you do not laugh, whether at these or at anything else. You are too good, my beautiful Wanda ; it is your sole defect. You have even inoculated this poor Marquis, who, after a few weeks upon the Szalrassee, surrenders Cochonette for the Chamber! My term of service comes round next month : if you will have me I will take the Tauern on my road to Gödöllo. I long to embrace you.'

'Olga will take pity on our solitude,' said Wanda von Szalras to her aunt. 'I have not seen her for four years, but I imagine she is little changed.'

The Princess read the letter, frowning and pursing her lips together in pretty rebuke as she came to the name of Cochonette.

'They have indeed lost all dignity,' she said with a sigh ; 'and something more than dignity also. Olga was always frivolous.'

'All her *monde* is ; not she more than another.'

'You were very unjust, you see, to M. de

Sabran ; he pays you the compliment of following your counsels.'

Wanda von Szalras rose a little impatiently.
'He had better have followed them before he
broke the bank at Monaco. It is an odd sort
of notoriety with which to attract the pious
and taciturn Bretons ; and when he was here he
had no convictions. I suppose he picked them
up with the gold pieces at the tables ! '

Olga, Countess Brancka, *née* Countess
Scriatine, of a noble Russian family, had been
married at sixteen to the young Gela von Szalras,
who, a few months after his bridal, had been shot
dead on the battlefield of Solferino.

After scarce a year of mourning she had
fascinated the brother of Egon Vàsàrhely, a
mere youth who bore the title of Count Brancka.
There had been long and bitter opposition made
to the new alliance on the part of both families,
on account of the consanguinity between
Stefan Brancka and her dead lord. But opposition had only increased the ardour of the
young man and the young widow ; they had
borne down all resistance, procured all dispen-
sations, had been wedded, and in a year's time
had both wished the deed undone. Both were
extravagant, capricious, self-indulgent, and unreasonable ; their two egotisms were in a perpetual collision. They met but seldom, and

never met without quarrelling violently. The only issue of their union was two little, fantastic, artificial fairies who were called respectively Mila and Marie.

At the time of the marriage of the Branckas, Wanda had been too young to share in opposition to it; but the infidelity to her brother's memory had offended and wounded her deeply, and in her inmost heart she had never pardoned it, though the wife of Stefan Brancka had been a passing guest at Hohenszalras, where, had Count Gela lived, she would have reigned as sovereign mistress. That his sister reigned there in her stead the Countess Olga resented keenly and persistently. Her own portion of the wealth of the Szalras had been forfeited under her first marriage contract by her subsequent alliance. But she never failed to persuade herself that her exclusion from every share in that magnificent fortune was a deep wrong done to herself, and she looked upon Wanda von Szalras as the doer of that wrong.

In appearance, however, she was always cordial, caressing, affectionate, and if Wanda chose to mistrust her affection, it was, she reflected, only because a life of unwise solitude had made a character naturally grave become severe and suspicious.

She did not fail to arrive there a week

later. She was a small, slender, lovely woman, with fair skin, auburn hair, wondrous black eyes, and a fragile frame that never knew fatigue. She held a high office at the Imperial Court, but when she was not on service, she spent, under the plea of health, all her time at Paris or *les eaux*. She came with her numerous attendants, her two tiny children, and a great number of huge *fourgons* full of all the newest marvels of combination in costume. She was seductive and caressing, but she was capricious, malicious, and could be even violent ; in general she was gaily given up to amusement and intrigue, but she had moments of rage that were uncontrollable. She had had many indiscretions and some passions, but the world liked her none the less for that ; she was a great lady, and in a sense a happy woman, for she had nerves of steel despite all her maladies, and brought to the pleasures of life an unflagging and even ravenous zest.

When with her perfume of Paris, her restless animation, her children, like little figures from a fashion-plate, her rapid voice that was shrill yet sweet, like a silver whistle, and her eyes that sparkled alike with mirth and with malice, she came on to the stately terraces of Hohenszalras, she seemed curiously discordant with it and its old world peace and gravity.

She was like a pen-and-ink sketch of Cham thrust between the illuminated miniatures of a missal.

She felt it herself.

'It is the Roman de la Rose in stone,' she said, as her eyes roved over the building, which she had not visited for four years. 'And you, Wanda, you look like Yseulte of the White Hand or the Marguerite des Marguerites; you must be sorry you did not live in those times.'

'Yes: if only for one reason. One could make the impress of one's own personality so much more strongly on the time.'

'And now the times mould us. We are all horribly alike. There is only yourself who retain any individuality amidst all the women that I know. "*La meule du pressoir de l'abru-tissement*" might have been written of our world. After all, you are wise to keep out of it. My straw chair at Trouville looks trumpery beside that ivory chair in your Rittersäal. I read the other day of some actresses dining off a truffled pheasant and a sack of bon-bons. That is the sort of dinner we make all the year round, morally—metaphorically—how do you say it? It makes us thirsty, and perhaps, I am not sure, perhaps it leaves us half starved, though we nibble the sweetmeats, and don't know it.

'Your dinner must lack two things—bread and water.'

'Yes: we never see either. It is all truffles and caramels and *vins frappés*.'

'There is your bread.'

She glanced at the little children, two pretty, graceful little maids of six and seven years old.

'*Ouf!*' said the Countess Zelenka. 'They are only little bits of puff paste, a couple of *petits fours* baked on the boulevards. If they be *chic*, and marry well, I for one shall ask no more of them. If ever you have children, I suppose you will rear them on science and the Antonines?'

'Perhaps on the open air and Homer,' said Wanda, with a smile.

The Countess Brancka was silent a moment, then said abruptly:

'You dismissed Egon again?'

'Has he made you his ambassadress?'

'No, oh no; he is too proud: only we all are aware of his wishes. Wanda, do you know that you have some cruelty in you, some sternness?'

'I think not. The cruelty would be to grant the wishes. With a loveless wife Egon would be much more unhappy than he is now.'

'Oh, after a few months he would not care, you know; they never do. To unite your fortunes is the great thing; you could lead your lives as you liked.'

'Our fortunes do very well apart,' said the Countess von Szalras, with a patience which cost her some effort.

'Yours is immense,' said Madame Brancka, with a sigh, for her own and her husband's wealth had been seriously involved by extravagance and that high play in which they both indulged. 'And it must accumulate in your hands. You cannot spend much. I do not see how you could spend much. You never receive; you never go to your palaces; you never leave Hohenszalras; and you are so wise a woman that you never commit any follies.'

Wanda was silent. It did not appear to her that she was called on to discuss her expenditure.

Dinner was announced; their attendants took away the children; the Princess woke up from a little dose, and said suddenly, 'Olga, is M. de Sabran elected?'

'Aunt Ottilie,' said her niece, hastily, 'has lost her affections to that gentleman, because he painted her saint on a screen and had all old Haydn at his fingers' ends.'

'The election does not take place until next month,' said the Countess. 'He will certainly be returned, because of the blind fidelity of the department to his name. The odd thing is that he should wish to be so.'

'Wanda told him it was his duty,' said Princess Ottilie, with innocent malice.

The less innocent malice of the Countess Brancka's eyes fell for a passing moment with inquiry and curiosity on the face of her hostess, which, however, told her nothing.

'Then he *was* Parsifal or Perceforest!' she cried, 'and he has ridden away to find the emerald cup of tradition. What a pity that he paused on his way to break the bank at Monte Carlo. The two do not accord. I fear he is but Lancelot.'

'There is no reason why he should not pursue an honourable ambition,' said the Princess, with some offence.

'No reason at all, even if it be not an honourable one,' said Madame Brancka, with a curious intonation. 'He always wins at baccara; he has done some inimitable caricatures which hang at the Mirliton; he is an amateur Rubenstein, and he has been the lover of Cochonette. These are his qualifications for the Chamber, and if they be not as valiant ones as those of *les Preux* they are at least more amusing.'

'My dear Olga,' said the Princess, with a certain dignity of reproof, 'you are not on

your straw chair at Trouville. There are
subjects, expressions, suggestions, which are
not agreeable to my ears or on your lips.'

'Cochonette!' murmured the offender, with
a graceful little curtsey of obedience and contrition. 'Oh, Madame, if you knew! A year
ago we talked of nothing else!'

The Countess Brancka wished to talk still
of nothing else, and though she encountered a
chillness and silence that would have daunted
a less bold spirit, she contrived to excite in the
Princess a worldly and almost unholy curiosity
concerning that heroine of profane history who
had begun life in a little bakehouse of the
Batignolles, and had achieved the success of
putting her name (or her nickname) upon the
lips of all Paris.

Throughout dinner she spoke of little save
of Cochonette, that goddess of *bouffe*, and of
Parsifal, as she persisted in baptising the one
lover to whom alone the goddess had ever
been faithful. With ill-concealed impatience
her hostess bore awhile with the subject; then
dismissed it somewhat peremptorily.

'We are provincials, my dear Olga,' she
said, with a very cold inflection of contempt in
her voice. 'We are very antiquated in our
ways and our views. Bear with our prejudices and do not scare our decorum. We keep

it by us as we keep kingfishers' skins amongst
our furs in summer against moth; a mere
superstition, I daresay, but we are only rustic
people.'

'How you say that, Wanda,' said her
guest, with a droll little laugh, 'and you look
like Marie Antoinette all the while! Why
will you bury yourself? You would only
need to be seen in Paris a week, and all
the world would turn after you and go back to
tradition and ermine, instead of *chien* and plush.
If you live another ten years as you live now
you will turn Hohenszalras into a religious
house; and even Mdme. Ottilie would regret
that. You will institute a Carmelite Order,
because white becomes you so. Poor Egon, he
would sooner have you laugh about Cochonette.'

The evening was chill, but beautifully
calm and free of mist. Wanda von Szalras
walked out on to the terrace, whilst her cousin
and guest, missing the stimulus of her usual
band of lovers and friends, curled herself up on
a deep chair and fell sound asleep like a
dormouse.

There was no sound on the night except
the ripple of the lake water below and the
splash of torrents falling down the cliffs around;
a sense of irritation and of pleasure moved her

both in the same moment. What was a French courtesan, a singer of lewd songs, an interpreter of base passions to her? Nothing except a creature to be loathed and pitied, as men in health feel a disgusted compassion for disease. Yet she felt a certain anger stir in her as she recalled all this frivolous, trivial, ill-flavoured chatter of her cousin's. And what was it to her if one of the many lovers of this woman had cast her spells from about him and left her for a manlier and a worthier arena? Yet she could not resist a sense of delicate distant homage to herself in the act, in the mute obedience to her counsels such as a knight might render, even Lancelot with stained honour and darkened soul.

The silence of it touched her.

He had said nothing : only by mere chance, in the idle circling of giddy rumour, she learned he had remembered her words and followed her suggestion. There was a subtle and flattering reverence in it which pleased the taste of a woman who was always proud but never vain. And to any noble temperament there is a singularly pure and honest joy in the consciousness of having been in any measure the means of raising higher instincts and loftier desires in any human soul that was not dead but dormant.

The shrill voice of Olga Brancka startled her as it broke in on her musings.

'I have been asleep!' she cried, as she rose out of her deep chair and came forth into the moonlight. 'Pray forgive me, Wanda. You will have all that drowsy water running and tumbling all over the place; it makes one think of the voices in the Sistine in Passion Week; there are the gloom, the hush, the sigh, the shriek, the eternal appeal, the eternal accusation. That water would drive me into hysteria; could you not drain it, divert it, send it underground—silence it somehow?'

'When you can keep the Neva flowing at New Year, perhaps I shall be able. But I would not if I could. I have had all that water about me from babyhood; when I am away from the sound of it I feel as if some hand had woolled up my ears.'

'That is what I feel when I am away from the noise of the streets. Oh, Wanda! to think that you can do utterly as you like and yet do not like to have the sea of light of the Champs-Elysées or the Graben before your eyes, rather than that gliding, dusky water!'

'The water is a mirror. I can see my own soul in it and Nature's; perhaps one hopes even sometimes to see God's.'

'That is not living, my dear, it is dreaming.'

'Oh, no, my life is very real; it is as real as light to darkness, it is absolute prose.'

'Make it poetry then; that is very easy.'

'Poetry is to the poetical; I am by no means poetical. My stud-book, my stewards' ledgers, my bankers' accounts, form the chief of my literature; you know I am a practical farmer.'

'I know you are one of the most beautiful and one of the richest women in Europe, and you live as if you were fifty years old, ugly, and *dévote*; all this will grow on you. In a few years' time you will be a hermit, a prude, an ascetic. You will found a new order, and be canonised after death.'

'My aunt is afraid that I shall die a free-thinker. It is hard to please every one,' replied the Countess Wanda, with unruffled good humour. 'It is poetical people who found religious orders, enthusiasts, visionaries; I wish I were one of them. But I am not. The utmost I can do is to follow George Herbert's precept and sweep my own little chambers, so that this sweeping may be in some sort a duty done.'

'You are a good woman, Wanda, and I dare say a grand one, but you are too grave for me.'

'You mean that I am dull? People always grow dull who live much alone.'

'But you could have the whole world at your feet if you only raised a finger.'

'That would not amuse me at all.'

Her guest gave an impatient movement of her shoulders; after a little she said, 'Did Réné de Sabran amuse you?'

Wanda von Szalras hesitated a moment.

'In a measure he interested me,' she answered, being a perfectly truthful woman. 'He is a man who has the capacity of great things, but he seems to me to be his own worst enemy; if he had fewer gifts he might probably have more achievement. A waste of power is always a melancholy sight.'

'He is only a *boulevardier*, you know.'

'No doubt your Paris asphalte is the modern embodiment of Circe.'

'But he is leaving Circe.'

'So much the better for him if he be. But I do not know why you speak of him so much. He is a stranger to me, and will never, most likely, cross my path again.'

'Oh, Parsifal will come back,' said Madame Brancka, with a little smile. 'Hohenszalras is his Holy Grail.'

'He can scarcely come uninvited, and who will invite him here?' said the mistress of Hohenszalras, with cold literalness.

'Destiny will; the great master of the

ceremonies who disposes of us all,' said her cousin.

'Destiny!' said Wanda, with some contempt. 'Ah, you are superstitious; irreligious people always are. You believe in mesmerism and disbelieve in God.'

'Oh, most Holy Mother, cannot you make Wanda a little like other people?' said the Countess Brancka when her hostess had left her alone with Princess Ottilie. 'She is as much a fourteenth-century figure as any one of those knights in the Rittersaal.'

'Wanda is a gentlewoman,' said the Princess drily. 'You great ladies are not always that, my dear Olga. You are all very *piquantes* and *provocantes*, no doubt, but you have forgotten what dignity is like, and perhaps you have forgotten, too, what self-respect is like. It is but another old-fashioned word.'

CHAPTER IX.

THE late summer passed on into full autumn, and he never returned to the little isle under the birches and willows. The monks spoke of him often with the wondering admiration of rustic recluses for one who had seemed to them the very incarnation of that world which to them was only a vague name. His talents were remembered, his return was longed for ; a silver reliquary and an antique book of plain song which he had sent them were all that remained to them of his sojourn there. As they angled for trout under the drooping boughs, or sat and dosed in the cloister as the rain fell, they talked together of that marvellous visitant with regret. Sometimes they said to one another that they had fancied once upon a time he would have become lord there, where the spires and pinnacles and shining sloping roofs of the great Schloss rose amidst the woods across the Szalrassee. When their grand prior heard them say so he rebuked them.

'Our lady is a true daughter of the Holy Church,' he said; 'all the lands and all the wealth she has will come to the Church. You will see, should we outlive her—which the saints send we may not do—that the burg will be bequeathed by her to form a convent of Ursulines. It is the order she most loves.'

She overheard him say so once when she sat in her boat beneath the willows drifting by under the island, and she sighed impatiently.

'No, I shall not do that,' she thought. 'The religious foundations did a great work in their time, but that time is over. They can no more resist the pressure of the change of thought and habit than I can set sail like S. Ursula with eleven thousand virgins. Hohenszalras shall go to the Crown; they will do what seems best with it. But I may live fifty years' and more.'

A certain sadness came over her as she thought so; a long life, a lonely life, appalled her, even though it was cradled in all luxury and strengthened with all power.

'If only my Bela were living!' she said, half aloud; and the water grew dim to her sight as

it flowed away green and sparkling into the
deep long shadows of its pine-clothed shores,
shadows stretching darkly across its western
side, whilst the eastern extremity was still warm
in the afternoon light.

The great pile of Hohenszalras seemed to
tower up into the very clouds ; the evening sun,
not yet sunk behind the Venediger range, shone
ruddily on all its towers and its gothic spires,
and the grim sculptures and the glistening
metal, with which it was so lavishly ornamented,
were illumined till it looked like some colossal
and enchanted citadel, where soon the magic
ivory horn of Childe Roland might sound and
wake the spell-bound warders.

If only Bela, lord of all, had lived !

. But her regret was not only for her
brother.

In the October of that year her solitude was
broken ; her Sovereign signified her desire to
see Hohenszalras again.   They were about to
visit Salzburg, and expressed their desire to pass
three days in the Iselthal.   There was nothing
to be done but to express gratitude for the
honour and make the necessary preparations.
The von Szalras had been always loyal allies
rather than subjects, and their devotion to the
Habsburg house had been proved in many ways
and with constancy.   She felt that she would

rather have to collect and equip a regiment of horse, as her fathers had done, than fill her home with the *tapage* inevitable to an Imperial reception, but she was not insensible to the friendship that dictated this mark of honour.

'Fate conspires to make me break my resolutions,' she said to the Princess; who answered with scant sympathy:

'There are some resolutions much more wisely broken than persevered in; your vows of solitude are amongst them.'

'Three days will not long affect my solitude.'

'Who knows? At all events, Hohenszalras for those three days will be worthy of its traditions—if only it will not rain.'

'We will hope that it may not. Let us prepare the list of invitations.'

When she had addressed all the invitations to some fifty of the greatest families of the empire for the house party, she took one of the cards engraved 'To meet their Imperial Majesties,' and hesitated some moments, then wrote across it the name of Sabran.

'You will like to see your friend,' she said as she passed it to her aunt.

'Certainly, I should like to do so, but I am quite sure he will not come.'

'Not come?'

'I think he will not. You will never understand, my dear Wanda, that men may love
you.'

'I certainly saw nothing of love in the conversation of M. de Sabran,' she answered, with
some irritation.

'In his conversation? Very likely not; he
is a proud man and poor.'

'Since he has ceased to visit Monte Carlo.'

'You are ungenerous, Wanda.'

'I?'

The accusation fell on her with a shock of
surprise, under which some sense of error stirred.
Was it possible she could be ungenerous? She,
whose character had always, even in its faults,
been cast on lines so broad? She let his invitation go away with the rest in the post-bag to
Matrey.

In a week his answer came with others. He
was very sensible, very grateful, but the political aspect of the time forbade him to leave
France. His election had entailed on him many
obligations; the Chamber would meet next
month, &c., &c. He laid his homage and regrets
at the feet of the ladies of Hohenszalras.

'I was sure he would say so,' the Princess
observed. It did not lie within her Christian obligations to spare the '*je vous l'avais bien dit.*'

'It is very natural that he should not jeopardise his public prospects,' answered Wanda herself, angrily conscious of a disappointment, with which there was mingled also a sense of greater respect for him than she had ever felt.

'He cares nothing at all about those,' said the Princess, sharply. 'If he had the position of Egon he would come. His political prospects! Do you pretend to be ignorant that he only went to the Chamber as he went to Romaris, because you recommended ambition and activity?'

'If that be the case he is most wise not to come,' answered, with some coldness, the châtelaine of Hohenszalras; and she went to visit the stables, which would be more important in the eyes of her Imperial mistress than any other part of the castle.

'She will like Cadiga,' she thought, as she stroked the graceful throat of an Arab mare which she had had over from Africa three months before, a pure bred daughter of the desert 'shod with lightning.'

She conversed long with her *stallmeister* Ulrich, and gave him various directions.

'We are all grown very rustic and old-fashioned here,' she said with a smile. 'But the horses at least will not disgrace us.'

Ulrich asked his most high countess if the Margraf von Sabran would be of the house party, and when she answered 'No,' said, with regret,

that no one had ever looked so well on Siegfried
as he had done.

'He did ride very well,' she said, and turned
to the stall where the sorrel Siegfried stood. She
sighed unconsciously as she drew the tufted hair
hanging over the horse's forehead through her
fingers with tenderness. What if she were to
make Siegfried and all else his, if it were true
that he loved her? She thrust the thought
away almost before it took any real shape.

'I do not even believe it,' she said half aloud,
and yet in her innermost heart she did believe it.

The Imperial visit was made and became a
thing of the past.

The state apartments were opened, the servants wore their state liveries, the lake had its
banners and flags, its decorated landing-stairs
and velvet-cushioned boats; the stately and
silent place was full for three days and nights
of animated and brilliant life, and great hunting
parties rejoiced the soul of old Otto, and made
the forests ring with sound of horn and rifle.
The culverins on the keep fired their salutes, the
chimes of the island monastery echoed the bells
of the clock tower of the Schloss, the schools
sang with clear fresh voices the Kaiser's Hymn,
the sun shone, the jäger were in full glory,
the castle was filled with guests and their servants; the long-unused theatre had a troop of

Viennese to play comedies on its bijou stage, the ball-room, lined with its Venetian mirrors and its Reseiner gilding, was lit up once more after many years of gloom; the nobles of the provinces came from far and wide at the summons of the lady of Hohenszalras, and the greater nobles who formed the house-party were well amused and well content, whilst the Imperial guests were frankly charmed with all things, and honestly reluctant to depart.

When she accompanied them to the foot of the terrace stairs, and there took leave of them, she could feel that their visit had been one of unfeigned enjoyment, and her farewell gift to her Kaiserin was Cadiga. They had left early on the morning of the fourth day, and the remainder of the day was filled till sunset by the departure of the other guests; it was fatiguing and crowded. When the last visitor had gone she dropped down on a great chair in the Rittersaal, and gave a long-drawn sigh of relief.

'What a long strain on one's powers of courtesy!' she murmured. 'It is more exhausting than to climb Gross Glöckner!'

'It has been perfectly successful!' said the Princess, whose cheeks were warm and whose eyes were bright with triumph.

'It has been only a matter of money,' said the Countess von Szalras, with some contempt.

' Nothing makes one feel so *bourgeoise* as a thing like this. Any merchant or banker could do the same. It is impossible to put any originality into it. It is like diamonds. Any one only heard of yesterday could do as much if they had only the money to do it with ; you do not seem to see what I mean ? '

' I see that, as usual, you are discontented when any other woman would be in paradise,' answered the Princess, a little tartly. 'Pray, could the *bourgeoise* have a residence ten centuries old ? '

' I am afraid she could buy one easily.'

' Would that be the same thing ? '   '

' Certainly not, but it would enable her to do all I have done for the last three days, if she had only money enough ; she could even give away Cadiga.'

'She could not get Cadiga accepted ! ' said Mme. Ottilie, drily. ' You are tired, my love, and so do not appreciate your own triumphs. It has been a very great success.'

' They were very kind ; they are always so kind. But all the time I could not help thinking, were they not horribly fatigued. It wearied me so myself, I could not believe that they were otherwise than weary too.'

' It has been a great success,' repeated the Princess. ' But you are always discontented.'

Wanda did not reply; she leaned back against the Cordovan leather back of the chair, crushing her chestnut hair against the emblazoned scutcheon of her house; she was very fatigued, and her face was pale. For three whole days and evenings to preserve an incessant vigilance of courtesy, a continual assumption of interest, an unremitting appearance of enjoyment, a perpetual smile of welcome, is very tedious work: those in love with social successes are sustained by the consciousness of them, but she was not. An Imperial visit more or less could add not one hair's breadth to the greatness of the house of Szalras.

And there was a dull, half conscious pain at the bottom of her heart. She was thinking of Egon Vàsàrhely, who had said he could not leave his regiment; of Réné de Sabran, who had said he could not leave his country. Even to those who care nothing for society, and dislike the stir and noise of the world about them, there is still always a vague sense of depression in the dispersion of a great party; the house seems so strangely silent, the rooms seem so strangely empty, servants flitting noiselessly here and there, a dropped flower, a fallen jewel, an oppressive scent from multitudes of fading blossoms, a broken vase perhaps, or perhaps a snapped fan—these are all that are left of the teeming life crowded here one little moment ago. Though one may be glad they are all gone, yet there is a certain sadness in it. '*Le lendemain de la fête*' keeps its pathos, even though the fête itself has possessed no poetry and no power to amuse.

The Princess, who was very fatigued too, though she would not confess that social duties could ever exhaust anyone, went softly away to her own room, and Wanda sat alone in the great Rittersaal, with the afternoon light pouring through the painted casements on to the damascened armour, and the Flemish tapestries, and the great dais at the end of the hall, with its two-headed eagle that Dante cursed, its draperies of gold-coloured velvet, its escutcheons in beaten and enamelled metal.

Discontented! The Princess had left that truthful word behind her like a little asp creeping upon a marble floor. It stung her conscience with a certain reproach, her pride with a certain impatience. Discontented! She who had always been so equable of temper, so enamoured of solitude, so honestly loyal to her people and her duties, so entirely grateful to the placid days that came and went as calmly as the breathing of her breast!

Was it possible she was discontented?

How all the great world that had just left her would have laughed at her, and asked what doubled rose-leaf made her misery?

No one hardly on earth could be more entirely free than she was, more covered with all good gifts of fortune and of circumstances; and she had always been so grateful to her life until now. Would she never cease to miss the coming of the little boat across from the Holy Isle? She was angry that this memory should have so much power to pursue her thought and spoil the present hours. Had he but been there, she knew very well that the pageantry of the past three days would not have been the mere empty formalities, the mere gilded tedium that they had appeared to be to her.

On natures thoughtful and profound, silence has sometimes a much greater power than speech. Now and then she surprised herself in the act of thinking how artificial human life had become, when the mere accident of a greater or lesser fortune determined whether a man who respected himself could declare his feeling for a woman he loved. It seemed lamentably conventional and unreal, and yet had he not been fettered by silence he would have been no gentleman.

Life resumed its placid even tenor at

Hohenszalras after this momentary disturbance.
Autumn comes early in the Glöckner and
Venediger groups.   Madame Ottilie with a
shiver heard the north winds sweep through
the yellowing forests, and watched the white
mantle descend lower and lower down the .
mountain sides.   Another winter was approach-
ing, a winter in which she would see no one,
hear nothing, sit all day by her wood fire, half
asleep for sheer want of interest to keep her
awake; the very postboy was sometimes de-
tained by the snowfall for whole days together
in his passage to and from Matrey.

'It is all very well for you,' she said pettishly to her niece.   'You have youth, you
have strength, you like to have four mad
horses put in your sleigh and drive them like
demoniacs through howling deserts of frozen
pine forests, and come home when the great
stars are all out, with your eyes shining like
the planets, and the beasts all white with foam
and icicles.   You like that ; you can do it ; you
prefer it before anything, but I—what have I
to do?   One cannot eat nougats for ever, nor
yet read one's missal.   Even you will allow
that the evenings are horribly long.   Your
horses cannot help you there.   You embroider
very artistically, but they would do that all for
you at any convent; and to be sure you write

your letters and audit your accounts, but you might just as well leave it all to your lawyers. Olga Brancka is quite right, though I do not approve of her mode of expression, but she is quite right—you should be in the world.'

But she failed to move Wanda by a hair's breadth, and soon the hush of winter settled down on Hohenszalras, and when the first frost had hardened the ground the four black horses were brought out in the sleigh, and their mistress, wrapped in furs to the eyes, began those headlong gallops through the silent forests which stirred her to a greater exhilaration than any pleasures of the world could have raised in her. To guide those high-mettled, half-broken, high-bred creatures, fresh from freedom on the plains of the Danube, was like holding the reins of the winds.

One day at dusk as she returned from one of these drives, and went to see the Princess Ottilie before changing her dress, the Princess received her with a little smile and a demure air of triumph, of smiling triumph. In her hand was an open letter which she held out to her niece.

'Read!' she said with much self-satisfaction. 'See what miracles you and the Holy Isle can work.'

Wanda took the letter, which she saw at a

glance was in the writing of Sabran. After some graceful phrases of homage to the Princess, he proceeded in it to say that he had taken his seat in the French Chamber, as deputy for his department.

'I do not deceive myself,' he continued. 'The trust is placed in me for the sake of the memories of the dead Sabran, not because I am anything in the sight of these people ; but I will endeavour to be worthy of it. I am a sorry idler and of little purpose and strength in life, but I will endeavour to make my future more serious and more deserving of the goodness which was showered on me at Hohenszalras. It grieved me to be unable to profit by the permission so graciously extended to me at the time of their Imperial Majesties' sojourn with you, but it was impossible for me to come. My thoughts were with you, as they are indeed every hour. Offer my homage to the Countess von Szalras, with the renewal of my thanks.'

Then, with some more phrases of reverence and compliment blent in one to the venerable lady whom he addressed, he ended an epistle which brought as much pleasure to the recipient as though she had been seventeen instead of seventy.

She watched the face of Wanda during the

perusal of these lines, but she did not learn anything from its expression.

'He writes admirably,' she said, when she had read it through; 'and I think he is well fitted for a political career. They say that it is always best in politics not to be burdened with convictions, and he will be singularly free from such impediments, for he has none!'

'You are very harsh and unjust,' said the Princess, angrily. 'No person can pay you a more delicate compliment than lies in following your counsels, and yet you have nothing better to say about it than to insinuate an unscrupulous immorality.'

'Politics are always immoral.'

'Why did you recommend them to him, then?' said the Princess, sharply.

'They are better than some other things— than *rouge et noir*, for instance; but I did not perhaps do right in advising a mere man of pleasure to use the nation as his larger gaming-table.'

'You are beyond my comprehension! Your wire drawing is too fine for my dull eyesight. One thing is certainly quite clear to me, dull as I am; you live alone until you grow dissatisfied with everything. There is no possibility of pleasing a woman who disapproves of the whole living world!'

'The world sees few unmixed motives,' said Wanda, to which the Princess replied by an impatient movement.

'The post has brought fifty letters for you. I have been looking over the journals,' she answered. 'There is something you may also perhaps deign to read.'

She held out a French newspaper and pointed to a column in it.

Wanda took it and read it, standing. It was a report of a debate in the French Chamber.

She read in silence and attentively, leaning against the great carved chimney-piece. 'I was not aware he was so good an orator,' she said simply, when she had finished reading.

'You grant that it is a very fine speech, a very noble speech?' said Madame Otillie, eagerly and with impatience. 'You perceive the sensation it caused; it is evidently the first time he has spoken. You will see in another portion of the print how they praise him.'

'He has acquired his convictions with rapidity. He was a Socialist when here.'

'The idea! A man of his descent has always the instincts of his order: he may pretend to resist them, but they are always stronger than he. You might at least commend him, Wanda, since your words turned him towards public life.'

'He is no doubt eloquent,' she answered, with some reluctance. 'That we could see here. If he be equally sincere he will be a great gain to the nobility of France.'

'Why should you doubt his sincerity?'

'Is mere ambition ever sincere?'

'I really cannot understand you. You censured his waste of ability and accession; you seem equally disposed to cavil at his exertions and use of his talent. Your prejudices are most cruelly tenacious.'

'How can I applaud your friend's action until I am sure of his motive?'

'His motive is to please you,' thought the Princess, but she was too wary to say so.

She merely replied:

'No motive is ever altogether unmixed, as you cruelly observed; but I should say that his must be on the whole sufficiently pure. He wishes to relieve the inaction and triviality of a useless life.'

'To embrace a hopeless cause is always in a manner noble,' assented her niece. 'And I grant you that he has spoken very well.'

Then she went to her own room to dress for dinner.

In the evening she read the reported speech again, with closer attention. It was eloquent, ironical, stately, closely reasoned, and rose in

its peroration to a caustic and withering eloquence of retort and invective. It was the
speech of a born orator, but it was also the
speech of a strongly conservative partisan.

'How much of what he says does he believe?'
she thought, with a doubt that saddened her
and made her wonder why it came to her.
And whether he believed or not, whether he
were true or false in his political warfare,
whether he were selfish or unselfish in his
ambitions, what did it matter to her?

He had stayed there a few weeks, and he
had played so well that the echoes of his music
still seemed to linger after him, and that was
all. It was not likely they would ever meet
again.

CHAPTER X.

WITH the New Year Madame Ottilie received another letter from him. It was brief, grateful, and touching. It concluded with a message of ceremonious homage to the châtelaine of Hohenszalras. Of his entrance into political life it said nothing. With the letter came a screen of gilded leather which he had painted himself, with passages from the history of S. Julian Hospitador.

'It will seem worthless,' he said, 'where every chamber is a museum of art; but accept it as a sign of my grateful and imperishable remembrance.'

The Princess was deeply touched and sensibly flattered.

'You will admit, at least,' she said, with

innocent triumph, ' that he knows how to make gratitude graceful.'

' It is an ex-voto, and you are his patron saint, dear mother,' said the Countess Wanda, with a smile; but the smile was one of approval. She thought his silence on his own successes and on her name was in good taste. And the screen was so admirably painted that the Venetian masters might have signed it without discredit.

' May I give him no message from you,' said the Princess, as she was about to write her reply.

Her niece hesitated.

' Say we have read his first speech, and are glad of his success,' she said, after a few moments' reflection.

' Nothing more? '

' What else should I say? ' replied Wanda, with some irritation.

. The Princess was too honourable a woman to depart from the text of the congratulation, but she contrived to throw a little more warmth into the spirit of it; and she did not show her letter to the mistress of Hohenszalras. She set the screen near her favourite chair in the blue-room.

' If only there were any one to appreciate it!' she said, with a sigh. 'Like everything else in this house, it might as well be packed up in a chest for aught people see of it. This place is not a museum ; the world goes to a museum : it is a crypt!'

'Would it be improved by a crowd of sightseers at ten kreutzers a head?'

'No : but it would be very much brightened by a house-party at Easter, and now and then at midsummer and autumn. In your mother's time the October parties for the bear-hunts, the wolf-hunts, the boar-hunts, were magnificent. No, I do not think the chase contrary to God's will ; man has power over the beasts of the field and the forest. The archdukes never missed an autumn here ; they found the sport finer than in Styria.'

Her niece kissed her hand and went out to where her four black horses were fretting and champing before the great doors, and the winter sun was lighting up the gilded scroll-work, and the purple velvet, and the brown sables of her sleigh, that had been built in Russia and been a gift to her from Egon Vàsàrhely. She felt a little impatience of the Princess Ottilie, well as she loved her; the complacent narrowness of mind, the unconscious cruelty, the innocent egotism, the conventional religion which clipped and fitted the ways of Deity to suit its own habits and wishes: these fretted her, chafed her, oppressed her with a sense of their utter vanity. The Princess would not herself have harmed a sparrow or a mouse, yet it seemed to her that Providence had created all the animal world only to furnish pastime for princes and their jägers. She saw no contradiction in this view of the matter. The small conventional mind of her had been cast in that mould and would never expand : it was perfectly pure and truthful, but it was contracted and filled with formula.

Wanda von Szalras, who loved her tenderly, could not help a certain impatience of this, the sole, companionship she had. A deep affection may exist side by side with a mental disparity that creates an unwilling but irresistible sense of tedium and discordance. A clear and broad intelligence is infinitely patient of inferiority ; but its very patience has its reaction in its own fatigue and silent irritation.

This lassitude came on her most in the long evenings whilst the Princess slumbered and she herself sat alone. She was not haunted by it when she was in the open air, or in the library, occupied with the reports or the requirements on her estates. But the evenings were lonely and tedious ; they had not seemed so when the little boat had come away from the monastery, and the prayer and praise of Handel and

Haydn, and the new-born glory of the Nibelungen tone-poems had filled the quiet twilight hours. It was in no way probable that the musician and she would ever meet again. She understood that his own delicacy and pride must perforce keep him out of Austria, and she, however much the Princess desired it, could never invite him there alone, and would not probably gather such a house-party at Hohenszalras as might again warrant her doing so.

Nothing was more unlikely, she supposed, than that she would ever hear again the touch that had awakened the dumb chords of the old painted spinet.

But circumstance, that master of the ceremonies, as Madame Brancka termed it, who directs the *menuet de la cour* of life, and who often diverts himself by letting it degenerate into a dance of death, willed it otherwise. There was a dear friend of hers who was a dethroned and exiled queen. Their friendship was strong, tender, and born in childish days. On the part of Wanda, it had been deepened by the august adversity which impresses and attaches all noble natures. Herself born of a great race, and with the instincts of a ruling class hereditary in her, there was something sacred and awful in the fall of majesty. Her friend, stripped of all appanages of her rank, and deserted by nearly all who had so late sworn her allegiance, became more than ever dear; she became holy to her, and she would sooner have denied the request of a reigning sovereign than of one powerless to command or to rebuke. When this friend, who had been so hardly smitten by fate, sent her word that she was ill and would fain see her, she, therefore, never even hesitated as to obedience before the summons. It troubled and annoyed her; it came to her ill-timed and unexpected; and it was above all disagreeable to her, because it would take her to Paris. But it never occurred to her to send an excuse to this friend, who had no longer any power to say, ' I will,' but could only say, like common humanity, ' I hope.'

Within two hours of her reception of the summons she was on her way to Windisch-Matrey. The Princess did not accompany her; she intended to make as rapid a journey as possible without pausing on the way, and her great-aunt was too old and too delicate in health for such exertion.

' Though I would fain go and see that great Parisian aurist,' she said plaintively. ' My hearing is not what it used to be.'

' The great aurist shall come to you, dear mother,' said Wanda. ' I will bring him back with me.'

She travelled with a certain state, since she did not think that the moment of a visit to a dethroned sovereign was a fit time to lay ceremony aside. She took several of her servants and some of her horses with her, and journeyed by way of Munich and Strasburg.

Madame Ottilie was too glad she should go anywhere to offer opposition ; and in her heart of hearts she thought of her favourite. He was in Paris ; who knew what might happen?

It was midwinter, and the snow was deep on all the country, whether of mountain or of plain, which stretched between the Tauern and the French capital. But there was no great delay of the express, and in some forty hours the Countess von Szalras, with her attendants, and her horses with theirs, arrived at the Hôtel Bristol.

The noise, the movement, the brilliancy of the streets seemed a strange spectacle, after four years spent without leaving the woodland quiet and mountain solitudes of Hohenszalras.

She was angry with herself that, as she stood at the windows of her apartment, she almost unconsciously watched the faces of the crowd passing below, and felt a vague expectancy of seeing amongst them the face of Sabran.

She went that evening to the modest hired house where the young and beautiful sovereign she came to visit had found a sorry refuge. It was a meeting full of pain to both. When they had last parted at the Hofburg ot Vienna, the young queen had been in all the triumph and hope of brilliant nuptials; and at Hohenszalras, the people's Heilige Bela had been living, a happy boy, in all his fair promise.

Meanwhile, the news-sheets informed all their leaders that the Countess von Szalras was in Paris. Ambassadors and ambassadresses, princes and princesses, and a vast number of very great people, hastened to write their names at the Hôtel Bristol.

Amongst the cards left was that of Sabran. But he sent it; he did not go in person.

She refused all invitations, and declined almost all visits. She had come there only to see her friend, the Queen of Natalia. Paris, which loves anything new, talked a great deal about her; and its street crowds, which admires what is beautiful, began to gather before the doors at the hours when her black horses, driven Russian fashion, came fretting and flashing like meteors over the asphalte.

'Why did you bring your horses for so short a time?' said Madame Kaulnitz to her. 'You could, of course, have had any of ours.'

'I always like to have some of my horses with me,' she answered. 'I would have brought

them all, only it would have looked so osten-
tatious; you know they are my children.'

'I do not see why you should not have
other children,' said Madame Kaulnitz. 'It is
quite inhuman that you will not marry.'

'I have never said that I will not. But I
do not think it likely.'

Two days after her arrival, as she was
driving down the Avenue de l'Impératrice, she
saw Sabran on foot. She was driving slowly. She
would have stopped her carriage if he had
paused in his walk; but he did not, he only
bowed low and passed on. It was almost rude,
after the hospitality of Hohenszalras, but the
rudeness pleased her. It spoke both of pride
and of sensitiveness. It seemed scarcely natural,
after their long hours of intercourse, that they
should pass each other thus as strangers; yet it
seemed impossible they should any more be
friends. She did not ask herself why it seemed
so, but she felt it rather by instinct than by
reasoning.

She was annoyed to feel that the sight of
him had caused a momentary emotion in her of
mingled trouble and pleasure.

No one mentioned his name to her, and
she asked no one concerning him. She spent
almost all her time with the Queen of Natalia,
and there were other eminent foreign person-

ages in Paris at that period whose amiabili-
ties she could not altogether reject, and she
had only allowed herself fifteen days as the
length of her sojourn, as Madame Ottilie was
alone amidst the snow-covered mountains of
the Tauern.

On the fifth day after her meeting with
Sabran he sent another card of his to the hotel,
and sent with it an immense basket of gilded
osier filled with white lilac. She remembered
having once said to him at Hohenszalras that
lilac was her flower of preference. Her rooms
were crowded with bouquets, sent her by all
sorts of great people, and made of all kinds of
rare blossoms, but the white lilac, coming in the
January snows, touched her more than all those.
She knew that his poverty was no fiction; and
that great clusters of white lilac in midwinter
in Paris meant much money.

She wrote a line or two in German, which
thanked him for his recollection of her taste,
and sent it to the Chamber. She did not
know where he lived.

That evening she mentioned his name to
her godfather, the Duc de Noira, and asked him
if he knew it. The Duc, a Legitimist, a recluse,
and a man of strong prejudices, answered at
once.

'Of course I know it; he is one of us, and

he has made a political position for himself within the last year.'

' Do you know him personally ? '

' No, I do not. I see no one, as you are aware ; I live in greater retirement than ever. But he bears an honourable name, and though I believe that, until lately, he was but a *flâneur*, he has taken a decided part this session, and he is a very great acquisition to the true cause.'

' It is surely very sudden, his change of front ? '

' What change ? He took no part in politics that ever I heard of ; it is taken for granted that a Marquis de Sabran is loyal to his sole legitimate sovereign. I believe he never thought of public life ; but they tell me that he returned from some long absence last autumn, an altered and much graver man. Then one of the deputies for his department died, and he was elected for the vacancy with no opposition.'

The Duc de Noira proceeded to speak of the political aspects of the time, and said no more.

Involuntarily, as she drove through the avenues of the Bois de Boulogne, she thought of the intuitive comprehension, the half-uttered sympathy, the interchange of ideas, *à demi-mots*, which had made the companionship of Sabran so welcome to her in the previous summer.

They had not always agreed, she often had not even approved him; but they had always understood one another, they had never needed to explain. She was startled to realise how much and how vividly she regretted him.

'If one could only be sure of his sincerity,' she thought, 'there would be few men living who would equal him.'

She did not know why she doubted his sincerity. Some natures have keen instincts like dogs. She regretted to doubt it; but the change in him seemed to her too rapid to be one of conviction. Yet the homage in it to herself was delicate and subtle. She would not have been a woman had it not touched her, and she was too honest with herself not to frankly admit in her own thoughts that she might very well have inspired a sentiment which would go far to change a nature which it entered and subdued. Many men had loved her; why not he?

She drew the whip over the flanks of her horses as she felt that mingled impatience and sadness with which sovereigns remember that they can never be certain they are loved for themselves, and not for all which environs them and lifts them up out of the multitude.

She was angry with herself when she felt that what interested her most during her

Parisian sojourn was the report of the debates of the French Chamber in the French journals.

One night the Baron Kaulnitz spoke of Sabran in her hearing.

'He is the most eloquent of the Legitimist party,' he said to some one in her hearing. 'No one supposed that he had it in him; he was a mere idler, a mere man of pleasure, and it was at times said of something worse, but he has of late manifested great talent; it is displayed for a lost cause, but it is none the less admirable as talent goes.'

She heard what he said with pleasure.

Advantage was taken of her momentary return to the world to press on her the choice of a great alliance. Names as mighty as her own were suggested to her, and more than one great prince, of a rank even higher than hers, humbly solicited the honour of the hand which gave no caress except to a horse's neck, a dog's head, a child's curls. But she did not even pause to allow these proposals any consideration; she refused them all curtly, and with a sense of irritation.

'Have you sworn never to marry?' said the Duc de Noira, with much chagrin, receiving her answer for a candidate of his own to whom he was much attached.

'I never swear anything,' she answered.

'Oaths are necessary for people who do not know their own minds. I do know my own.'

'You know that you will never marry?'

'I hardly say that; but I shall never contract a mere alliance. It is horrible—that union eternal of two bodies and souls without sympathy, without fitness, without esteem, merely for sake of additional position or additional wealth.'

'It is not eternal!' said the Duc, with a smile; 'and I can assure you that my friend adores you for yourself. You will never understand, Wanda, that you are a woman to inspire great love; that you would be sought for your face, for your form, for your mind, if you had nothing else.'

'I do not believe it.'

'Can you doubt at least that your cousin Egon——'

'Oh, pray spare me the name of Egon!' she said with unwonted irritation. 'I may surely be allowed to have left that behind me at home!'

It was a time of irritation and turbulence in Paris. The muttering of the brooding storm was visible to fine ears through the false stillness of an apparently serene atmosphere. She, who knew keen and brilliant politicians who were not French, saw the danger that was at hand for France which France did not see.

' They will throw down the glove to Prussia,
and they will repent of it as long as the earth
lasts,' she thought, and she was oppressed by
her prescience, for war had cost her race dear ;
and she said to herself, ' When that liquid fire
is set flowing who shall say where it will
pause ? '

She felt an extreme desire to converse with
Sabran as she had done at home ; to warn him,
to persuade him, to hear his views and express
to him her own ; but she did not summon him,
and he did not come. She did justice to the
motive which kept him away, but she was not
as yet prepared to go as far as to invite him to
lay his scruples aside and visit her with the old
frank intimacy which had brightened both their
lives at the Hohenszalrasburg. It had been so
different there ; he had been a wanderer glad of
rest, and she had had about her the defence of
the Princess's presence, and the excuse of the
obligations of hospitality. She reproached herself at times for hardness, for unkindness ; she
had not said a syllable to commend him for that
abandonment of a frivolous life which was in
itself so delicate and lofty a compliment to herself. He had obeyed her quite as loyally as
knight ever did his lady, and she did not even
say to him, ' It is well done.'

Wanda von Szalras—a daughter of brave

men, and herself the bravest of women—was conscious that she was for once a coward. She was afraid of looking into her own heart.

She said to her cousin, when he paid his respects to her, 'I should like to hear a debate at the Chamber. Arrange it for me.'

He replied: ' At your service in that as in all things.'

The next day as she was about to drive out, about four o'clock, he met her at the entrance of her hotel.

' If you could come with me,' he said, ' you might hear something of interest to-day; there will be a strong discussion. Will you accept my carriage or shall I enter yours? '

What she heard when she reached the Chamber did not interest her greatly. There was a great deal of noise, of declamation, of personal vituperation, of verbose rancour; it did not seem to her to be eloquence. She had heard much more stately oratory in both the Upper and Lower Reichsrath, and much more fiery and noble eloquence at Buda Pesth. This seemed to her poor, shrill mouthing, which led to very little, and the disorder of the Assembly filled her with contempt.

' I thought it was the country of S. Louis!' she said, with a disdainful sigh, to Kaulnitz, who answered :

'Cromwell is perhaps more wanted here than S. Louis.'

'Their Cromwell will always be a lawyer without clients, or a journalist *sans le sou* !' retorted the châtelaine of Hohenszalras.

When she had been there an hour or more she saw Sabran enter the hall and take his place. His height, his carriage, and his distinction of appearance made him conspicuous in a multitude, while the extreme fairness and beauty of his face were uncommon and striking.

'Here is S. Louis,' said the ambassador, with a little smile, ' or a son of S. Louis's crusaders at any rate. He is sure to speak. I think he speaks very well ; one would suppose he had done nothing else all his life.'

After a time, when some speakers, virulent, over-eager, and hot in argument, had had their say, and a tumult had risen and been quelled, and the little bell had rung violently for many minutes, Sabran entered the tribune. He had seen the Austrian minister and his companion.

His voice, at all times melodious, had a compass which could fill with ease the large hall in which he was. He appeared to use no more effort than if he were conversing in ordinary tones, yet no one there present lost a syllable that he said. His gesture was slight, calm, and graceful; his language admirably chosen, and full of dignity.

His mission of the moment was to attack the ministry upon their foreign policy, and he did so with exceeding skill, wit, irony, and precision. His eloquence was true eloquence, and was not indebted in any way to trickery, artifice, or over-ornament. He spoke with fire, force, and courage, but his tranquillity never gave way for a moment. His speech was brilliant and serene, in utter contrast to the turbulent and florid declamation which had preceded him. There was great and prolonged applause when he had closed with a peroration stately and persuasive; and when Emile Ollivier rose to reply, that optimistic statesman was plainly disturbed and at a loss.

Sabran resumed his seat without raising his eyes to where the Countess von Szalras sat. She remained there during the speech of the minister, which was a lame and laboured one, for he had been pierced between the joints of his armour. Then she rose and went away with her escort.

'What do you think of S. Louis?' said he, jestingly.

'I think he is very eloquent and very convincing, but I do not think he is at all like a Frenchman.'

'Well, he is a *Breton bretonnant*,' rejoined the ambassador. 'They are always more in earnest and more patrician.'

'If he be sincere, if he be only sincere,' she thought: that doubt pursued her. She had a vague sense that it was all only a magnificent comedy after all. Could apathy and irony change all so suddenly to conviction and devotion? Could the scoffer become so immediately the devotee? Could he care, really care, for those faiths of throne and altar which he defended with so much eloquence, so much earnestness? And yet, why not? These faiths were inherited things with him; their altars must have been always an instinct with him; for their sake his fathers had lived and died. What great wonder, then, that they should have been awakened in him after a torpor which had been but the outcome of those drugs with which the world is always so ready to lay asleep the soul?

They had now got out into the corridors, and as they turned the corner of one, they came straight upon Sabran.

'I congratulate you,' said Wanda, as she stretched her hand out to him with a smile.

As he took it and bowed over it he grew very pale.

'I have obeyed you,' he murmured, 'with less success than I could desire.'

'Do not be too modest, you are a great orator. You know how to remain calm whilst you exalt, excite, and influence others.'

He listened in silence, then inquired for the health of his kind friend the Princess Ottilie.

'She is well,' answered Wanda, 'and loses nothing of her interest in you. She reads all your speeches with approval and pleasure; not the less approval and pleasure because her political creed has become yours.'

He coloured slightly.

'What did you tell me?' he said. 'That if I had no convictions, I could do no better than abide by the traditions of the Sabrans? If their cause were the safe and reigning one I would not support it for mere expediency, but as it is——'

'Your motives cannot be selfish ones,' she answered a little coldly. 'Selfishness would have led you to profess Bakouinism; it is the popular profession, and a socialistic aristocrat is always attracted and flattering to the *plebs.*'

'You are severe,' he said, with a flush on his cheek. '.I have no intention of playing Philip Egalité now or in any after time.'

She did not reply; she was conscious of unkindness and want of encouragement in her own words. She hesitated a little, and then said:

'Perhaps you will have time to come and see me? I shall remain here a few days more.'

The ambassador joined them at that moment, and was too well bred to display any sign of the supreme astonishment he felt at finding the Countess von Szalras and the new deputy already known to each other.

'He is a favourite of Aunt Ottilie's,' she explained to him as, leaving Sabran, they passed down the corridor. 'Did I not tell you? He had an accident on the Umbal glacier last summer, and in his convalescence we saw him often.'

'I recollect that your aunt asked me about him. Excuse me; I had quite forgotten,' said the ambassador, understanding now why she had wanted to go to the Chamber.

The next day Sabran called upon her. There were with her three or four great ladies. He did not stay long, and was never alone with her. She felt an impatience of her friends' presence, which irritated her as it awoke in her. He sent her a second basket of white lilac in the following forenoon. She saw no more of him.

She found herself wondering about the manner of his life. She did not even know in what street he lived; she passed almost all her time with the Queen of Natalia, who did not know him, and was still so unwell that she received no one.

She was irritated with herself because it compromised her consistency to desire to stay on in Paris, and she did so desire; and she was one of those to whom a consciousness of their own consistency is absolutely necessary as a qualification for self-respect. There are natures that fly contentedly from caprice to caprice, as humming-birds from blossom to bud; but if she had once become changeable she would have become contemptible to herself, she would hardly have been herself any longer. With some anger at her own inclinations she resisted them, and when her self-allotted fifteen days were over, she did not prolong them by so much as a dozen hours. There was an impatience in her which was wholly strange to her serene and even temper. She felt a vague dissatisfaction with herself; she had been scarcely generous, scarcely cordial to him; she failed to approve her own conduct, and yet she scarcely saw where she had been at fault.

The Kaulnitz and many other high persons were at the station in the chill, snowy, misty day to say their last farewells. She was wrapped in silver-fox fur from head to foot; she was somewhat pale; she felt an absurd reluctance to go away from a city which was nothing to her.　But her exiled friend was recovering health, and Madame Ottilie was all alone; and though she was utterly her own mistress, far more so than most women, there were some things she could not do.　To stay on in Paris seemed to her to be one of them.

The little knot of high personages said their last words; the train began slowly to move upon its way; a hand passed through the window of the carriage and laid a bouquet of lilies of the valley on her knee.

'Adieu!' said Sabran very gently, as his eyes met hers once more.

Then the express train rolled faster on its road, and passed out by the north-east, and in a few moments had left Paris far behind it.

END OF THE FIRST VOLUME.

For Spiritu Santo, *wherever so printed, read* Espiritu Santo.